Praise for
Rooted in Sunrise

"In the blue grass of Kentucky, Beth Dotson Brown ignites a heartfelt tale of family and faith in the worst of circumstances. When a tornado hits Lexington, and destroys Ava Winston's house, she looks at her life with new eyes. She redefines love and the relationship with her daughter, ex-husband and a beloved aunt. Ava must decide to stay and rebuild or pursue a new life. A loving coming-of-age story for women in mid-life. Brava!"

—ADRIANA TRIGIANI, Author of *The Good Left Undone*

"Beth Dotson Brown, in her debut novel *Rooted in Sunrise*, captures the true meaning of resilience—something so many women strive to know in the depths of their inner-self. It is not just being able to 'bounce back' after a trauma, but rather to engage in a journey of self-discovery that finds the gifts within—and feels fulfilled. The beautiful description by Aunt Lila of Ava captures this fullness of resilience, 'You're the night sky, Ava.' Perplexed Ava asks, 'What do you mean?' As both of them looked up to the night sky, Aunt Lila responded, 'If the sky were filled with stars, then none of them would shine brilliantly enough to stand out among the rest. You're one of those hundreds of millions of particles that are content to stay dark so the stars around you can shine.' A must-read for every woman."

—SISTER ROBBIE PENTECOST, OSF former Executive Director of the New Opportunity School for Women

"A brilliant and beautiful account of tragedy followed by the finding of home, *Rooted in Sunrise* stands as a creative and compelling metaphor of the idea that tomorrow brings newfound hope and possibilities."

—EMILY H. KEEFER, Author of *The Stars on Vita Felice Court*

"*Rooted in Sunrise* is a beautifully written debut novel by Beth Dotson Brown. When a tornado pushes Ava out of her small, but safe world, she is forced to face her regrets and fears, and forge a new path. This work of fiction has many truths that will resonate with anyone facing a crossroads in life, either chosen or forced."

—ANGELA CORRELL, Author of *Restored in Tuscany*

"Beth tells an inspirational story about perseverance, courage and the importance of family. This story will inspire you to take your own future into your hands."

—KATRINA MACKRIDES, Author of *The Salty Swan*

"*Rooted in Sunrise* follows a woman's journey in rebuilding after a tornado upends her life and leaves her questioning everything she thought her future would look like. As Ava digs through the rubble, she uncovers new possibilities afforded by the blank slate, proving that silver linings are always waiting when you have the courage and resilience to look."

—RACHEL STONE, Author of *The Blue Iris*

"*Rooted in Sunrise* is grounded in a strong sense of place (small town and rural Kentucky) and a time of life when it would be easy to slide into one's golden years. Brown brings the reader along in the journey of the protagonist as she ventures outside the confines of her physical and emotional safety, examines the choices and circumstances that led to her current situation, and charts a new course for her future. Brown also weaves threads of other female characters' arcs into a tidy story."

—JAN CAPPS, Author of *Bird's Eye View*

"Experience a tale of resilience and renewal in this captivating novel where a woman's life is uprooted by a tornado. With unforgettable characters and a comfortably paced narrative, the story beautifully explores themes of strength and community. A truly inspiring story, *Rooted in Sunrise* will stay with you long after the last page is turned."

—ANN E. LOWRY, Author of *The Blue Trunk*

"Beth's story is both motivating and inspirational! This is the very essence of the quote 'You can't change the direction of the wind, but you can adjust your sails.' An excellent read for the value of family."

—JEFFREY A. WHITE, Executive Director, The Nest - Center for Women, Children & Families

"Beth Dotson Brown has a fine talent for showcasing everyday characters and how they navigate catastrophic circumstances with solid wit. Beth's new book *Rooted in Sunrise* narrates the bonding and cohesion among women in a rural Kentucky family. A family saga that includes neighbors, *Rooted in Sunrise* is a story of coping against adversity, taking recourse in the mutual support of women, and reckoning with your childhood dreams that were hidden behind the daily routine. Everybody has dreams and talents not fulfilled. What can be done about that later in life? A tornado disaster shows Ava how to transform herself.

"*Rooted in Sunrise* is filled with succinct female characters. Along the pages, a number of women drop their masks and face the music. It's a treat to read a book with normal, real-life characters. And one of them owned that mysterious suitcase. Read the book, and find out what's in it."

—ANNELISE MAKIN, Owner, iMAKINations

Rooted in Sunrise

by Beth Dotson Brown

© Copyright 2024 Beth Dotson Brown

ISBN 979-8-88824-448-7

All rights reserved. No part of this publication may be reproduced, stored in a retrieval system, or transmitted in any form or by any means—electronic, mechanical, photocopy, recording, or any other—except for brief quotations in printed reviews, without the prior written permission of the author.

This is a work of fiction. All the characters in this book are fictitious, and any resemblance to actual persons, living or dead, is purely coincidental. The names, incidents, dialogue, and opinions expressed are products of the author's imagination and are not to be construed as real.

Published by

3705 Shore Drive
Virginia Beach, VA 23455
800-435-4811
www.koehlerbooks.com

Rooted *in* Sunrise

A Novel

Beth Dotson Brown

VIRGINIA BEACH
CAPE CHARLES

To my parents, who always encouraged me to do what would make me happy.

Chapter 1

It should have been a normal evening.

The microwave dinged, drawing Ava's attention from the steady rain outside the window. She draped a kitchen towel across her palm. The first time she'd cooked a bag of the off-brand popcorn, she'd grabbed it by the bottom and immediately dropped it, her skin a hot red where the oil seeped through. This time Ava shook the bag and delicately pulled open the top, backing away from the steam. She caught the luscious smell of butter. *Ah.* The perfect treat to help her forget the day.

She pushed on the window above the sink to make sure it was shut, then drew the curtains closed. The rain was pounding now.

It was her boss who had made her job unbearable. After all, she'd been at Kentucky Ventures for twenty years before he showed up. They did good work to help people improve their skills, health, and housing. She'd hung in there through the switch to new accounting software, the staff restructuring, and moving offices. Even at her age, she appreciated the challenge of learning.

Since the last restructuring, however, where they'd added a layer of management and hired an empty-headed boy who ran the finance department with daily basketball analogies, everything was circling the rim. This newcomer didn't understand the rules around spending federal grant dollars. Nor did he know how to motivate an experienced staff. If the board didn't do something about him, the next audit could close the agency.

But this evening, she wouldn't worry about that. She stretched out on the couch and turned on the television. If she was lucky, she might find a game show or an old movie—maybe one with Bette Davis or Audrey Hepburn.

A red ticker flowed across the bottom of the screen. Before Ava could read it, the weatherman replaced the game show. He pointed to a map of funnel cloud locations. Almost simultaneously, the rain outside became torrents, hitting the house in gusty intervals. The tornado siren erupted in the distance, and her phone buzzed, both sounds pricking an internal alarm that set her pulse pounding in her ears. She shoved her phone in her pocket, then snatched her popcorn and a knitted afghan to keep her company in the basement.

Ava hurried down the stairs. Assuming this would be a quick false alarm, she sank into her demoted couch, huddled under the afghan, and turned on her old TV. It showed a blank screen. She pulled out her phone to text Juniper. Her daughter had no TV service at the farm to warn her. Ava hit SEND and willed the message to go through. Instead, NOT DELIVERED glared at her.

Debris pummeled the small basement windows. Then the lights went out. Ava felt like she couldn't breathe. She pushed deeper into a corner of the couch and put a pillow over her head. Something upstairs shattered. The house trembled, shaking her with it. She couldn't help thinking that if it all came down on her, no one would find her beneath the destruction.

A freight train roared overhead, a noise so loud that she covered her ears with her fists like she had as a child during thunderstorms. She braced for impact.

Then it was still.

Early twilight reached Ava in her basement hiding place. She pushed the throw aside. A damp spot from her tears grazed her hand.

Ava's pulse continued to reverberate in her ears. She took a deep breath, then another.

Rain tapped overhead. A lavender haze settled in her mind, the same haze she worked through every morning to determine whether she was still dreaming or it was truly time to get out of bed. But it wasn't morning, and she wasn't in her bedroom.

She pinched the skin on her forearm. It was what she had done at her mother's funeral to confirm that she, Ava, was still walking the earth even as she felt absent from her body. The slight pain jarred her senses, sharpening the smell of spring rain that she shouldn't have been able to detect through closed windows.

She clutched the pillow to her chest as she climbed the stairs, taking cautious steps and then stopping to listen. A pitter-patter persisted though the torrents were gone. She stepped, then stopped, stepped, then stopped, until she reached the top and tentatively emerged into the kitchen.

The space that had been the kitchen.

The rain drizzled on her face as she looked up. The roof was gone. At her feet, ripped vinyl flooring stood upright. She absorbed every inch of the scene before her, taking baby steps around the piles of rubble.

Ava turned in a circle, an invisible rope tightening around her throat as she absorbed the new landscape. Only the southwest triangle of her house remained. She let out a small cry when she saw that the rolltop desk her grandfather had bought at an auction so many years ago stood untouched in the corner. Next to it, a striped burgundy-and-ivory curtain hung from a now vertical rod still held up by one nail.

Everything else in the main floor had been toppled or carried away to someone else's street, someone else's yard, someone else's life. She used the pillow to wipe her face, then hugged it tighter.

A picnic basket lay on its side where her television had stood. She'd never owned such a thing. She pictured Dorothy Gale in her flying house, holding Toto close with one arm and using the other hand to fling Auntie Em's belongings to the ground in hopes that lightening the load could somehow save her.

Maybe she had a point.

Ava hurried back down the steps to trade the pillow for the afghan. Upstairs, she covered her grandfather's desk with it. She then stepped around the remaining corner and into the littered yard. Her feet, clad in yellow slippers, sank into a cold puddle.

Ava clasped her palms together to calm their shaking. Her eyes darted here and there until she closed them, overwhelmed by the destruction. But she had to open them. She couldn't just stand there in the rain, light as it was. When she opened her eyes, they landed on her car, which appeared untouched.

The sirens blared: one, then two, and then Ava couldn't tell how many or where they were coming from. Police, life squads, fire crews—they must all be scouring Lexington for those in immediate danger.

Ava searched her property for any stubborn item that might have refused to go. A leather-covered photo album had landed next to a puddle, which rippled in the slight wind. She didn't recognize it. Picking it up, she opened the cover. There was Bernadette O'Donnell as a young woman, adjusting her wedding veil. They had gone to school together, and the O'Donnells lived a mile or so away. The album's presence didn't bode well for their home. Ava carried it to the back seat of her car and put it on the floorboard to deliver later.

She walked the perimeter of her house's foundation. The shrubs were gone, leaving behind lonely patches of dirt. The one tree she and her husband had planted, when Juniper was five, sprawled on its side, roots exposed. Ava had a deep urge to lie down next to it and hug it, to pause and take in the reality before her, comforted by the one thing that might have some of its previous life yet flowing through it; but Connie and Marvin Gaines were approaching with the pitying expressions of neighbors who weren't friends and still had a house.

"Helluva thing, Ava," Marvin said, crossing his arms over his chest. "You and the Pedigos. No one else on the street touched besides a few shingles blown off."

Ava turned to see that the house catty-corner to her backyard was gone. The Pedigos must not have been home. They weren't out and surveying the debris in their yard.

She looked up the street and wondered if anyone there would miss her. In her grandparents' time, the neighbors would've come together to help her rebuild. That was not how it worked anymore. Marvin would offer a bid on rebuilding. Larry McBride would ask to see her insurance to determine whether he could do better with a new policy. Perhaps Ellen and Louise Slater would offer a few pots and pans they no longer used. But there wouldn't be a frame-raising party or the offer of a room to stay in until her home was complete.

Ava had lived on the street for twenty-six years. Now that her house was gone, it didn't feel a bit like home.

"I'm so sorry, honey," Connie said. She'd put on her face like she always did before leaving the house. The woman had kept one makeup company after another in business for years. Ava wondered if Connie had considered that makeup wasn't required in the aftermath of a natural disaster.

"How are you taking it, Ava?" Connie said. She stepped closer and put her hand on Ava's arm.

"Apparently I'm homeless and possession-less, except for the desk and anything I might find around the yard."

"I don't know how you're holding it together," Connie said.

Ava felt her eyes narrow at her neighbor. She couldn't take back the reaction. Connie stepped away and bit her lip, maybe stopping herself from saying something else in the midst of obliteration that she would then realize was stupid.

"We can help," Marvin offered, spreading his arms to encompass the yard. "Looking for anything in particular?"

"Anything that's mine. But I'll take care of it. I appreciate you stopping by."

Marvin nudged Connie back toward their house. His wife ignored him and pointed at Ava's feet.

"You must be freezing with those wet slippers. What size do you wear?"

Ava looked down at the dirty, soaked yellow fuzzies. It would be easier to walk if the mud weren't sucking at her slippers with each step.

"Size six."

Connie gazed around the yard and nodded. "I'll find something and be back."

Left alone, Ava wished she had her throw wrapped around her like a papoose.

In the basement, she had been sure the wind would pull her up into its vortex. However, nothing in the basement went. Thanks to Donovan, she was still alive.

When they'd checked out houses, Ava and Donovan had been married for two years. Juniper was on the way, and Donovan insisted they couldn't bring her home to an apartment. They needed a house with a backyard and a basement to provide shelter from tornadoes. Ava found another house she liked better, one with a loft that would be ideal for Juniper's high school parties. Donovan said no. He insisted on a storm shelter.

He'd been gone for eleven years, yet he had saved her life.

Ava registered the louder sirens. She ignored them and squished over to the fallen tree. Something blue was lodged between the cracked branches. She skirted broken plates and an iron skillet, none of which were hers, and discovered a suitcase. She dragged it toward her, bending a branch but not breaking it.

Wet leaves clung to the blue leather American Tourister, circa 1980 or so. Her older cousin, Lizzie, had received a set for her high school graduation. This one's tag showed a name she didn't recognize, but maybe there was someplace for Ava to turn it in so the owner could locate it. And if not, there might be clothes inside that fit her.

Clothes. She had no idea what she would wear to work the next day. The day before, Ava had worn her oldest blouse and pants, all but daring one of the younger women to mention her appearance.

"Ma'am, do you need a place to stay tonight?"

Ava turned toward a police officer who was neatly turned out in his dark shirt and trousers, not a hair out of place in his short black mane. The tornado had clearly skipped over him. Beyond him, people milled around on the street, staring at the pile of splintered lumber and memories in her yard but not walking onto the property.

Ava's attention returned to the officer.

"Maybe. I don't know. I need to call my daughter."

He nodded and handed her a card with a phone number on it.

"Do you have a phone?"

"That's one thing I took with me," Ava said, patting her front pocket. She pointed toward the hole leading to her basement. "Do you think it's safe to go down there? I came up that way. I might be able to find clothes, at least."

"Let me see if I can get some firemen up here to check it out. I wouldn't want to send you down there without knowing."

Ava appreciated his effort and hoped he would hurry. Dusk was creeping onto the scene, not content to let the storm get the last hurrah of the day.

"The vultures will come with the dark," Ava said to herself. Enough had already been taken from her; she wouldn't let them take anything else.

Chapter 2

Juniper answered the phone after three rings.

"My text didn't go through. Are you okay?"

"Sure, why wouldn't I be?"

The pulsing in Ava's ears slowed. One worry unfounded.

"Do you have someone out at your place who can bring a pickup truck to haul your grandpa's rolltop desk?"

"Why, Mom? I thought you liked it."

"It's the only thing left, Juni. The tornado got the house."

Ava heard nothing from her daughter.

"Are you there, Juni?"

Juniper's voice came back louder, pushed to the edge between speaking and screaming.

"The tornado got our house? You didn't tell me that first?"

"It did, and that's done. I want the desk, which is the one intact thing left except whatever's in the basement. On a night like this, there's bound to be looters out, and I won't leave them the desk."

Ava felt her voice waver as the tears gathered in her throat. She wouldn't turn into a slobbering mess while talking with her daughter.

"Are you okay, Mom?"

"I'm not hurt. I just want my desk. And to know you're okay, which is what it sounds like."

There was silence, a deep breath, Juniper ratcheting down to speaking volume.

"We had wind and rain, no catastrophes. We're fine. I'll get

Washington's truck and be right there. And I guess I'll bring him with me. It's probably heavy."

Ava cleared her throat. "Thank you, Juni. I don't plan to go anywhere."

After she hung up, Ava wondered if Juniper interpreted that to mean her mom wanted to stay in that spot, to continue living there. It might be hard for Juniper to lose her homeplace. Nonetheless, Mother Nature's wicked sister had snatched it away.

At least Juniper's farm was safe. She was buying it with four friends who had started a farming cooperative. It seemed to Ava more like a hippie commune than a business, except that she didn't really know the difference between a co-op and a commune. When Juniper first got involved, Ava thought it must be for the love of Washington. But as far as Ava could tell, he had stayed firmly in the ex-boyfriend camp while offering his mechanical and building expertise to improve the long-neglected property.

As for the business, she admired the kids' gumption, their ability to imagine beyond every problem they encountered to the day when they could all afford health insurance and vacations. She'd expected that with her good college education, Juniper would graduate to a traditional steady job. Still, Ava trusted her daughter to decide for herself what to do with her life.

There was Connie Gaines heading Ava's way again, shoes and socks in hand and a towel over her bony shoulder. This time Marvin stayed in the street, talking with Louise Slater while tracking Connie. Connie's eyes roved the property, then focused on Ava.

"Here you go, Ava. Sit down and put these on so you don't get sick." Connie touched her hand to Ava's back and guided her to the tree, where she could sit. Mud splattered Connie's rain boots.

Ava pulled off the mucky slippers and left them on the ground. She used the towel to clean off her feet as best she could, digging in between each toe like she did when she got out of the shower. Then she squinted at the white shoes and white socks.

"Connie, if I put those on, I'll ruin them. Look at this yard. They'll be covered with mud."

"Oh, honey, it doesn't matter. Sometimes things get ruined, but they aren't as important as the rescue."

Ava turned that sentence over in her mind and wondered what Connie knew about rescues. She also wondered at her age. Maybe sixty, though it was hard to tell with the makeup.

A big gray pickup parked at the curb, and Juniper jumped out. She glanced at her mother, then stared at their remaining corner, paralyzed, unable to tear her eyes from the devastation. Ava thanked Connie and crossed over to Juniper, flinging her arms around the young woman.

To Ava, Juniper was five again, crying over the inflatable pool that had sprouted a leak. Ava rocked her as she sobbed, smoothing the frizzy curls that poured onto her shoulders.

Then Juniper was thirteen, incredulous at the idea of her father leaving for Colorado—until the day he got in the car and drove away.

And now she was twenty-five, unable to bear the loss of her childhood home.

Only a mother's love could dam Ava's own tears so she could steady her weeping daughter. As long as Ava had Juniper, the world would be okay.

When Juniper finally pulled away, she wiped her face on her sleeve and kept her eyes on her mother's as if afraid to let them stray to the fatally wounded house. "The desk?"

"This way."

They walked together over the garbage-strewn yard and onto the floor of the former living room. Ava removed the afghan and folded it. The desk stood solid as always, like nothing had changed.

Washington rolled a blue dolly up to it.

"Well, look at that. You must have all sorts of tools out at that farm," Ava said.

"We'll get it, Mrs. Winston. And anything else you want us to take. We've got an extra bedroom to set you up in."

Juniper and Washington studied the desk from various angles and moved the dolly from one place to another. Juniper was five foot eight, and Washington towered over her with beautiful posture that enhanced his muscular shoulders. Ava felt better about the farm, knowing he was there.

They loaded the desk onto the dolly and wheeled it down the front sidewalk with Ava following.

"They gave me a number to call for a place to stay," Ava said, holding out the card the police officer had given her.

"Mom, you're coming with us. I know you think the farm is a freak factory, but we want you there. No arguing."

When Juniper got that look, Ava knew further words were useless.

"Excuse me, ma'am." A fireman wearing a yellow jacket approached her on the sidewalk. "You wanted something from your basement?"

"I'd be happy to find clothes down there since my closet is gone. Is it safe enough?"

"I checked it out. It's fine, but make it quick. Someone will be here tomorrow to help you get the rest."

Ava motioned to Juniper to follow her, but barely a step down, Ava halted as if she had glue on the soles of her shoes.

Juniper stopped behind her.

"Mom? He said make it quick."

Ava sensed that this was what it was like for a victim to return to the scene of a crime, fear senselessly blocking progress. Another tornado wasn't going to blow in while they were down there. A deafening roar would not sweep in and take the basement. She had to summon her common sense, make herself move, and find what she needed, then get out of there.

Juniper stepped around Ava to continue down. Ava followed.

"What should I look for?" Juniper said. She reached for the pillow on the couch and tucked it under her arm.

"I should have one of those plastic tubs with clothes in it. It'll be labeled. They might be summer clothes, but that'll have to do."

Ava stared at the shelves Donovan had built, which were filled with orderly plastic tubs. She leaned closer to read the labels in the fading light: Christmas tree, Christmas ornaments, Christmas lights. Albums. Tax records. Pitchers.

Juniper stood next to her mom, peering into the same shelves. "Are those photo albums?"

"Record albums."

"I remember you playing them when I was little." Juniper pulled the tub off the shelf, put it on the floor, and snapped open the top. She flipped through a few square cardboard album covers before replacing the lid. "We'll take these. We have a turntable at the farm. You can listen if you want."

Ava hadn't owned a turntable for years. A hippie farm did seem like a logical place to find one.

Next Juniper pulled out the pitcher tub. "These are Grandma's, right?"

Ava nodded.

"They go too. We don't want anyone taking them."

"I can't wear a pitcher to work. I need clothes, Juni. I hope I didn't throw them out in a fit because they were too tight."

"Are they behind something?"

Juniper removed a box to search behind it. It was too dark to make out anything except a general shape.

"Is that your safe, Mom? The one with all your papers?"

Ava glanced over Juniper's shoulder. Her head was throbbing.

"I'll need that," she said as Juniper scooted it out.

There were too many boxes, too many decisions. The boxes jumbled together as if Ava were seeing the scene through a kaleidoscope. She stepped back and found a tub to sit on. Dropping her head into her hands, she closed her eyes, not sure how much longer she could hold it together.

A light brightened the storage space. Washington stood behind them, shining a flashlight at the stack of bins.

Juniper pushed a few more tubs out of the way. Finally, Ava spotted the clothes bin. That was all she needed—maybe all she wanted.

By the time they got to the farmhouse, it was going on nine o'clock. They put the tubs and the desk in the guest room on the first floor. The only furniture already in the room was an iron-framed twin bed.

Ava took in the kitchen, with its old-fashioned wooden cabinets painted butter yellow and a deep two-sided sink. It was the kind of house Ava's parents had gone to college to get away from. Get a college education and don't come back to the farm, her grandfather had told her dad. Her mom had heard much the same at home. Education and a neat ranch-style house defined progress for her grandparents' generation.

Ava was glad of it because she had never been able to grow anything in her yard, even flowers. If she'd had to raise her own food, she would have starved by now, and Juniper would never have made it to adulthood. Had Donovan possessed a green thumb, they still would have been in trouble. All the peeling and chopping that went with fresh vegetables didn't appeal to Ava one bit; those tasks presented far too many opportunities to cut her fingers. She always kept bandages in her silverware drawer.

Ava did like baking. She thrived on those precise measurements of flour, sugar, and baking powder. If you followed a recipe correctly, it turned out every time.

But one couldn't live on hummingbird cake.

Ava collapsed onto the bed. The headache had dulled, and the pulse in her ears had faded somewhat. She longed for the silence of home. People mumbled in the kitchen outside the guest room. Maybe Juniper had gathered her housemates to explain why her mom was staying with them. Ava didn't want to cause problems for Juni. She would stay one night, then find somewhere else.

She stretched her limbs away from her body, pulling at her bones and muscles to open spaces between them. She'd felt this desire before, the urge to make room for her bones to breathe before they resettled into a different groove, one that might feel familiar or totally new. It was like she had flipped the TV to a new season of a show she no longer recognized. Mrs. Brady had grown out her hair, and Jan got braces. Greg looked more like a man than a boy. Who were these people? It would take a while to get used to this iteration of her favorite television family.

She'd felt something similar two months after she lost the baby. Donovan had lain next to her every night, arms around her, softly singing Dean Martin tunes until she fell asleep. If he drifted off before Ava, she still listened to him. She cataloged the songs in her mental library so she could pull them out to hear on repeat until she finally drifted off.

They'd had to settle into their new season.

It happened again when they brought Juniper home from the hospital. There was so much to do, and Ava knew she was the worst mother in the universe. She couldn't get the diaper changed before it was soaked or send thank-you notes to everyone who attended the shower. She didn't know how they would manage when she went back to work, which she had to do since she was the one with company health insurance for the family. Donovan was exploring yet another business idea while delivering newspapers to bring in money for the house payment.

Regardless, they managed. Donovan embraced more of the parenting responsibilities. He developed the touch for getting Juniper down for her afternoon nap. And once in a while, he cooked a stew for supper.

They wrote their new season and moved on.

Twelve years later came the day when he told her about the opportunity in Colorado. Despite so many entrepreneurial failures, Donovan and his business partner convinced an investor of their potential. The man operated a marketing firm and was certain they would sell their product. Donovan wanted to sell the house, buy one in Boulder, start the life for them that he'd long promised.

The problem was that none of Donovan's business ideas had come to fruition. Ava's was the steady income. She'd been thrilled when he got the job at the grocery store; it came with benefits. It lasted until Donovan was ready to launch his electric luggage carrier, which failed within the first three months.

Besides that, Ava's vision for their life took place in Kentucky. She'd never wanted to move from Lexington. The constant for Ava during her own childhood was gathering at her grandparents' farmhouse with the rest of the family, celebrating every holiday with her cousins. A child needed family. Ava needed family.

She couldn't leave. Donovan could and did.

The channel changed, and she shifted again.

There was a knock on the guest room door. Juniper walked in. She sat on the corner by her mom's feet until Ava opened her arms and Juniper stretched out beside her. They hugged each other like they had in those months after Donovan left, trying to close that empty space. A welcome stillness overcame Ava. Juniper was all she needed.

Too soon, Juniper rolled back to her feet and stood next to the bed. Ava tugged at the cover to replace Juni's warmth.

"Do you want anything else for the night?"

"I'm not sure what I need, Juni. It's going to take some time to figure it out."

Juniper nodded, understanding in her soft eyes.

"What about you, Juni?"

Juniper took the elastic band from her wrist and pulled her thick hair back into a ponytail at the nape of her neck.

"It's a strange feeling to know it's not there anymore. Even though I have this place, it's not home in the same way."

Their house was the sole other place Juniper had lived, except for her college dorm.

Juniper shifted her weight. "I'll be doing morning chores when you wake up. Vivienne gets up a little later, so she might still be around. Anyway, help yourself to breakfast."

Ava sat up. "I need to be at work at eight."

"Mom, I don't think anyone would expect you to be at work tomorrow."

Ava considered the idea. She couldn't remember when she last missed work.

"I suppose there are other things I should do. Go back to the house, call the insurance company, that kind of thing."

"I'll be back before lunch, and I can help you with whatever," Juniper said.

She shuffled toward the door, then looked back.

"Mom, I'm so glad you weren't hurt. I don't know what . . ."

She shook her head.

"I'm here, Juni. I'm here."

Juniper nodded, her expression as solemn as it had been when her dad told her he was leaving. Ava's chest squeezed. To have a daughter was to always be connected with her heartbreak, big or small.

Juniper closed the door behind her, and Ava reached into her pocket for her phone. She needed to let her boss know she wouldn't be in.

"I NEED TO TAKE A SICK DAY TOMORROW," she texted.

She put the phone on the bed, not expecting him to respond immediately. Ava rarely contacted her boss outside of work hours. Poor health wasn't her burden in life, so she'd amassed weeks of sick days during her years with the agency. Then there was all her unused vacation time. She could probably take off a couple of months, if they allowed that sort of thing.

Her phone dinged.

"WE HAVE TWO GRANT REPORTS TO COMPLETE."

"A TORNADO BLEW MY HOUSE AWAY. I'M HOMELESS. I NEED TO TAKE A SICK DAY."

"Sorry to hear it. When will you return?"

Ava squeezed her phone to stop herself from throwing it.

"Don't know."

Ava turned off the phone and closed her eyes. Amid the room's quiet, the sounds of sirens filled her head. It didn't matter that there were none outside; they had embedded themselves. She needed to clear her mind.

She didn't have a house. Most of her belongings were gone or buried in the rubble. Surely it was a sign. But of what?

Her grandfather had been a watcher of signs. He planted by the moon. He took possible coincidences as signals that God was encouraging him in a specific direction.

"How do you know it's a sign, a real sign?" Ava had once asked him during her teen years.

He fixed her with his steady blue gaze before turning it toward the apple trees outside the window. "You have to slow down long enough to ponder. If it's a true sign, you'll know."

Ava turned onto her side and pulled her knees to her chest. Not having a house could slow her down. Or it could speed her up if she hurried to put everything back like it was.

It was up to her.

Ava snuggled into the pillow. She had only to close her eyes to feel Donovan's arms around her and hear him singing, "When the moon hits your eye like a big pizza pie, that's amore."

Light had settled softly into the day by the time Ava awoke. She eased out of bed and pulled back the gauzy curtain to see a blue sky with white cloud puffs here and there. Nary a breeze touched the massive tulip poplars standing like guardians in the yard.

Ava went to the rolltop and ran her palm along the curve of the desk, feeling each rib as she traveled from top to bottom. For half of

Ava's life, it had sat in the corner of her grandparents' living room. At four o'clock every afternoon, her grandpa came in from the farm, showered, then sat at the kitchen table for supper. Grandma joined him, along with anyone else who happened to be in the house. They all remained at the table until he had finished his dessert—either banana pudding, apple pie, or coconut cream cake. While Grandma cleaned the kitchen, he opened the top of the desk and got back to work.

Ava's earliest memories were of sitting on his lap at that desk. Sometimes she peered into the cubby holes where he stored pens, pencils, postage stamps, envelopes, receipts, writing paper, and bills. At other times, she watched him write in his diary and record his jobs for the day: "fenced the south field," "cut hay," "helped Paddy vaccinate the cows." Then he opened his ledger to record the day's purchases and bills paid. That was how Ava learned her numbers.

When Ava and Donovan bought their house, Grandpa gave her the desk. She could still smell his pipe tobacco and feel his whiskers on her cheek when he kissed her good night.

Ava pulled herself away from the rolltop. There was a lot to do. She needed a list. However, she first needed a strong booster shot for the day. *Coffee.*

A woman about Juniper's age with two thick blond braids falling over her shoulders sat at the kitchen table, scrolling through her phone.

"Coffee?" Ava asked and pointed at the girl's mug.

The girl nodded toward the counter. There sat the same complicated machine that one of Ava's coworkers had brought into the office. It required tiny plastic cups of coffee grounds that, in this case, hung neatly on a carousel, boasting names like Caramel Dream Delight, Café Italiano, Smoky Black.

"Plain black coffee. The old-fashioned stuff. Do you have any of that?"

The girl pointed to the other end of the counter.

"Washington makes it strong," she said.

"God bless him."

Ava poured a cup and sat at the table to introduce herself.

"I'm Vivienne," the girl replied.

She fit Juni's description, wearing a cheery pink apron and red lipstick as if a television crew would show up to film her as she made the farm's value-added products. Vivienne had developed a menu of miniature quiches that they sold to a handful of Lexington restaurants. Next, she intended to concoct jams.

"Are you cooking today?" Ava said.

"Yes. It's also time for the health inspectors to come around, so I need to make sure the kitchen is up to standards. Not my favorite part of the job, but no one else wants to do it."

Ava sipped her coffee and wondered how well Vivienne fit in with the other partners.

"Do you work on the farm?"

"I take care of the chickens. The eggs are my responsibility from conception to table." Vivienne pursed her lips. "Don't worry yourself. We have it together here."

Ava mentally threw up her hands. She hadn't intended to pry; she simply wanted to make conversation. Maybe Vivienne mainly conversed via technology and didn't have in-person conversational manners.

"Do you have a pen and paper? I need to get myself organized."

The curvy young woman went to the drawer under the coffee pot and returned with a Farmers for Life notepad and a pen in Kentucky blue. Vivienne picked up her phone again. Ava created her list.

Call insurance company.

Call HR for leave of absence.

Locate Bernadette O'Donnell.

Find a place to stay.

Return suitcase to owner.

Ava stepped back into the guest room to call human resources, though she had no illusion that the room gave her privacy. She sensed in Vivienne the kind of woman who listened to every conversation, then put her own spin on it.

Ava wasn't concerned about the work going undone while she was out of the office. She'd been training Shadiqua on reporting, and they had the drafts completed for the two grants that were due. Shadiqua could handle it without her.

"We've never had an employee who lost her house to a natural disaster," Mrs. Alvarado said.

"I should have enough sick and vacation time to take a month or two. How long does the agency allow?"

"It's three months for family leave. However, it does depend on the circumstances. I don't know if that applies in your situation. I'll look into it and call you back this afternoon."

Ava disconnected and threw her phone on the bed. If a long-loyal employee needed time off, the company should provide it, no questions asked. This wasn't a time for anyone to tell her what she could and could not do. This was real life, her real life—a life blown away that she'd have to figure out how to restore or rebuild, or maybe invent anew, no matter how much time it took.

Conversation on the other side of the door drew Ava back to the kitchen. Juniper, Washington, and Vivienne had gathered around a few envelopes on the kitchen table. Juniper opened one and held up a check.

"Our first subscriber!"

Vivienne laughed. Juniper and Washington exchanged high-fives.

Washington picked up another envelope, opened it, and waved it above his head. "And our second."

Juniper turned to Vivienne. "Have you checked our account?"

Vivienne picked up her phone and went through a few screens before she looked at them and laughed. "Two more here. We really are in business!"

Ava watched them join hands and dance, swirling in a circle like a strengthening whirlpool. She could imagine the three of them as carefree children playing in a sprinkler under the summer sun.

Vivienne spotted Ava. "Maybe you brought us good luck."

Juniper bounded over to her mother and hugged her. "It's happening, Mom. We really have a business. We have people who want us to deliver vegetables to them this summer!"

Ava wondered who she could recruit to add to their subscribers.

Ava checked in with emergency management headquarters to locate Bernadette O'Donnell. She also asked about Natalya Kerminskaya, the name on the suitcase. They didn't have her listed.

She found Bernadette at the Circle Road Inn, sitting on the motel's second-floor balcony and staring at the parking lot. Ava called to her and held up the photo album.

"I found something that's yours."

"Come up," Bernadette said, pointing toward the stairs at the end of the building.

It wasn't the sort of place Ava would have pictured the O'Donnells. The family lived in a large two-story house on one of the nicest streets in Lexington. Their two oldest children, a boy and a girl, were on their own. They still had a daughter in college and two sons in high school. Ava didn't see any of them around.

"I heard it hit you too," Bernadette said when Ava reached her. They hugged, and Ava handed her the album. Bernadette's eyes moistened.

"Well, I never."

She opened the cover to the first page and ran her palm across it.

"Not even much water damage. God must have wanted me to have this."

Ava settled into the second plastic chair on the balcony. Country music and the smell of cigarettes wafted from below.

Bernadette's dark hair was styled and sprayed as always, yet she had dark rings around her eyes from her runny mascara.

"Where's your family?"

"The boys went to school. They couldn't wait to tell their big tornado story. Joe insisted on going to the office. Erin was at the university, so she hasn't seen it yet. Sheila was with me earlier. She's my sweetheart. Knows when her mama doesn't want to be alone."

"And Patrick?" Ava asked, knowing he and his wife lived next door to Bernadette.

"He's repairing his ruined roof. He lost a third of it or more. It's okay because we're all safe."

Bernadette sniffled and pulled a handkerchief from her pocket. It had been years since Ava had seen one of those, maybe since the two of them were in elementary school together at St. Agatha's. Bernadette's had an edge tatted in pink.

"No, actually, it's not okay," Bernadette said. She cleared her throat. "I sit here and I imagine our house as it was when we moved in. I was pregnant with Patrick. I wasn't like you, Ava, or so many of our classmates who went to college. All I ever wanted was to raise a family and care for them, make a comfortable home and a beautiful life for the people I love. I knew Joe and I would grow old in that house with all of our memories of where the kids took their first steps. And now . . ."

Bernadette let the tears flow, and Ava gave her the time. Ava had never pictured that for herself—living in her house as an old woman with memories. She hadn't truly visualized her life beyond Juniper graduating from college. Maybe that was why she'd been frustrated at work. She didn't know if she was where she should be.

Bernadette sniffled and wiped her eyes with her handkerchief. "You know Linda Mueller lives next to me?"

Ava squirmed in the chair, trying to get comfortable. The hard plastic pushed into her back, annoying her much as her memories of Linda Mueller.

"She of the perfect ninth-grade English scores? The one who never shows up at class reunions and isn't at church except on Christmas?"

"She's still spritzed with gold. The storm gave her one broken window. That's it. She'll probably turn that into a scene for her next book."

"How many has she written now?"

"I haven't kept up. Twenty? Thirty?"

Ava shook her head. While Linda had been raising two children and writing books, what had Ava done? It felt like nothing, absolutely nothing.

Bernadette dabbed at her nose. "Will you rebuild?"

The insurance company still had to visit the site, but they'd already told Ava her policy would cover at least a portion of rebuilding. Or she could take the money and go elsewhere, maybe not even buy. She could rent until she made a decision. That would remove lawn maintenance from Ava's chore list. It would certainly leave more time for sitting at her grandfather's desk, waiting for a sign to guide her.

"I don't know, Bernadette. Building takes months and so many decisions. I don't know if I want to spend my energy on that. I might be better off looking for where I want to spend the second half of my life, which is probably in a different neighborhood."

"Joe's contacting builders today. We'll be back, but we need to find a place in the meantime. The boys are in the room next door, and I do not trust them to be even that little bit on their own." She threw up her hands and motioned at the space around her. "I can't do this for a year."

"I might be your neighbor soon. I stayed at Juniper's last night. I'm sure I'm in her way. I don't want to cause her problems."

Bernadette nodded.

"What does Juniper think about rebuilding?"

"I didn't ask."

Ava had left the question intentionally untouched. She wasn't ready for that conversation.

"Maybe you should come with me to my place, Bernadette—see if anything else there is yours."

Bernadette stood. "I'll feel better if I do something." She looked at the parking lot, then back at Ava. "Did you say something about the second half of your life? Are you planning to live another fifty years?"

Ava rose as well. "I don't see why not. I'm healthy. I'll be happy, too, if I can figure out what to do with myself. Anyway, you follow me to the house, and we can sift away."

Bernadette turned to go inside for her purse.

"Wait a minute. I forgot something," Ava said. She pulled a slip of paper from her pocket. "Do you know someone named Natalya Kerminskaya? I found a suitcase in my yard, and her name was on the tag."

Bernadette went pale beneath her curls, but her expression didn't change.

"Natalya?"

"Kerminskaya."

"I don't believe I've ever met anyone by that name. Surely I would have remembered."

Ava hesitated, waiting for Bernadette to say more. The other woman remained silent.

"If you come across her, let me know. I'd like to return the suitcase."

As Ava pulled up to the curb, she spotted a person lying on the downed tree, their arms hugging the trunk. Juniper's strawberry-blond hair draped to the side. She lay on her stomach, her head turned so her cheek could feel the bark. Ava wasn't close enough to see tears or to hear whether Juniper was talking to the tree.

Juniper's victory at the farm wasn't enough to ease the pain of her loss.

Ava swallowed hard. This loss would hit Juniper differently. Ava's intelligent, courageous daughter was so much more sentimental than Ava had ever been. And this was her childhood home. It held her firsts, along with the daily meals and baths and their holiday celebrations—and their losses. Of course the destruction pierced her at her core.

Ava glanced in her rearview mirror. There was Bernadette, pulled up behind her and waiting for Ava to get out of the car. Ava stepped out into a damp, not-quite-muddy yard.

"Help yourself," Ava said. She motioned to the heaps of belongings scattered among bricks and shingles.

Bernadette nodded toward Juniper. "I see you have someone else to tend to. I'll be fine on my own."

Ava slogged through the yard to Juniper, who hadn't moved. She whispered Juni's name and put her palm on her daughter's back.

Juniper remained so still that if Ava hadn't felt her lungs expanding and emptying, she would have shaken her to make sure she was alive.

Juniper stirred and sat up. Ava took a seat next to her.

"Mom, will you rebuild exactly as it was?"

Her voice was so quiet, so faint. She sounded like a little girl again. Still, her words froze Ava. *Exactly as it was? No.* That was a world away from what she was thinking.

"I would like it to be the same," Juniper said.

"I don't know, Juniper. The insurance company will visit, then tell me what they can do."

"Dad's coming. He wants to see it."

Ava stiffened. Donovan had come for Juniper's college graduation, with his sisters, but outside of phone calls regarding Juniper, the two of them hadn't had a moment alone since he left. His absence from her life relieved Ava of the anxiety she felt every time she thought about him. There was an unease about the end of their relationship that had heightened over the years; the farther she got from their marriage, the more she wondered whether their decision to divorce—her decision to divorce—was the wrong one.

Nonetheless, they had split, and that was that. If the tornado was a sign to start a new season of her life, she didn't want someone from seasons past trespassing. Even if it was her first, and maybe only, true love.

"I found a kettle," Bernadette called across the yard. She held it up like a trophy, then pulled her handkerchief from her pocket and wiped the dirt from her kettle.

Juniper gazed at the scene as if seeing their home as it had been.

"We had a good life here. It was a happy place to grow up," she said.

"Who was that girl down the street who you insisted was your long-lost sister during middle school?"

"Luisa Morales. Oh, what a good friend she was. I missed her so much when she moved."

"We all move on."

It landed between them like a seed that neither of them chose to water. At least, not yet.

Chapter 3

Bernadette glowed as she held out the box of items she'd found in the yard. Ava rose to meet her, leaving Juni on the tree.

Among other things, the box held white wedding china, all of which was broken except for one delicate tea cup that hadn't even lost its handle. Bernadette picked up one of the broken pieces, saying she would make a mosaic in her new home. Then there were the candlesticks Patrick brought back from Ireland. Bernadette carried the box to her car and returned to find Ava holding forth a green sweater that was soaked through and caked with dirt.

"Look at it, Ava. You might think it's ruined, but not to worry. I'm going to save it. I wore that for Kevin's Eagle Scout ceremony."

Bernadette twisted it until water dripped just beyond her toes before carefully folding it.

Ava had no desire to find the trail of her own belongings. At least Juniper hadn't expressed an interest in that.

"Ava, Bernadette," Connie called as she crossed the street. In all the years Ava had lived there, the only other time she could remember Connie and Marvin in her yard was when they all lost power during a snowstorm the year Juniper was fourteen. Now it was three times in forty-eight hours, and today, Connie was solo.

"Come over to the house and have something to drink. It's the least I can do."

"I appreciate it, Connie, but no," Bernadette said. "Now that I've found at least part of the path, I intend to follow it to see what else

I can recover."

Bernadette headed to her car with the sweater. Connie followed, opening the door to the back seat and pulling out a plastic shopping bag for Bernadette to place the sweater in.

"Ava, you coming?" Bernadette said.

"You go on," Ava said.

"Do you want something to drink?" Connie offered Ava.

"No, though I appreciate the offer," Ava said.

Connie approached anyway, phone in hand. "What's your number, Ava? I'll need to get your slippers back to you."

Ava gave her the number, and Connie hurried back to Bernadette's car, apparently not content to return to the safe arms of her own whole home.

Ava's phone jingled. It was Mrs. Alvarado.

"Ava, I can get you six weeks, but your boss is asking that you either come in for a final training with Shadiqua or be on call to answer her questions."

That man. She thought she'd already made it clear that Shadiqua could handle the work.

"I can answer her questions; it's not a problem. What if I need more than six weeks? Between my sick time and vacation time, I have at least eight I could take."

"Come in this week, and we'll take care of the paperwork, whenever it's convenient for you. I am sorry, Ava."

Ava shifted and sighed.

"I appreciate that. The problem isn't you. I understand."

"Is there any way we can help?"

"Let Shadiqua do the work. She's a brilliant young woman."

Ava slid the phone into her pocket and realized her neck had stiffened during the conversation. She dropped her head to the right, to her left, then rolled her shoulders.

Juniper remained perched on the tree trunk, glowering at what had been their home. Ava decided to forge ahead with the painful truth, even if her daughter didn't want to hear it.

She settled next to Juniper. She wove her fingers together, then pulled them apart.

"Juniper, I don't know if I want to rebuild."

Juniper whipped her head toward her mother, her brown eyes staring as if at a stranger.

"Why not? It's our place, our home."

Her voice cracked, and Ava made herself stop, made herself think before she responded. She didn't want to further break her daughter's heart. Yet she couldn't promise what Juniper wanted.

"It was our home. Look at it, baby. It is no more. It's gone."

They both looked at the one remaining corner. It would never be what it had been.

Ava turned back to Juniper. "Maybe it's time for me to move on to something else."

"Something else? What are you talking about, Mom?"

Juniper jumped to her feet and faced her mother. Her emotions colored her cheeks.

"If you wanted to move on to something else, then we could have gone with Dad to Colorado all those years ago."

There it was, the one thing between them that would continually be the rock in Ava's shoe. Juniper had eventually understood that the choice to stay was her mother's. Her father had always wanted them.

"It was complicated. You're old enough to understand that now."

"Mom, you're afraid to go anywhere. You won't get on a plane. You've never driven farther than a state away. That's why we didn't go with Dad. That's what I can see from my adult point of view. Is there any chance the tornado blew away all your ridiculous fears?"

Ava pulled in a breath that felt more like a pitchfork to her center. *Ridiculous fears.* Maybe they were ridiculous. Still, she didn't want her daughter jabbing that pitchfork.

"I hope it did blow them all away. I hope it blew some kind of courage into you so you'll do something that will make you happy.

Do you think I can't see how much you hate your job?"

Ava blinked three times, then turned a puzzled expression to her daughter. She rarely mentioned work to Juniper.

"How did you pick up on that?"

"We have dinner together every Sunday night. Or we did."

Juniper again glanced at the absence before turning back toward her mom, her hands on her hips.

"When I get to the house, you're so happy. You've baked a fabulous Mom dessert, you're buzzing with all the news about Aunt Lila or Fawn or Uncle Jarvis. You ask me all about the farm, and we eat a good meal. By the time I'm ready to go home, by the time you realize Monday's coming, you've transformed into this expressionless zombie."

"Maybe that's because I look forward to seeing you, so when you're going home, it's a letdown."

"I'm not it. It's the idea that in less than twenty-four hours, you'll have to go back to work. And you don't want to. Maybe if you had applied for the management job, you wouldn't be so unhappy."

It was true that Ava thought she could do a better job than that man. And she should have applied, yet at the time, she didn't realize her years at the agency had helped her develop the skills she needed to lead the work. If she had been part of the inner circle, if she'd had a champion at the agency, someone would have pointed that out to her. They would have invited her to apply.

Juniper took a long, slow breath and recomposed herself. She dropped her arms to her sides.

"This isn't all about your job. It's about the house. You'll still need a home, Mom. We'll need a home. Our home would make me happy."

Ava intertwined her fingers again and pulled them apart.

"Juni, you have a home on your farm. And you'll always have a home wherever I am. I don't know where that will be."

Juniper stared at Ava, shrugged, then headed to her car. Ava rose, her daughter's anger lingering like a too-hot breeze. Ava wanted to stop her, to refresh things before Juniper drove off. Yet if the only way to make things right was to agree to rebuild, she couldn't do that.

Juniper drove away. *Oh, Juniper.* That girl was the best thing Ava had done in her life—the center of her existence, the reason she had gotten out of bed for so many years.

Without her, what would life be?

They'd gone through the slow, natural separation that happened when a child headed off to college, but even that didn't change much about their dynamic. Ava had felt so lucky when Juniper decided to begin her independent adulthood at home instead of moving across the country. Although Juni continued to grow her autonomy, Ava was still a part of her life. She always would be to some degree.

This decision shouldn't determine that degree.

A moving van pulled into Juniper's spot. Two men emerged. They scanned the remains on the lot, then spotted Ava and strode her way.

"Hello, ma'am. Is this yours?"

Ava nodded. "All that's left is in the basement."

"We're here to move it to a storage facility for you. They're giving you three months free." The man handed her a card with the name and address of the storage facility, plus a unit number and a key. "If you can meet us there, we'll deliver all of it."

Ava studied the men, clean cut and in their sixties. They didn't appear to be thieves. Still, scammers loved disaster zones.

"Why? I mean, it's not your stuff. And that's a lot of work."

The taller man laughed lightly. "Makes us feel good, I suppose. We volunteer through our church, First Southern Praise House." He reached into his pocket and pulled out another card for Ava. "We'd be happy for you to join us on Sunday."

Ava read the address. She had seen that church. Apparently, she'd been lucky enough to get true love-your-sister volunteers rather than grifters.

"I appreciate that, but I do already have a church."

"Not a problem, ma'am. You're still welcome."

With that, four other people appeared. They all trooped into the basement, and the leader put them each to work in different parts of the remaining space. Ava wondered if she should help, though truthfully, she might not want all of what was down there. After all, it was there because she didn't use it. Maybe she should leave it to ruin. But they were already carrying up the first tubs. She followed them to the curb.

Ava looked at her car. She had nowhere to be. They weren't expecting her at work. No dishes were waiting in the kitchen sink. She could go wherever she wanted, do whatever she wanted, for at least six weeks.

Ava got in her car and typed the storage facility address into her phone. She wasn't familiar with the street, but it didn't matter to her where it was located; she had plenty of time to get there. Instead of following the directions, she meandered through the neighborhood until it morphed into another.

Away from her house, the city seemed largely as it had two days earlier. A woman with a mass of red hair got out of her car in front of Gillian's Music. Ava wondered if she was going in to choose an instrument, to take up playing something she'd never touched, or maybe to dust off her old skills. Ava admired musicians, but it wasn't a talent she'd ever discovered in herself.

On the playground of the elementary school, children scampered, their high-pitched shouts and laughter seeping through her barely opened car window like a sip of hot chocolate. Ava would like to find the adult version of that kind of abandon. She couldn't remember the last time she had been consumed by something that was so much fun that she lost track of where she was or the time of day.

Children naturally knew how to escape.

At the stoplight, a teenager walking a fat dog tugged impatiently at the leash. Maybe Ava needed a pet. Donovan had been allergic, or so he said, and it wasn't something she felt strongly enough about to fight. In a new place, she might want a spunky companion, the right puppy, or a soft, playful kitten.

Ava wandered through neighborhoods she rarely visited. She perused the 1950s brick homes on one street and wondered what life would be like inside. She didn't need much space for one person, so a smaller place might feel cozy. Did a house retain some spirit of its original owners? She wasn't thinking of ghosts so much as a feeling—maybe a room that encouraged rest or a kitchen where Ava would feel like trying new recipes because the chef of the house had left behind a creative essence.

After her mother died when Ava was a teenager, Ava's father moved them into a house in an older, established neighborhood like this. The new place wasn't smaller than the house William and Jeannie had bought when Ava was starting school, but it was different, a place to start a life without the person who had brought them sunshine daily. William moved into the smallest bedroom and gave the largest one to Ava's little brother, Jarvis. He was still in middle school and had a race car set with a track that filled the spacious floor.

The house never felt like home to Ava. Jeannie had been the creative one, the fun one, the one everyone wanted to be around. When Ava and Jarvis were little, Jeannie would take them on what she called big adventures—walks through the woods where they hunted for Big Foot's tracks but usually ended up tracking deer or the occasional fox. It didn't matter what they pursued because Jeannie made it fun.

Even on rainy days, when they stayed in the house, Jeannie found something for them to do. They made face paint (was that out of face cream and food coloring?) and became animals, clowns, trees, and flowers. When William came home, he had to guess what each of them were. They turned the house into a museum by creating paintings and sculptures, grouping them by theme, then displaying them in each room. Everything with her mom had been fun.

But then she and two girlfriends booked a private plane to a resort in Missouri. It was supposed to be a birthday celebration. They crashed on a farm in western Kentucky, and the three of them, along with the pilot, all died.

Juniper called Ava's fears silly. She couldn't understand the way that accident debilitated the teenage girl who remained.

Their dad had lasted another twelve years, long enough to get both of his children through college, to see Ava married, to witness the birth of his granddaughter. Losing Jeannie left William without his spark. He kept his family safely on the ground, never driving above the speed limit or allowing a utility or house payment to be late. When he had to fly for work, he checked the safety rating of the carrier and flew only on the major airlines in large planes, even when it meant driving to Louisville or Cincinnati to fly out instead of leaving from Lexington.

Jarvis had gone to college in California, met Emma and married her, then stayed in the golden sunshine. He rarely came home. Dad was gone, and Jarvis never felt the connection to the family farm that Ava did. He'd become a Californian. Since Ava refused to fly, she never visited him—hadn't attempted to drive out for his wedding. She had three California nephews who she'd never met. She contented herself with stories heard during her weekly calls with Jarvis and Emma.

A church bell rang, and Ava realized she had lost track of time. She went back to her phone to reroute herself and located the storage facility. She'd always wondered who used those places. She once heard a rumor about a large family camping out in one for months because it was cheaper than rent.

As she waited for the moving van, Ava pulled the card with the housing number from her pocket and dialed. All the available rooms were booked. They would call her when one became available.

In the meantime, she didn't want to stay in her storage unit or return to Juniper's. She could sleep in her vehicle. At sixty-three, her great-uncle Walt had sold his house and everything that couldn't fit in his car, then drove to the Navajo reservation to volunteer with the Franciscans, sleeping in his back seat along the way. Ava wouldn't be the first in the family to choose her car for temporary shelter.

She could probably drive to Cincinnati or Louisville and find a hotel room. *What would I do there? Eat alone at restaurants when I should be saving money until I make decisions about my future?*

Or she could go somewhere that always felt good to her: Aunt Lila's.

"Oh, honey, I had no idea." Aunt Lila's voice was like butter melting on freshly baked bread. "You come right over. I'll have Lizzie's room ready for you when you get here."

"That sounds like exactly what I need."

They chatted a few more minutes until the moving van pulled up with a car behind it. Ava unlocked the door to the unit, and the army of four men and two women unloaded her belongings. "Should we arrange it any way in particular?" the tall man asked.

"Any way works."

The group was so well organized that Ava couldn't have inserted herself into the flow had she tried. Quicker than she could catch up, they were stacking bins, inserting a shelf, carrying in a lamp they had wrapped in a blanket so it wouldn't break. Then they asked if she would like to join them in prayer.

The group gathered in a circle. Ava felt the people on either side encase her hands with a reassuring clasp. The man she'd spoken with previously asked them to bow their heads.

"Oh Father God, we want to thank you for the health and safety of your beloved daughter, who survived a terrible ordeal. She's here, she's healthy, and thanks to you, we're here with her. As we fulfill our task today, we ask you to continue to guide and protect our sister as she makes a new way through the coming days. You are the way, the truth, and the light that will lead her forward. In your holy name we pray."

"Amen."

After the chorus of amens, they each nodded to her reverently, as though leaving a funeral. Then they got into their vehicles while Ava stood in the doorway and stared at the hodgepodge of stuff. It was everything from the basement—enough to live on, really. There was the couch (where she'd fallen asleep plenty of times), television, end table, lamps, and recliner. There was a box of her grandmother's china, so she did have something to eat on. She even had the mini-fridge that Juniper used in college.

The rest of it, well, why did she have it? There were boxes and bins that Ava hadn't opened for years. *If it won't help me reestablish a home, what's its point?* she asked herself. Her mother might have turned those things into art or a game or boxes to give away to a local shelter. All Ava could think was that at least it hadn't ended up strewn across someone else's block like the rest of her stuff. It had the good manners to stay put.

Ava turned off the light and closed the door behind her. As the metal lock clicked into place, something inside Ava opened, a startling new space that was nearly empty, yet not quite. There was a faint tapping, of something wanting to burst out to live untamed, to spontaneously explore the world. Ava looked to the sky, almost expecting to see her own heart flying high in search of a new experience.

She turned back for another glance at the closed storage unit and pictured a flock of strangers peering inside, deciding how much to bid for what they assumed were someone's treasures. She would leave them to it while she tested how far this new feeling could take her.

Although she wanted to let things cool with Juniper, she had to return to the farm to get her few belongings. Really all she needed to retrieve was the plastic bin of clothes and that stranger's suitcase, which she had yet to open. Juni would probably let her keep the desk at her house as long as Ava didn't stay with it.

As she drove up to the farm amid the first tinge of the April dusk, the bright lights from the kitchen ahead made Ava imagine a hearty evening meal with a tableful of chattering young people. She parked and went to the kitchen door but stopped when she heard Juniper's voice. The kitchen windows were open, exchanging the evening air for the conversation.

"I don't know how long she'll be here. She's trying to figure out what she wants to do."

"What do you mean? She's an accountant, isn't she?"

It was Vivienne, derisive as she had been in the morning.

"Yes. But this has turned her world upside down. She doesn't act like herself at all. She's thinking of not rebuilding."

"She can't live here. We don't need someone coming in to tell us how to do things."

"You are so paranoid, Vivienne. Have you considered that maybe, for a change, this isn't about you? It's actually about my mom needing a place to hang while she figures things out. And it's about me. I lost my childhood home, the only home I've known outside of this place."

The voices stopped, but Ava heard what sounded like a knife hitting a cutting board. She pictured Vivienne with her blond braids swaying across her back as she chopped onions for her quiches.

"She'll calm down in a few days and go back to her job, decide to rebuild or not. What else would she do? She's old," Juniper said.

Old? From Juniper's vantage point, Ava supposed she did seem old. She was approaching her fifty-fifth birthday. *Is that old?*

She did not feel it. In fact, Ava felt younger than she had the previous week, when she was cemented to her computer, plugging numbers into spreadsheets. The cleanliness of a row of numbers used to make Ava feel like all was well in the world. She didn't know when that feeling had left her.

Something inside had shifted, and she couldn't say precisely when. She always had been a late bloomer. Maybe this milestone would be an opportunity to flower anew as she considered where to live, what to do with her life. Those questions were typically the purview of a young person. For Ava, they were much more interesting to ponder than whether the grant was on target to spend all of its money.

Ava saw a frame expanding before her, changing the unspoken

boundaries she had long lived within. Possibilities from outside could now step in where Ava might see them and claim them for herself. Maybe she could be a manager if she moved to another agency. Perhaps she could grow something if she tried it another way. Maybe she would even subscribe to the co-op's service and learn to love creating a meal from fresh produce. The possibilities were so boundless that she wasn't sure whether her frame was the average rectangle or an outrageously large octagon.

Inside the house, another voice joined Juniper's and Vivienne's. Ava knew she didn't fit into the frame Juniper had built around this portion of her life. It would be better not to insert herself again.

Ava turned to leave. She would text Juniper to tell her she'd be by tomorrow for her things. Aunt Lila would have whatever Ava required for the evening.

Aunt Lila's was the one place in the world where Ava still felt like a child, in a good way. Lila was the middle sister in her mom's family, the stabilizer between Maud, the bossy oldest, and Jeannie, the firecracker youngest. Growing up, Ava was endlessly thankful that Maud wasn't her mother.

After Ava's grandparents died, Aunt Lila and Uncle Frank moved into the family farmhouse where the three sisters had grown up. The house remained the centerpiece of extended family get-togethers. For two Christmases, they celebrated with a hole in the wall between the living room and the kitchen. Aunt Lila had taken a sledgehammer to it in a bid to convince Uncle Frank that they needed to get rid of it. Uncle Frank's answer was to leave the hole and ignore it. Aunt Lila eventually won. That wall turned into a breakfast bar that opened the rooms into one giant space.

Ava spent countless weekends and summer days at the house with her cousins Lizzie and Fawn. Ava and Fawn had been in the same class at school. They both liked riding their bikes, helping Aunt Lila in her garden, watching movies, and dreaming about the cute guys who starred in them.

Lizzie was four years older and had always been glamorous in Ava's eyes. She was tall, like Aunt Lila, with the family's trademark strawberry-blond hair that had skipped Ava. Lizzie was the first family member to go to college, get married, move into her own home. She did it all with such panache that she made life beyond their family look like a blockbuster movie.

Fawn and Lizzie had both eventually moved away, Fawn to Indianapolis with her husband, Beau, and their children, Brad and Florence. Lizzie and her husband, Max, moved from city to city as Max ascended the corporate ladder. Lizzie had a miscarriage, then another. They never adopted.

Although Lizzie's sadness about her losses was real, Ava admired her efforts to give back to her community. But every time Lizzie became chair of an organization's board or got comfortable with a volunteer role, Max moved them again.

Ava turned onto the tree-lined lane to Aunt Lila's house. Pink-and-white dogwoods stood welcomingly along the gravel road, making it resemble the entrance to a country castle. Then the lane opened to a large lawn surrounding the white two-story farmhouse.

Ava instinctively glanced to her right to see how the apple grove was doing. As children, she and her cousins had played tag under those trees. In the fall, they helped Aunt Lila make the best pies on the planet, which were even better when Uncle Frank cranked out ice cream to go with them.

A small garage sat thirty feet or so from the house. One of the apple trees had fallen on it and crumpled one wall of the old building. Ava hoped there wasn't a car inside. Besides a few limbs scattered across the yard, Ava didn't see any other storm damage.

Aunt Lila stood on the porch, her white hair framing a face still soft enough to welcome and stern enough to prod when needed. In

Ava's memory, none of the women in that family had ever been the quiet, gentle types.

"Welcome, sweetie," Aunt Lila said, reaching for Ava's hand and squeezing it. "I am so sorry about what happened."

Ava pulled away and motioned toward the garage. "I see you got a little of it."

"Practically nothing next to what you got." Aunt Lila peered at Ava's car. "Do you have bags in the car you need help with?"

"Nothing. I rescued a bin of clothes but left it at Juniper's. I don't think she wants to see me tonight. I can get it tomorrow."

"You know that's not a problem. Lizzie's room still has some of her clothes in it. Fawn took everything she owned when she and Beau married. Of course, she didn't have nearly as much as Lizzie. I believe that girl could open a secondhand store and stock it with all of her own things."

Aunt Lila laughed as she led Ava inside. Ava knew she wouldn't fit into Lizzie's old clothes unless they were stretchy T-shirts. She had never been that slender.

The open living space didn't at all appear like something that belonged in an old farmhouse. Aunt Lila had decorated in violet and butter yellow. The couch had small, subtle flowers strewn across its upholstery. A hand-crocheted afghan draped the recliner, and fresh flowers sat on the table next to it.

"I would offer you a cup of tea, but if I remember right, you're a coffee woman."

"I don't have the elegance required to drink tea, and it's too late in the day for coffee."

Aunt Lila raised her eyebrows. "Bourbon?"

Ava sat on a stool at the breakfast bar. "Serve it up!"

Aunt Lila laughed, a shiny tinkle that brightened the room.

"Do you have any guests right now?" Ava said. After Uncle Frank died and her daughters moved away, Aunt Lila fulfilled her need to caretake by offering the extra bedrooms through an online rental agency. The success pushed her to develop a full-fledged bed-and-breakfast. Her location twenty minutes outside of Lexington made it an ideal place for any traveler seeking the rolling green hills of central Kentucky while staying close enough to Lexington to attend a basketball game, a play, or the races at Keeneland. Word of her warm hospitality and comfortable home had spread online, and in her third business year, she was booked for 80 percent of her available days.

"No one at the moment, though I called emergency management to offer rooms if they ran out for the tornado victims."

"Anyone who knows this place would choose it over one of the chain hotels."

Aunt Lila set the bourbon in front of Ava and slid onto the seat across from her. As Ava sipped the rich liquid, she imagined it speeding through her body to give her the courage to face the upcoming days and the clarity to see what she most needed. Instead, it combined with Aunt Lila's warm presence and made her sleepy. She wanted to fall into the comfort of Lizzie's room as if she were a teenager who could sleep until noon.

"You can stay as long as you want, honey. I'll be happy for your company."

Lizzie's bedroom was the one Aunt Lila kept solely for family. The space looked familiar yet updated. Lizzie's high school graduation photo hung on the wall next to a self-portrait she had painted. The bedspread was new, a quilted lilac-and-white spread a shade darker than the walls.

Ava glanced at the dresser, where a necklace caught her eye. The silver chain still shone, attesting to the amount of money Ava's mother had paid for it. The heart pendant had a small ruby in its center.

"Every young woman needs at least one precious stone," her mother had said. She'd raided the family vacation fund that winter to buy each of the cousins a necklace with their birthstone—a ruby for Lizzie, sapphire for Fawn, and pearl for Ava. The three of them had worn them every day of that Christmas vacation.

Lizzie probably left it behind because it was no longer good enough for her. Her husband went to a fine jeweler every year for her birthday. On her fiftieth, he'd given her a diamond-and-ruby ensemble from Tiffany's.

Ava delicately lifted the necklace and imagined she was holding her own pearl. She touched her collarbone, and a sharp pain jabbed her throat. She would never see her necklace again. Like anything of her mother's she had kept—the photo album Ava stored in her dresser drawer, the wristwatch that hadn't worked for years. All gone.

She could tell people she wasn't sentimental and it didn't matter that all of her belongings were gone. It wasn't fully true. Those remnants of her mother, they had been precious.

She went to the window and turned the old metal lock, then pushed up on the wooden frame to let in a lilac-scented breeze. She settled into her cousin's old bed, pulled the covers over her, and inhaled deeply.

A few raindrops pinged off the metal roof, and Ava held the cover tighter to her. A brisk wind blew the curtain up and whistled into the room as the rain intensified. Another storm, too soon. Fear paralyzed her like in a nightmare where she knew she must escape but her body wouldn't obey her. She couldn't make herself move to get out of the bed and hide downstairs in a safe inner room with no windows.

Then she remembered there was no need to fear. If there was a tornado, Aunt Lila would wake her. Aunt Lila would take care of her.

It was nearly lunchtime the next day when Ava awoke to the dinging of her phone. Juniper's message said, "Dad wants to see you. At the house?"

Juniper couldn't accept the reality that the house was no longer there. The only place to meet on that lot was at the fallen tree.

"Bring him to Aunt Lila's."

"With your things?"

"Yes."

Ava sat up and squinted at her reflection in Lizzie's mirror. Lizzie hadn't left any of her glow in that reflection. Ava appeared as plain and middle aged as she did when she stepped into the bathroom on her way to her office each morning. Short, dull brown hair, slight bags under her green eyes. Was that an age spot on her cheek? She rubbed at the brown spot. It didn't go away. That must be why Juniper insisted Ava wear sunscreen daily. Even the winter sun was strong enough to reach her through the driver's-side window.

Donovan had been her husband, so he knew what she looked like at her best and at her worst. But that had been in the days when her youth naturally outshone her flaws. Now that trick would require makeup, a mask to give her the confidence to face him.

She knew one person who could help: Connie, she of the consistent makeup mask. Ava reached for her phone.

"I don't want to be overdone," Ava told Connie on the phone. "I did used to be married to the man, but I was young and dewy then. At that age, you can fool a person into thinking what they see is beauty."

"Stop it, Ava. You're an attractive woman. Donovan will remember that the minute he sets eyes on you."

Or he'll remember that yelling fit about the move. Or the ugliness of serving him divorce papers. There were so many things Ava wished she could take back.

Ava gave Connie the address, then waited, berating herself for reaching out. She could call her back, cancel. Ava studied herself in the mirror again. No, she wouldn't do that. It would take a miracle worker, and Connie was the closest she knew.

Connie arrived with a massive bag that she placed on the bed. She inspected the light at the vanity before scanning the room, searching for better illumination. The jewels on her ears and neck sparkled with her slightest movement as she set up her workstation. There was a vitality about her that Ava hadn't observed previously.

"I miss you already," Connie said as she pulled masses of small boxes from her bag. "I look across the street, and it's wrong."

"Did anyone hear from the Pedigos?"

Connie paused her organizing. "They'd gone to a pizza place for their son's birthday. Imagine what they felt like when they got home."

Ava didn't have to imagine, and she didn't want to go there.

Connie pulled mascara, blush, and lipstick out of the small boxes. She examined the colors and arranged groups of products on the bed before choosing what to use.

"I'm going to leave a lot of this for you," Connie said. "This should replace what you lost and keep up the look we're going to give you."

Ava didn't bother to tell Connie she had never owned that much makeup. She thanked her but didn't figure on changing her personal care habits. Maybe the lipstick. That was easy.

Ava sat on Lizzie's stool and stared at herself, wondering what Connie saw.

"You don't mind a little plucking?" Connie asked.

There was such eagerness in Connie's voice that Ava couldn't turn her down. They had slipped into Connie's world, and Ava was at her mercy.

Connie pulled back Ava's hair in a headband before running a moistened cotton ball over her skin. Ava remembered going to the department store at the mall once as a teenager. She and Fawn had wanted to look glamorous in their school photos, so they decided a makeover at the cosmetics counter would do the trick. The woman worked her magic on each of them, though Ava couldn't truly see much difference in the mirror. Ava had squirmed when the woman listed the prices. Between them the cousins had enough money to buy one mascara and one lipstick to share. That was sufficient to get them the free gift bag and split what was in it.

"You have beautiful skin, Ava," Connie said as she dotted on a citrus-scented cream. She spread the cool substance around with a light touch.

"I'm glad something's still good."

"Honey, you obviously have no idea what some women struggle with. Hair growing where it shouldn't, acne into their forties and their fifties, sallow skin that doesn't brighten up no matter what they eat. You're one of the lucky ones."

Connie hummed a few bars of a song that pricked at something in Ava's memory, but she couldn't place it.

"Where did you learn all this, Connie? Did you go to beauty school?"

Connie stopped what she was doing. Ava glanced at her in the mirror and saw a darkness pass over Connie's expression, as if the question had pulled her out of her fairy-godmother trance. She took an obvious breath before putting the blush brush to Ava's cheek.

"Mother taught me. She insisted that a woman's looks were all she really had in life. She never left the house in a wrinkled blouse or skirt, and she certainly wouldn't step outside without her earrings and necklace, and a scarf over her hair if it was windy."

Ava thought of her own mother, who hadn't worn a bit of makeup or had much concern about her clothes, except on special occasions. Perhaps Connie had enough years on Ava that her mother came from another generation.

"Look at yourself," Connie said, standing behind her. "You are going to make him wonder why he left."

Ava raised her eyes to the mirror. There was a woman with the confidence to face the past before stepping into her new future.

Juniper entered the house with an expression uncommon for her. Ava so rarely saw Juniper with her father that she had forgotten how her daughter would cock her mouth sideways when she was sure she had the upper hand, precisely like Donovan.

There it was, that certainty widening her eyes and setting her mouth so it was nearly pursed.

Juniper carried the stranger's suitcase upstairs. Donovan followed with the plastic tub of clothes. His hair had slight silver touches at both temples; the rest remained black and thick. He wasn't a man who had to worry about going bald.

Donovan returned to the main floor, went to Ava, and took her hands in his before she had a chance to back away. He leaned in and kissed her on the cheek. The woodsy scent of his aftershave followed him.

"Ava, I'm so sorry. Juni took me to see it."

Ava nodded because she didn't trust herself to say anything. She should thank him for saving her life. She wanted to say it the right way, with some measure of self-confidence rather than like a puppy that had been carried away from its home and didn't know how to get back.

"Juniper told me you sheltered in the basement," he said. He crooked his mouth to the side, sending Ava's thank-you to the back of her throat, where she swallowed it.

Ava pulled her hands from his and motioned to the bar stools. Juniper sat next to her dad.

"Dad says I have the right to rebuild," Juniper said as she took a seat.

"Juniper, I don't think I—"

"Ava, did you forget? Our divorce agreement gave my half of the house to Juni. Now that she's over eighteen, she's half owner and can make her own decision about what to do."

He was right. She had forgotten. For all those years, Ava had controlled her daughter's interest in the house and took care of all the expenses. She would never have predicted that, given a situation like this, they would disagree about what to do.

Ava looked at both of them before standing to pace between the breakfast bar and the window. She was a grown woman who had been on her own for years. She could not imagine Juni having a say in where she lived. Had Ava's existence come to mean so little that she didn't have control over where she would call home?

Ava wandered to the corner of the living room where Washington had delivered her grandfather's desk earlier in the day. Juniper and Donovan chuckled at something. Ava gazed at the desk. In her grandfather's later years, Aunt Lila had taken over paying the bills. Uncle Frank oversaw the little work they still did on the farm. They rented out most of the hundred acres to a cattle farmer, yet Grandpa still saw it as his land.

Grandpa would sit at the desk, his hands on the ink blotter open as if someone might hand him a check to sign or a letter to read. He would stare at the small compartments. Ava wondered if he might be remembering, telling himself stories about his life so he wouldn't forget them—or maybe trying to make sense of them.

On the outside, he seemed to be fading. His skin stayed gray all year instead of tanning to a summer brown. His eyes lost their sharp edges and became misty pools. His voice, once so strong and crisp, dwindled to a softer tone.

Was Ava already beginning to fade? She had obviously lost some of her luster. Juniper and Donovan carried on in her absence as if they didn't remember she was in the room.

Surely she had more years before she would be totally invisible.

Ava put her palm on the desk, feeling the ribs of the rolltop. Her grandfather had been such a strong man, in body and in will. She had discerned how to be strong from him as she studied about budgets and paying bills. He would never stand for anyone, not even Ava's daughter, and especially not her ex-husband, telling Ava what she had to do.

Ava walked back to the breakfast bar, and they fell silent.

"Juniper, it's not your decision alone. We each have an interest in the house, and I hold the insurance, which I have paid for beyond your eighteenth year. We can make this decision together; however, I will not simply bend to your whims."

"My whims? I'm not a hormonal twelve-year-old, Mom. I am a college graduate who is running her own business. I don't operate on whims."

"Not usually, but in this case, you've made a decision with your heart. You have every right to do that. But you haven't looked at any of the practicalities, including the fact that I might not want to live there any longer."

The expression on Juniper's face morphed from anger to disbelief. Donovan sat as a passive bystander. Ava caught something in his eye—maybe a glimmer of respect?

Ava's phone interrupted. It was her boss, so she picked it up.

"Yes?... No, I can't come in... You know that Shadiqua can do the report. She's perfectly capable... You don't have to threaten me. I quit."

Ava disconnected, turned off the phone, and shoved it into her pocket, her hand trembling. This time when she lifted her eyes, it was Donovan who wore an expression of disbelief.

Chapter 4

"Mom, what did you do?"

Juniper walked to her mother and settled an arm around her. Ava leaned into her daughter's solidness. Then she saw Donovan still staring at her and stood straighter, planting her soles like the roots of a hundred-year-old oak tree.

"I quit my job." She wanted it to come out boldly, but it landed soft as a cotton ball.

"I was right. You do hate it," Juniper said.

Ava knitted her fingers together, then pulled them apart. She moved away from Juniper and returned to pacing.

"Couldn't they at least give me a week? Mrs. Alvarado said I could have six weeks. That pretty boy they put in charge of my department knows so little about what he's doing that he thinks he can't do it without me. Which I suppose he can't."

"Ava, maybe you should call them back. I'm sure they owe you vacation time, a leave of absence," Donovan said.

He had always been the one who acted on impulse, repeatedly jeopardizing their financial future. For the years they were married, Ava had to be rational for both of them.

She no longer had to do that.

"I'll call Mrs. Alvarado and work things out so I get what they owe me, but I'm not going back to that job."

Juniper smiled. "I think that storm really did blow away something that was holding you back."

Ava locked eyes with her. "Maybe that's why I don't want to rebuild the house."

Juniper stepped back toward her dad. When he didn't say anything, she refocused on her mom. "Just a minute ago it was maybe you didn't want to rebuild. Now you've already decided?"

"Let's give it six weeks, Juni. A big decision like this requires research."

"Research that we can each do on our own. I think we need to take time away from each other to figure this out," Juniper said.

Ava walked to the window and back, her steps a steadying rhythm. *Six weeks without Juniper?*

Ava had always been careful, methodical. She didn't have to toss that out the window.

Ava went again to the desk. She also wanted to wait for the signs. But she wasn't going to say that to Juniper and Donovan; they would definitely think she had lost it.

Ava returned to her seat across from them.

"It requires . . . contemplation. We can't act on raw emotion. Do you think we have to do that on our own?"

Juniper nodded.

"It'll be hard, but okay. Let's take the time on our own. Then we'll meet and make a decision," Ava said.

"What are you going to do in the next six weeks?" Juniper said.

Ava threw her hands toward the ceiling.

"I'll stay here with Aunt Lila. Or maybe I won't. Maybe I'll go visit Fawn in Indianapolis."

"You could go to California to see Uncle Jarvis and his family. Or you could visit Lizzie in the Dominican Republic."

"I didn't know she was living overseas," Donovan said.

"Oh yes, in a swanky gated community with its own beach. Mom's never even seen the ocean. Mom, you need to experience the blue of the Caribbean."

Ava regarded them both. She'd had enough of Juniper and

Donovan for the day. She needed to be alone. She wanted to be still so that all of what had happened could wash over her, could sink into her tiniest crevices and sting her with her new reality. Then she could figure out what to do next. Only then.

"Juniper, you know I don't do airplanes. I'm not going out of the country. And I don't care about the ocean. Don't you think that going to Indy will take enough out of me?"

"Mom! If you're going to do something different, then go all the way. Rest when you come home from Indy, then go see Lizzie. You don't have a job to go to. You don't have a house to take care of. Geez, enjoy yourself for a change."

Juniper crooked her mouth to the side. She'd reclaimed the upper hand.

"Enjoy your six weeks, Mom."

She gave Ava a quick hug and avoided eye contact before heading toward the door. She glanced back at her dad.

"I'll be there in a minute," he said.

Donovan resettled onto the bar stool, leaning toward Ava as if he planned to stay.

"Sometimes she reminds me of you, and sometimes she reminds me of my mother," Ava said. "That scares me."

"I wish I had known your mother."

"I wish you had too. Then she wouldn't have died so young. And maybe . . ."

"Maybe what?"

Ava met Donovan's gaze, and he reached across the bar for her hand. His warm palms cradled hers, one below and one above.

"Nothing." Ava closed her eyes and shook her head. His touch took her back to those happy days when Juni was a baby. When she could tell him anything. He might have been irresponsible, but he always listened, even when he didn't fully grasp what she was trying to say.

"I'm such a wreck, Donovan. I honestly didn't know I was until now, until that idiot demanded I go back to work. And until Juniper came in here so decided. It's ridiculous that a woman's daughter can make her feel like this."

"Like what?"

"I don't know—small, foolish, timid. We're usually so in tune, but when we're not, it's bad."

"And your boss?"

"Oh, that's ridiculous, don't you think? He can't get along without me for two days?"

Donovan didn't say anything to reassure her, not even to acknowledge that he heard what she said. Maybe it had been too many years and he didn't get her any longer. She was still following the safest, easiest-to-navigate side streets of life while he flew along the highway without a map.

Or maybe they had flipped places.

"I can stay for a few days, Ava. Help get the property cleared, whatever would be useful to you."

Ava wondered what that would mean. Complications, most likely. If he could passively be there to call on if she needed him, that could be helpful. But she knew it wouldn't be like that. He would be back to see her again, even if she needed to be alone. He would wiggle into a fracture in her heart. Then he would pull away, and she would be solo again.

Ava slid her hand from his.

"What are you doing here, Donovan? We've spoken, what, maybe four times in the past six years? Why are you here now?"

His eyelashes fluttered like they always had when something wasn't going as planned.

"Juni called me. I was in Indianapolis, and I was worried about you, Ava. It was our house you were in. We had some good years in that house."

He stood and planted his feet comfortably yet firmly. She saw the expectation on his face, the waiting for an answer to his offer.

Ava rolled her shoulders to loosen them. Donovan stepped

behind her and massaged her tight muscles, his hands applying the perfect pressure to release the tension in warm waves. Ava closed her eyes and sighed.

He stopped and circled around to face her, taking her hands in his before she could do anything else with them.

"I won't stay unless you need me. I'll be in Indy next week for business. If you get to Fawn's and want to have dinner, let me know."

He kissed her cheek and left.

The door closed, and a loneliness she hadn't felt for years gripped her. Ava rubbed her palms to warm herself. He would have spent the day with her, called the insurance company, carried some of the load. Instead, his car's engine hummed, then faded as it headed toward the road.

Ava found a pink sweater on a hook by the back door and pulled it on as she walked out. There wasn't anything she had to do. No one was expecting her; nothing needed her attention. Her daughter had made it clear that she didn't want to hear from her.

It was a little bit like summer vacation when she was a child, except that the April wind chilled Ava even as the sun beckoned her to keep strolling the mown path around the farm.

She'd spent an enormous amount of time on the farm as a girl. She loved the people, though she didn't particularly like the farm itself. If Ava saw a bee, she would race inside. She couldn't remember ever being stung; the fear came from simply knowing it could happen, like it had to Lizzie. Lizzie once spent an afternoon in tears because a bee had stung her on the nose. It was red, swollen, and not the kind of mark a pretty little girl wanted at school.

So, Ava didn't like insects. What she did like was the way her grandfather had divided the farm into neat squares and rectangles. The corn grew in such straight rows. Another field held all the garden vegetables, with a stake at the end of each strip. He spent Saturdays hoeing the weeds that sprouted between the plants.

The chickens would peck around a small square area with a henhouse in one corner. For a few years they had sheep in another neatly fenced rectangle. Then there were the cows. They moved from field to field, some with fences so far apart that Ava couldn't take them all in with one glance.

When her mother died, Ava liked to escape their newly quiet house to visit the farm and see the chickens. They didn't hover and ask how she was or what she was going to do without her mom. She threw them food, and they pecked. It was the natural order of things.

That was long in the past. Ava didn't see any planting happening in the divided fields now. She listened for chickens and cows and heard only a crow. Yet the farm felt like home. It had never asked anything of her. It welcomed her.

A bird trilled repeatedly, a beautiful sound next to the crow's caw. Ava stopped at the tall tulip poplar and searched for the singer. There were two cardinals, a male and a female. They flitted from branch to branch, landing in a spot where the sun brightened the male's feathers.

I need to find a spot like that—where the sun will shine on me, she thought. A spot where the light could reveal the little beauties hidden within her otherwise ordinary self. Her mother had told her that when all was not right with the world, Ava had a river of pearls running through her that would push her along. She had to settle in and allow it to carry her to where she needed to be.

Back in Lizzie's room, Ava found that Juniper had deposited the mystery suitcase on top of the bed. Ava might not yet know where her own pearl river was, but if she searched within, she might find a strand that would lead her to Natalya.

It looked like an ordinary suitcase, old and scuffed but whole. Ava unzipped the top and opened it. A brown velour sweat suit was neatly folded and tucked into one half. Ava picked it up and found a soft, peach-colored sweater below it, then underwear and socks, plus a nightgown. There was also a yellowed blouse with a tatted collar that appeared older than everything else in the luggage.

Natalya must be a woman of a certain age. Young women like Juniper wore stretched-out T-shirts to bed, not a granny nightie.

The other half of the suitcase held a pair of dark-blue jeans, a small, bulging toiletry bag, and a manila envelope. Ava picked up the envelope and undid the metal clasp. Pushing her hand into it, she pulled out black-and-white photos and a faded handwritten letter.

Dear Natalya.

I am so proud my beautiful American daughter make a fine match. Good man equal good family. I wish he treat you well and give you babies to love. It was sad day when I return home to nurse father. I would not see you again. Now I leave you in care of your new family. We do what we must for family. I pray your safety and happiness every day.

Love, Mother

The photos showed a dark-haired woman holding a bright-eyed infant and standing beside a pretty little girl. In the largest photo, the little girl was sitting in her mother's lap and gazing up at her. The photos all had the soft, unfocused edges that showed up so often in old pictures. Ava wondered if the women of that time were as beautiful in real life or if the lack of clarity added romance to the images.

Ava examined the pictures again and noticed a date on the corner of the first photo. June 1947. Ava assumed Natalya was the girl, who looked about eight years old. That would likely put her in her eighties.

She returned to the letter in search of a date. It wasn't there.

Ava tenderly put the photos and letter back into the envelope. She searched through the suitcase again. This belonged to a woman with a family, a woman who had been loved. There had to be another clue to lead Ava to the owner.

"There you are," Aunt Lila said as she walked in. "Went to the grocery so I could make us meatloaf and macaroni tonight. Should we invite Juniper?"

"We're on a Juniper-requested separation for the next six weeks until we decide what to do with the property."

Aunt Lila glanced at the suitcase, then sat next to it on the bed.

"I don't understand. I know she's your daughter, but it's your decision."

"It's not. She's half owner."

"Donovan?"

Ava nodded. She took a seat in the rocker in the corner.

"Does he still have that charm?"

"Oh yes. He said very little, but the charm inflates even the silence."

Ava shook her head as if that would blur the picture of him. She pointed to the suitcase.

"That blew onto my property, and I need to find the owner."

Ava rose again to show Aunt Lila the clues. Aunt Lila ran her hands around the perimeter of the suitcase and found an attached zippered bag. Opening it, she drew out a white business-sized envelope. She handed it to Ava, who pulled out the money and counted it. Five 100-dollar bills.

"It's a go bag," Aunt Lila said. "I've had a few women from the shelter come stay here. The experienced ones who've left their husbands before have a go bag with at least one change of clothing, toiletries, one or two treasures, and money."

"In that case, I can't find her soon enough."

Aunt Lila read the tag on the handle. "Russian? Lordy, I hope the poor woman wasn't one of those mail-order brides. Mac Lozelle got one from the Philippines. He brought her to church with him, though she never said a word."

"What happened to her?"

"They had three children, two boys and a girl. Sweet kids. Mac had a heart attack, a bad one, and he wasn't the same after. Couldn't work. So she up and moved them to Illinois where she had a cousin. I heard she started a custom embroidery business. She might have been quiet, but she had spirit, which didn't show itself until Mac got sick."

"Maybe the best of us doesn't come out until we need it."

Ava wandered to the mirror and glanced at herself, which made her eyes widen. She'd nearly forgotten how Connie had remade her, and she looked, well, not bad, though Aunt Lila hadn't mentioned it. She wondered if Donovan had noticed. Even Juniper hadn't commented. Maybe the change was only in her head.

She turned back to Aunt Lila, who was still studying the name on the tag.

"Of course, that might be a maiden name, or something made up," Lila said.

Ava retraced the outside of the bag with her hands as her aunt had, hoping for another clue. She didn't find a thing.

"It'll give me something to do while I'm stewing."

Lila stood and put her arm around Ava. "Don't stew too much, sweetie. Get out there and live. The world is waiting for you."

"What's waiting for me? One minute I feel a freedom that I don't know I've ever felt, like I could soar into the sky and see the world. The next minute, I feel lost, like I'm at a crossroads in the country, there are four directions to choose from, but there are no trees, no houses, no scarecrow to point me in the right direction."

"Sweetie, you've never had a choice like this. Of course it's not clear," Aunt Lila said.

She was right. She immediately went to work after college. There had been no casting about for the perfect job to fulfill her dreams.

Then Ava and Donovan had married. It was more like "The rent is due next week, and we don't have anything left to pay it with, so take what work you can get."

"Give it time, and don't be hard on yourself," Lila continued. "It'll come if you slow down and let it."

"Are you telling me to wait for a sign? That's what Grandpa would say."

"I bet you believed signs were real when you were a child. So be that child again, honey. Feel that freedom. I'm here to catch you if you fall."

Ava sat across the desk from Mrs. Alvarado, who was neat as always, with her hair in a barrette at her neck and a forest-green jacket over her white blouse. The office was stark in its simplicity. Two framed Rocky Mountain landscape photos hung on the wall by Mrs. Alvarado's service plaque. There were no family photos—not even a coffee mug with a lipstick stain.

"You've had such a respected career here at Kentucky Ventures. I know you must be under a lot of stress because of the storm. Mr. Moehler told me you said you quit. He doesn't want you to go. We would need a resignation in writing."

Ava sighed. It had felt good to say she was quitting. It was what she wanted to do because she was angry. But Donovan was right; she shouldn't jeopardize her financial security.

"Ava, it's been three days since the storm. Give it a week or two, or the whole time you can take. You're on leave anyway. If at the end of your leave you still want to resign, you can give me a letter."

Mrs. Alvarado looked professional, her expression betraying no emotion. She sounded like a kindergarten teacher trying to be patient with a student who wasn't catching on. While she was one of the few people who had been with the agency nearly as long as Ava, they didn't know one another well.

"Did he tell you to get me to stay?"

Mrs. Alvarado plucked a pen from her desk and held it steady between her hands.

"That's not it. As a human resource professional, I want to help our employees benefit from their employment here like the organization benefits from the work you put in. Truly, Ava, this is in your best interest."

Ava took in every orderly item on Mrs. Alvarado's desk: pens, Post-Its, phone. The woman operated like Ava did in her own work, lining everything up to serve its purpose.

"We've done a lot of work over the years that made a difference," Ava said. "That always made me proud."

"It's one of the benefits of employment with a good agency."

"Are we still a good agency?" Ava leaned forward, hoping Mrs. Alvarado could let down the professional screen and be real with her.

"Why wouldn't we be?"

"I see where the money goes now that we have an entire new layer of management."

Mrs. Alvarado put her pen back on her desk. "Organizations experience growing pains now and then. In the end, it will serve our clients well, I think."

There was a hesitation in her voice.

So, Mrs. Alvarado had seen it too.

"Something's happened to me, Mrs. Alvarado. Maybe I'm still in some post-trauma state, though I don't think so."

Ava couldn't keep motionless any longer. She stood and paced, making herself stay quiet. The answers would come if she let them. She cast an eye over Mrs. Alvarado's desk again, contemplating the certainty of having everything in its place. Mrs. Alvarado waited like a patient counselor.

"The day after the tornado, some people came to my house to pack up my stuff from the basement and take it to a storage unit. They did all the work, loaded it into a truck, then unloaded it into the space. I stood and watched. And when I closed that door and clicked the lock, I felt free."

Mrs. Alvarado wrinkled her brow.

Ava halted and rested her hands on the back of the chair. "I don't quite get it either, but I know that it felt good. Like, like . . ." Ava motioned to Mrs. Alvarado's hair. "Do you ever wear your hair down, without the barrette? I think every time I've seen you in all these years, your hair has always been the same."

Mrs. Alvarado reached back to touch the barrette.

"It makes getting ready for work easy."

Ava nodded. "I think I'm okay with things not being easy for a while if the tradeoff is feeling possibilities again, feeling, like . . . I don't know how to say it. I know that it felt right to close that door on the past. I don't want to go back. I want to see what else there is for me."

Mrs. Alvarado's skepticism played across her brow.

Ava didn't want to give it up, felt like she couldn't.

"Maybe if you take out that barrette, you'll understand how I feel."

"Ava, you're clearly suffering from some kind of post-storm trauma. You would never come in here and ask me about my hair."

"Yet I did ask you about your hair. That's the problem here. You're seeing me as I was. Everyone is. I'm not the same person."

Mrs. Alvarado's expression remained placid.

Ava sat again. "It's okay. I'll do as you say. I'll sign whatever you need me to sign for the leave, then be on my way."

"You'll get paid for your weeks of leave. If you do decide quitting is best, this additional time will help you end on better terms so we can give you a good recommendation for your next position."

"Maybe there won't be a next position," Ava said. It was out of her mouth before she had fully formed her ideas. A week ago, the possibility would have terrified her.

"You would retire early?"

"Well, no. I couldn't do that. Still, I'm feeling like maybe there's another way for me."

Ava opened her purse and extracted a stack of postcards. She handed them to Mrs. Alvarado.

"They're about my daughter's business. Would you share them?"

Mrs. Alvarado glanced at them and nodded.

Ava stood and offered her hand.

"I appreciate your support," Ava said. "I do have a few personal things at my desk I'd like to get."

"I'll call back there. Unless you want me to gather them for when you return?"

If Ava didn't need everything from her basement, she didn't need what was on her desk either. She changed her mind and took her leave.

"I'll be in touch."

Ava meaningfully tapped the nape of her neck as she looked at Mrs. Alvarado's hair again, then left the office.

Her job now was to find Natalya Kerminskaya.

Chapter 5

Ava woke to the sunrise painting the sky outside her window. The scent of cinnamon wafted upstairs from the kitchen. *Aunt Lila remembered!* Her favorite breakfast at Lila's had always been cinnamon french toast with whatever fruit was in season.

That's when it hit her. *The Baker's Bible. Betty Crocker. Artisan Bread. Bravetart.* All gone.

The books Ava could replace. It was those random recipes she stored between their pages that were lost. The oatmeal, peanut butter, and chocolate chip cookie recipe she'd cut out of the newspaper years ago. They didn't even publish recipes in the newspaper these days. She'd made those cookies so many times that she could remember most of the amounts, yet one minor alteration could ruin them.

Then there was the gluten-free coffee cake she'd ripped from a magazine. A week before the tornado, she'd decided to go ahead and invest in the ingredients—almond flour, coconut sugar, coconut oil. At the cost of those foods, she would only be able to afford baking once a month. No wonder the recipe author was able to lose fifty pounds.

She could find another recipe if she ever decided to gather the ingredients again.

Her grandmother's coconut cake. That's what she craved—the sweeping arches of her grandmother's handwriting on the index card with a drop or two of dried vanilla in the corner. So moist, so pretty, with the white icing made with shortening that she finished in curling peaks. Ava could never resurrect the experience of replicating the cake from her grandmother's handwriting.

Ava wiped the sleep from her eyes. *No time to wallow in self-pity.* Her grandmother certainly wouldn't have stood for that if she were around. She would tell her to experiment, find her own way to make the cake. Ava didn't need *Betty Crocker* or the rest. It was all inside her, baked into the cells of her life. When she needed to access it, she simply had to relax, let it flow into her fingertips and brain, and trust that it was right.

That sure would be a different way of living, and why not? A failure or two wouldn't hurt her. Start again and make it better this time. Make it her own.

Ava showered and put on a pair of black pants from her bin. She preferred her favorite jeans, all worn in and soft in the way years-old jeans could be. But by now dirt clung to the hem, and they smelled stale.

She gathered her small pile of dirty clothes and carried them downstairs to the laundry room, where she dumped them into the washer. Then she followed the smell of breakfast to the sun-brightened kitchen.

"You're my favorite aunt, now and forever," Ava said.

Aunt Lila turned from the stove.

"Nice as that is, I know that compared to Maud, I wouldn't need to do much."

They both laughed.

"She's coming to see you."

Ava gulped. It didn't seem to matter how old Ava was. Aunt Maud always made her feel like an awkward eleven-year-old.

"This morning?"

"Sometime today. I told her I didn't know if you had plans. I'll be here because we have guests checking in."

"Do you need me to vacate the room?"

"That's the room I keep for family and friends. It's yours for as long as you want it."

Aunt Lila flipped the french toast. Ava grabbed the orange juice from the refrigerator and poured glasses for both of them. Filling a mug with steaming coffee, she sat at the table.

"I went into work yesterday to talk with HR about my resignation, or my leave," Ava said.

"What do you mean?"

"Mrs. Alvarado made a good case for why I should wait until I finish my leave before I officially turn in my resignation. She thinks she shouldn't take seriously what I say because I'm suffering from post-tornado trauma."

"That is a possibility," Lila said. "It's also possible that change has been lurking in your mind and you needed something to push you toward it. So what's next, Ava?"

"I've been thinking about that. I need to be around someone who understands that leaving my job while I'm also homeless isn't a terrible thing for me to do."

"You're not exactly homeless," Lila said as she nudged the almonds around with a spatula. "You have a home as long I'm here."

Ava breathed deeply. She had believed that to be true, yet it felt better to hear Lila say it.

"I will take you up on that. I've also been thinking about visiting Fawn if it won't be an imposition on her."

"She'll be thrilled, honey."

The doorbell rang. The door opened. Ava heard heavy steps.

Aunt Maud came to Ava first and lightly touched her shoulder, the best acknowledgment of her niece's loss that she could express. She then pulled out the chair on Ava's right and let her weight fall into it.

"Bad luck, it was. I don't know what else to call it since your neighbors are okay. I drove by and saw it," Maud said, her eyes not leaving Ava. She scrutinized her niece, perhaps looking for signs of shock or grief on her face. If Ava had any of that, she would not share it with Maud.

"No need to call it anything. It just is," Ava said.

"Maud, do you want french toast?" Aunt Lila asked.

"Already had breakfast, though that smells scrumptious. Maybe one piece."

Ava searched for something to say, a direction to set the conversation that wouldn't bring down Maud's judgmental wrath, but she couldn't get there quick enough.

Aunt Maud flattened both of her palms on the table and squinted. Ava had long wondered whether Maud needed glasses and was too vain to admit it.

"Now, Ava, what about rebuilding? Is that your plan? I assume the insurance would cover it?"

Ava sighed. Maud's steady blue gaze didn't offer an out.

"I don't have a plan yet. Juniper has a say because she's half owner of the house. She's in favor of rebuilding."

"Her childhood home. I suppose she would want to keep it. Still, a girl telling her own mother what to do," Maud said, almost to herself. Then she turned back to Ava. "She could buy you out if the girl had any money. And you could go find an efficiency apartment, or buy a condo. Apartment living is the way to go, I say. It's so much easier to clean than an entire house. Every time there's an open apartment at my place, I try to get Lila to apply. She's too stubborn."

Aunt Maud ended her statement with a squint at her sister.

Ava couldn't picture Aunt Lila anywhere except in this house where she grew up.

"Wouldn't you miss the place, Aunt Maud? It's the family home, for all of us," Ava said.

"Well, I don't see the family over here taking care of it. I saw that tree fallen over on the garage. You planning to do that repair, Ava?"

Ava sat back in her chair to create distance from her aunt. Her morning could have been so pleasant.

"I can't say that's my skill set, but Washington could do it. He's been fixing up all kinds of stuff out at the farm."

"And charge an arm and a leg?" Aunt Maud said.

Aunt Lila brought over a plate of french toast topped with blueberries and almonds and set it in front of Ava. She quickly returned with butter and syrup. Ava poured on the syrup, determined not to allow Maud to sour this plate of sweetness.

Lila placed a plate with one piece in front of Maud.

"I need some powdered sugar."

Lila handed her the oversized shaker, and Maud dusted the bread.

"Whatever he charged would be fair. Washington is a good, honest man," Ava said.

"So, Juniper's still wasting her college education out at that farm. I'm surprised she's not gone broke yet."

Ava shoved a piece of toast into her mouth to avoid speaking. She cut another piece and dragged it through the thick syrup.

Aunt Lila joined them at the table. "Juniper is a smart girl, and she's following her heart and using her talents. I admire that," she said.

"If that girl's like her daddy, she won't follow that direction for very long."

As Donovan's ex-wife, Ava had permission to point out his faults. Aunt Maud did not. If Ava didn't redirect the conversation, she might not be able to stay civil with this woman.

"How are your children, Aunt Maud? I haven't seen Kim and Bob for ages," Ava said.

"They're both still down in Atlanta, doing fine. I might go down there this spring. I found a bus I could take so I don't have to drive. Of course, hard to know what I would have to sit next to on a public bus."

Neither Ava nor Aunt Lila responded.

"You could drive me, Ava. Then I wouldn't have to do the bus."

"I'm not built for a drive that long," Ava said, knowing she also wasn't built to spend that much time with Maud.

"I suppose you'll be back to work soon anyway. Someone in your family has to earn an honest living."

Revealing that she had quit her job was sure to provoke a tirade Ava didn't want to handle early in the morning. Lila glanced at her as if to say, "Hold your tongue and don't tell her anything more."

"Lila told me you found a suitcase, Ava. Any clues on that?"

"The name on the tag. She's not on the city's emergency list, so I'm not sure how to find her."

"Did you try the phone book? I know it's a skinny thing compared to what it was before these cell phones took over the world, but you might find her in there."

Ava had not considered the phone book. Perhaps Maud had made her visit worthwhile.

Lila went to a corner cabinet and pulled out a stack of old phone books. Picking up a dish towel, she dusted off each of the four tomes before she brought them to the table.

"What's the name?" Lila asked.

"Kerminskaya."

Ava reached for a book. Lila shooed her hand away.

"I'll look. You finish eating."

Maud had finished her french toast, so she pushed the plate back and took a book.

"With a 'K' or a 'C-h'?"

"K."

Ava watched them both as she chewed the last few bites of her breakfast, then reached for the third book.

"Keminsky. Any chance she might have changed her last name?" Maud said.

"What's the first name?" Ava said.

"Walter and Eleanor."

It sounded like too much of a reach.

Ava delicately turned the nearly brittle pages. This one was so old that even if they found her name, there was no guarantee the woman would still be at that number. So many landlines were gone.

Karr. Keith. Keller. Kemper. Kerby. Knight. Kohl.

No Kerminskaya.

"She could be dead," Aunt Maud said. "I had a friend whose sister died when she was seventeen. Years later, when their mother died, they found suitcases filled with the sister's things, as if the mother planned to carry them to heaven with her and deliver them to her daughter."

"Sad, so sad," Aunt Lila said. "But this is a go bag. I feel like this woman is alive and needing it."

"Maybe she'd already done her going and was staying with a friend when the tornado took it," Maud said.

Either way, the woman needed her things. Ava had to find another way to locate her.

Fawn's enthusiasm burst through the phone like the first shower of spring.

"Opening night is next Friday. Can you get here early enough to go to the play with us?"

Ava dragged the chair in her room to where she could see the blue sky outside. She settled into it.

"What play?"

"My play!"

"Since when did you become a playwright?"

"Oh, sweetie, you have not spent time with my family for too long. Florence went through an *Annie* stage. She made me turn her hair into ringlets so she could audition, and when I refused to let her dye it red, she used Kool-Aid."

Ava laughed. The idea of anyone using Kool-Aid to dye their hair was funny enough. Imagining Fawn dealing with a determined daughter was funnier.

"How did it look?" Ava asked.

"Not so bad. Her hair's dark like mine, so it turned into a dark red that shimmered under the lights."

"Did she get the part?"

"She was named Lara McIntosh's understudy, which thrilled her because Lara is two years ahead of her in school, and everything Lara does in theater, Florence wants to do. Lara did Florence a huge favor by losing her voice on the final night of performances."

"I bet Florence was a star."

"She missed a few lines but was quick on her feet and filled in. She's got such charisma that no one noticed. So, she's the one who led me to playwriting, even if she's moved on to making YouTube movies with a couple of friends. And my first ten-minute play to be produced in this fair city will debut next Friday night as part of the Hoosier Ten Festival. Are you in?"

"Do I have to get dressed up?"

Fawn laughed. "The theater is above a restaurant bar, and I don't think they've ever sold out a show. Wear your sweats if you want."

"That's the theater for me."

"Listen, Ava," Fawn said, her voice lowered to a more serious register. "I'm so sorry about your house. I can't imagine."

Ava saw the devastation again. The picture was lodged in her memory even though she didn't want it there.

"The strange thing is that it took everything except the corner where Grandpa's desk was. It wasn't touched."

"The rolltop where he used to hide his cigarettes?"

Ava had forgotten about that. Her grandmother couldn't abide smoking.

"That one. He gave it to me when I got married. And I've been thinking, do you remember how he used to always talk about the signs?"

"Sure, like if your palm itched, then you were going to get some money. That worked for me once. My palm itched when I was going to sleep, and the next day at school, they announced the winner of the poetry contest. I won first place and fifty dollars."

"So you believe that there are signs for things? Because we both know you won that contest because you were a good poet."

"And probably only three or four students even entered poems. I'll say it's fun to notice signs. And who's to say they aren't there? Maybe Grandpa's desk is a sign that your family is your strongest support during a catastrophic loss."

Ava hadn't considered that. That was the thing about signs; they could mean something different to everyone.

She gazed at the blue sky, bringing herself back to the task at hand.

"I've felt more like the whole tornado thing is a sign to me that I need to do something different with the rest of my life. Maybe drastically different."

"Then you are coming to the right place. Our home is filled with more than enough creativity to give you ideas."

"I'll see you on Thursday if that's good."

"Your guest room awaits."

Ava wandered through the racks of clothes, wishing for a personal shopper. Though she appreciated the discount the store had offered the tornado survivors, she would have paid full price for someone else to make the choices and send them to Aunt Lila's.

She pulled a pair of navy-blue pants off a rack. Not exciting; her wardrobe never had been. Which was exactly why she needed something else, something she wouldn't have bought before. She put the pants back on the rack.

The next rack over was filled with leggings. Ava had avoided the recent trend, thinking leggings might not be appropriate for the workplace, though the younger women wore them. Still, she remembered sporting them in the nineties. Oh, they were comfortable.

A pair with a leather stripe down the side caught Ava's eye. They were black, yet the embellishment made them something she wouldn't have chosen before, showing better taste than she usually displayed. If she got leggings, this should be the pair. She grabbed them in three different sizes, unsure which would be suitable for something so tight.

"Ava, hello!" Bernadette strolled toward her with a bundle of clothes over one arm. She looked like her pulled-together self, wearing a soft, pastel-green sweater and dark-blue jeans. She could have come straight from a salon, and she wore a necklace and matching earrings like she did when she helped at Sheila's antiques shop.

"Finding much? I have a pile to try on."

"I've started," Ava said. "Shopping isn't my favorite thing. I need something new. I'm going to see Fawn's play premiere, and I don't want to embarrass her."

"I can help you," Bernadette said. "What's your favorite color?"

"Orange, but not to wear."

"Blue, maybe? Or pink?" Bernadette turned to sort through a rack of flowered blouses. Ava preferred plain colors rather than prints, but the other woman shifted the pile on her arm to pull a blue shirt with pink roses off the rack. She handed it to Ava.

"I don't think it's me."

"Try it, Ava. And let me get you a couple more."

Before she knew it, Ava was following Bernadette into the dressing room with her own heap.

Ava tried on the clothes and considered each ensemble in the mirror. The blouse with the flowers actually looked good, making Ava feel younger. The leggings did the same thing. Maybe they would add a bounce to her step.

Ava stared at the clothes before settling on the dressing room chair. She was already accumulating things again. Maybe she didn't want to. The new Ava wanted to feel unencumbered.

"How you doing, Ava?" Bernadette called. "Got an outfit for the theater?"

"Almost there, Bernadette."

Ava held up each of her possible choices again. She chose two pairs of pants and three shirts. That would get her through a visit with Fawn, even if she had to wash something and wear it again.

Ava exited the dressing area, and there was Sheila, Bernadette's daughter. She had the eye-shifting appearance of someone desperate to avoid trouble.

"Help my mom, please," Sheila said. Her voice was so low that Ava moved closer to hear. "Ten pairs of pants. Eight sweaters. It won't even be sweater season for that much longer. It's barely sweater season now."

"Just today?"

"Yes. The trunk of the car is already full. All the way full. We'll have to put these bags in the back seat."

"Did she always buy so many clothes?" Ava kept her voice quiet as they both gazed toward Bernadette, who was perusing yet another rack. While Bernadette always dressed nice for church on Sundays, Ava never got the impression that she wore something new every week.

"She mostly shopped for stuff for the house and helped me find antiques for the store." Anxiety cracked Sheila's voice. Her pleading expression made Ava want to help her. "Now there's no house, so it's clothes. And it's like this at every store."

"How many have you been to?"

"This is number four. Two more on the list."

"Oh, mercy," Ava said. She pictured the bags taking over the small room where the O'Donnells were staying.

Sheila's face smoothed out, and Ava turned to see Bernadette heading their way with half as many clothes as she had carried into the dressing room.

"All of those, Mom?"

"Yes, dear. Remember we get the deep discount, and what isn't right for the season, I'll wear next winter. I'll be prepared."

"Bernadette, do you really have space for all that in your hotel room?" Ava said.

Bernadette stood tall, her back straight, indignant as she had been as a child when the teacher told her the answer she gave was wrong.

"I'll certainly make room for what's important. Clothes make a woman. They're an expression of who I am. Don't take that away from me too."

Bernadette sniffled, then pulled a handkerchief out of her pocket and wiped her nose.

Hysteria had infected both of them. For Bernadette, it showed up in her shopping. For Ava, it pushed her to be rid of her job. Ava wondered how many people across the city were acting out of character.

Ava turned to Sheila and shrugged before suggesting they all get lunch together.

Bernadette nodded, clutching her selections to her chest on the way to the checkout.

As Ava folded her new clothes to fit into the suitcase she bought, her mind returned to Natalya.

An online search had yielded nothing. She checked in again with the emergency management center, which still didn't have Natalya's name on a list of those affected by the storm. All Ava knew was that what had ended up in her yard came from the direction of Bernadette's neighborhood.

Ava spent an afternoon tracing the path of the tornado through the city. It had hit houses on ten different streets, a couple at a time, as it traveled on a diagonal path. Some homes retained a wall or a corner, like Ava's. Others had become piles of rubble, like the O'Donnell home.

Ava parked in front of the O'Donnells' and got out, leaning back on her car as she stared at the splintered lumber, broken glass, overturned tables. That anyone had survived was amazing.

A car slowed as it drove by, and Ava glanced behind her. The placard on the car door read BETTER BUILDERS. Marvin Gaines's company. She had been right about him. He must be cruising the destruction to see what business he could drum up.

She could call him for a quote on rebuilding. Rebuilding and returning would be the easiest choice.

The sound of hammering pulled Ava's attention next door. Bernadette's son Patrick was on his roof with a pile of shingles. Ava approached the house and called up to him.

He stood and waved. "Not as bad as your house, I hear. I'm sorry about it, Mrs. Winston."

"Well, such is life," she said. "Did your mom tell you about the suitcase that ended up in my yard?"

He shook his head.

"I'm trying to find the owner. Her name is Natalya Kerminskaya. Ever heard of her?"

"I would've remembered that name if I'd met her," he said.

"Not a worry. Good luck."

Ava turned back to her car, and the hammering resumed. A woman wandered over from the other side of the O'Donnell property. It was Linda Mueller, every blond hair in place and as trim as she had been as a high school tennis player. The rubble stood in contrast to everything she represented to Ava.

"Oh, Ava, I was devastated when I heard about your house." Linda went directly to Ava, her arms open wide. They'd rarely seen each other since high school. Ava stepped back from the offered embrace, and Linda's eyes opened wide before she rearranged her expression to something less emotional but still helpful. It reminded Ava of how Linda had always been able to reform herself to the task at hand—the always obedient teacher's assistant, the perky French club president, the sneaky flirt who wore short shorts under her skirts so she could make a quick getaway after school.

"Don't worry about me, Linda. I'll be okay."

"Oh, I know you will be. You're a survivor." Her tone was admiring of this brave, down-on-her-luck soul. Ava didn't need that.

"Still, is there anything I can do to help?" Linda said. She glanced from Bernadette's home to her own, which was still standing, with flowers blooming from the rains. "Anything, Ava, for you or for Bernadette. I mean, I don't know what it's like to go through what you're both experiencing. Regardless, I'm here."

"I don't think so," Ava said. Linda was fishing for something. She didn't remember Linda ever oozing with empathy. Maybe she wanted to know Bernadette's plans.

"Do you want to come to my house? We could sit and chat, catch up."

Ava reflexively looked at her wrist. A watch could be handy for more than the time.

"I have to move on, Linda," Ava said.

Then she realized that Linda might be the person to know someone with a foreign name. "Do you know someone named Natalya Kerminskaya? Her suitcase ended up at my house, and I would like to return it to her."

Linda repeated the name without asking to hear it again.

"Did you look inside?"

It seemed important to protect Natalya's privacy, so Ava didn't answer, instead saying, "I want to find her so I can return it."

Linda smiled, all of her teeth gleaming an unnatural white. "She sounds like a good character for my next novel."

"That won't help me," Ava said.

"Give me your number, and I'll do some digging, some research, then get back to you if I can identify her. In the meantime, you could write a post on social media and ask your friends to share it. If she's around, someone will tell you."

Having found nothing so far, Ava didn't think it would be that easy.

Chapter 6

Ava had driven to Indianapolis once before, when Juniper won tickets to see the Indianapolis 500. Thankfully, Fawn and her family went also, so all Ava had to do was get to Fawn's house, then let them do the driving through the race-day crowds.

The entire city had been on fire with racing spirit, but the west side near the track held the heart of the celebrations. They parked in a church lot nearly a mile away and hiked past yards filled with checkered flags, life-sized cutouts of drivers, lawn chairs, and coolers of beer. Despite the early hour, the aroma of grilling hot dogs and sausages followed them down the sidewalk.

Gatherings of this magnitude were new to Ava. She'd been to horse races at Keeneland, but that was a kindergarten crowd compared to this. They wove through clusters of college students, some of whom already had open beer cans raised high. Young couples held hands, and the older folks carried bags, coolers, and cushion seats. There were so many people; Ava knew that if she lost sight of Fawn or Juniper, she wouldn't find them again. And in such a crowd, it could happen as quickly as a bee sting.

In the middle of their walk, Ava stopped on the sidewalk and held tightly to Juniper's hand. Fourteen-year-old Juniper pulled free. She and her cousins ran ahead.

"Not farther than we can see you," Beau called.

"We'll never get back. This is too far and too confusing," Ava said. She closed her eyes and put her hands to her face, the purple haze of disorientation creeping over her.

Fawn curled an arm around her waist. Her voice was soft like it had been with her infant children. "Not to worry, Ava. We've done it before. We'll get you there."

Ava shook her head and didn't open her eyes. "We're not even to our seats yet. There are so many ways we could get lost."

Fawn pinched Ava's forearm. Ava's hands flew away from her face, and she gawked at her cousin. "Fawn!"

A group of people parted as they walked through them.

"Ava! It's Indy 500 day. You need to snap out of it. You know we won't lose you. We never have."

Fawn had been with her when she got the news about her mother, when her world crashed without warning. And Fawn had spent time with her every day, even when Ava didn't say a word. Fawn was the person who taught Ava the pinching trick to shock her body beyond the funk that tried to overtake her when a situation felt out of control.

Ava focused on the people ambling past her. She scanned ahead and saw Beau with the three kids, waiting for Ava and Fawn by the gate. The crowd sounded like a symphony—a cackle here, a high-pitched squeal there, then the crescendo of laughter. A man pulling a wheeled cooler rumbled along the route. The sun stood naked against the blue May sky, and Ava willed it to burn away her lingering haze.

They'd continued, catching up with Beau and the children. Once they were in their seats, the excitement of the crowd lifted Ava so she felt at one with them as they listened to Jim Nabors sing "Back Home Again in Indiana," the playing of taps, the overhead flight of the fighter jets, and "Start your engines," followed by a roar so unlike that of horse hoofs. And once the cars got going, the speed was intoxicating. Ava didn't know why anyone needed beer when the racing was so thrilling. The cars flew by them, driving nose to tail, then strategically darting around to pass.

She had watched the race every year since. Maybe she could get tickets this year so she and Juniper could go.

Except that their weeks apart wouldn't yet be finished.

And the tickets wouldn't be free this time.

Even if Fawn were with her, it wouldn't be as much fun without Juniper.

After that initial trip to Indy, Juniper had begged to move to the city, where she could go to school with her cousins. Indianapolis was too far for Ava. At least for a permanent move.

Oh, Juniper. It had been more than a week since they'd spoken. Neither had Ava heard from Donovan, though she didn't expect to. He had opened an invitation, and it was up to her to make the next move.

Ava wondered how things were going on the farm. Washington had agreed to inspect Aunt Lila's storm damage on the garage, which Ava had arranged without talking to Juniper. She was used to updates at least a couple days a week. She so wanted Juniper and her friends to succeed. When Juniper spoke about the farm, the cadence of her voice changed as if she were about to break into song. Her skin took on a happy pink like she was still a teenager, flushed about a boy she had a crush on. But it wasn't a boy; it was her work, which seemed all the better.

Ava didn't know what they had planted this week or what they had harvested or which piece of machinery needed a repair or which housemate had a crisis. Usually the crises belonged to Vivienne, which, after meeting her, did not surprise Ava.

Focus on what's ahead, not what's behind. She repeated the mantra as the interstate highway stretched toward the horizon. Something out there was waiting for her, something better than what she'd been doing since Juniper moved out. After all, there had been plenty of good things in the first half of her life. Certainly her daughter topped that list. Donovan was also up there, for a while. She wouldn't trade the fine years she had with him. Or her work. It had been fulfilling most of the time. They'd helped a lot of people.

Focus on what's ahead, not what's behind.

The road to Indy was easy to drive—few hills or curves, just straight ahead to the city. Once she had gotten through the snarl of Louisville traffic and over the bridge, the cars diminished. Yet even in the soft light of spring, Ava's muscles tensed as she searched for road signs to tell her where she was. If she needed to stop for food or gas, she didn't know what towns offered possibilities. The unfamiliarity hardened Ava's shoulders. She wanted a shell to insulate her like the ancient turtle who could choose to stick his head out when he was ready.

Ava kept her eyes focused as she wandered into this strange territory, watching the mile markers guide her to Indianapolis. The sun descended, and the gray of a cloudy evening emerged. When she got to the city, Ava grew anxious. One wrong turn could put her in a neighborhood where she didn't want to land.

She had put the address into the navigator on her phone and periodically glanced at the printed directions on the seat next to her. She would drive east around 465 until she reached Allisonville Road. Then there was a long series of left, right, left, straight, left, right to their neighborhood on the northeast side of town. At that point, if she found their street, it wouldn't be hard to find the house.

She had to get that far first.

"Turn right onto Key Lane in one hundred feet," the navigator announced.

Ava wasn't spatially gifted, so she assumed that would be the next turn. There was a gas station, a fast food restaurant. She was close enough to stop and ask Fawn to meet her if she got too lost.

She let her head drop back against her headrest. A masseuse had once told her the headrest was designed to cradle the head, and if she let it do its job, her shoulders wouldn't get so tense. Too late for that.

The phone glowed in the twilight as the voice continued to guide her. She could trust the directions, the definite steps she needed to take. When Ava turned onto Laurel Lane, she knew she would make it.

Ava pulled into the wide driveway. Fawn opened the front door and skipped to the car with an "Ohhhhhhh!" It was the way she had greeted Ava since they were children.

Ava climbed out and rolled her shoulders. Fawn wrapped Ava in her arms, then walked her around in a small circle as they embraced, finishing with a kiss on each cheek.

"Finally, finally. It's been many gray hairs since I've seen you," Fawn said.

"And more today for me. I don't know why I didn't leave earlier so I could get here before dark. I was so afraid I would end up downtown instead of at your house."

Fawn patted Ava's cheek and put on her baby-talk voice. "Look at what you did all by yourself. You're such a big girl, Ava Marie."

Ava warmed at the familiarity of her full name. Her mother was the one person who had used it regularly until Fawn picked up the habit after high school.

They walked inside, and Ava followed Fawn down a hallway. She looked for gray in Fawn's hair and saw an errant strand or two. Her cousin seemed younger than Ava. Maybe it was the clothes. Or the fact that she still had children at home to keep her spry.

They went into a room with a desk, television, recliner, and a couch pulled out and made up as a bed. Fawn placed the suitcase next to the bed, and Ava put her purse on the end table. That's when she remembered she was holding the box of cookies Aunt Lila had sent.

"This is full," Ava said as she handed it to her. "Your mom made everyone's favorites."

Fawn opened the top. "Chocolate for Florence. Oatmeal raisin for Brad and Beau." She picked up the third type, a chocolate chip cookie. "Shortbread is my favorite, but I see none. I love my mother, who is still living in, oh, I don't know, 1985?"

"Not true, because you didn't yet have a husband or children then."

"Point to you."

She replaced the box lid.

"Cookies for you, or another snack? Wine?"

"Red, please. And cheese and crackers? You know how I am with travel. My stomach is in knots, so I can't eat much."

"I will take care of you. Let me go put together an indulgent snack tray. This is Ava-pampering night."

Ava followed Fawn to the living room and sank into the deep couch. She could imagine it sucking her in and not spitting her out until she was more like Fawn—energetic and enthusiastic in the way of a person who truly loved life. A new family portrait printed on canvas hung in the middle of the wall, with individual portraits of the children on both sides. So beautiful, all of them.

Fawn returned carrying a tray filled with three kinds of cheese, two kinds of crackers, cashews, pistachios, and dark-chocolate-covered almonds. She then disappeared again and came back with two wine glasses, which she filled.

Fawn raised her glass to Ava. "To surviving the storm."

"To kick-starting life."

They clinked glasses.

"How's it feel to have a home no longer?" Fawn's eyes stayed steady on Ava, not flitting away to her phone or anything else in the room. Fawn was like Aunt Lila in her ability to devote all her attention to the person in front of her.

"Strangely lightening," Ava said.

She had to pause, trying to gather the right words to convey what she had been feeling the past ten days.

"In some ways, it's not bad at all. It's almost like I was carrying this huge box of stuff I didn't need. Because I'm still here. I'm perfectly healthy. Life goes on."

Fawn's eyebrows raised. "That doesn't sound to me like an Ava thing to say."

"I did say 'in some ways.'"

Fawn sipped her wine, then picked up a few cashews.

"And in other ways?"

Ava chose a cracker.

"Things come to me out of the blue. Like the baby pictures of Juni that hung on the living room wall. There were pictures of her all the way through college graduation. I had an album in the basement with photos, but that's not the same. I would look at those portraits every time I walked through the room, like it was a reminder of why I was there, of why I existed. To give that beautiful girl life and a home and love."

"The sap has risen in your veins," Fawn teased.

"That's another thing. You would have never called me sentimental before. What is that about?"

"Hormones? Do you have that stuff going on too?"

"Maybe. My body is transitioning in fits and starts. My emotions are another thing. It seems like I'm going along, and everything is okay. I'm calling the utility company to make sure that's all shut off. Or I'm on the phone with the insurance agent. It's stuff I can do. Then I do something crazy, like quit my job. I was proud of myself; I wasn't even sorry I did it. That doesn't make sense. It's not logical."

"Hurray for you breaking out of that box." Fawn sipped her wine. "We're human. Humans don't always make sense. And women humans get more leeway in my book. We've got more going on. And on top of all that, now you have a destroyed home to contend with."

Fawn selected another nut.

The front door opened, and Florence, taller now, marched straight to Ava.

"Oh, oh, you're here!"

Florence opened her arms wide, and Ava stood to hug her, then stepped back to take in Florence's current get-up—hair bobbed to her chin with bangs, a sweater set in pink, and narrow, dark-pink pants that would have been called pedal pushers in another decade.

"Give me a few more seconds. I'll get it," Ava said. The last time she'd seen Florence had been on a video chat when she was perfecting her Bette Davis look. This was definitely someone sweeter.

Florence stood back and posed, opening her eyes wide and tucking her hands under her chin. It was always a classic movie actress she was emulating. Florence would dress up a certain way for a month or so until she discovered another look she wanted to try.

"She sings as well as acts?" Ava said.

Florence smiled and nodded.

"Doris Day."

"Ding, ding, you are the winner!"

Florence perched on the end of the couch, and Ava returned to her seat.

"And thank you for getting it right. Because I'm a brunette, most people guess Annette Funicello or Mary Tyler Moore. I wish people could get out of their boxes."

Ava and Fawn exchanged nods. Boxes must be the theme of the night.

"And oh, wait till you see the dress I'm wearing to school tomorrow. I found it at a vintage clothing store downtown, and it looks like it came from the costume department at Warner Brothers. It even has a matching jacket and hat."

"That sounds very Doris. Have you learned any of her songs?"

"*Gonna take a sentimental journey. Gonna set my heart at ease,*" Florence sang.

"Sounds like you have her. So why Doris? She's so . . . frothy," Ava said.

"I think we need frothy these days. Let us not turn to the ugliness of politics, global climate change, and the irresponsibility of social media."

Ava took in a deep breath. She'd always admired Florence's boldness and confidence, traits she'd gotten from her mother and magnified. The strong-woman gene had definitely been passed down in this branch of the family.

Florence settled next to Ava and kicked off her shoes, curling her legs under her.

"I'm sorry about your house," Florence said. "Do you wish the storm had blown you to Oz?"

"Maybe it did. I am at your house now."

"Does that mean your rainbow is coming out?"

"You are a rainbow, dear girl," Ava said. "But what's really coming out is mystery. A suitcase landed in my yard with a tag that says it belongs to Natalya Kerminskaya, who I've never heard of."

Ava told them about the contents, including the photos and the letter.

"Did you put it on social media? Take a photo and put it everywhere with the name. I'll help you while you're here," Florence said.

"I didn't take a photo."

"I'll call mom and ask her to do that and send it. Even she can manage a photo," Fawn said.

Her daughter shifted so she was on her knees, bouncing with excitement. "We'll be the Triple Threat Detective Agency. Oh, what smart actress plays a movie detective? That should be my next character."

Florence's phone dinged. She pulled it out of her pocket, then excused herself. Ava watched her leave, wishing she had some of Florence's enthusiasm. She couldn't remember when she was last that passionate about something. Sure, she liked old movies; but they didn't give her that spark.

What does excite me? she asked herself. Everyone had something. She loved numbers, which she knew classified her as a nerd. But her number excitement might have been buried under other people's stuff in her yard, uninterested in coming out to play any longer. There must be something amid the rubble that called to her like Doris called to Florence.

Ava awoke early to the sounds of Florence, Fawn, and Beau in conversation in the kitchen. Their voices braided together into a warm muffler that wrapped around their home.

Everything first-rate landed at Fawn's doorstep; it had never been the same for Ava.

Ava scolded herself. Fawn was like her sister, and of course she wanted her to be happy. She had even bent uncomplainingly to Fawn's will and worn that hideous peach bridesmaid dress for her wedding. Meanwhile, as everyone expected, Fawn could have been on a runway at a bridal show. That was no vacant smile lighting her face; Fawn had been deeply joyful and thrilled about the future she and Beau would build together.

And their years of marriage had proved they were meant to be joined. The one genuine disagreement Fawn ever shared with Ava had been about Brad being more interested in the outdoors than sports. Beau had been a good athlete, and he saw that same ability in his son. He pushed Brad to participate, while Fawn defended her son's right to sit out. Eventually, Brad found a compromise with golf, which put him outside and gave his dad a sport to cheer. A college student now, Brad still joined his dad for tournaments and leisurely weekend games.

Ava rolled onto her back and stretched. She couldn't picture herself at the breakfast table again with Donovan. Early in their relationship, his creativity and bravery in trying the unknown had thrilled Ava. He felt like exactly what she needed. Yet rather than loosening Ava's constraints, Donovan had tightened them without realizing what was happening.

Ava sat up on the side of the bed. There was no need to go there again. She'd been through it so many times, trying to figure out how it could have turned out differently. The kind of kitchen table Fawn presided over wasn't likely to ever show up in Ava's home again, wherever it might be. Ava hadn't gotten pregnant again after Juniper, and she was okay with that. Donovan was the one who wanted a van full of kids. She was surprised he hadn't remarried and started a second family with a younger woman. Instead, they were both unlikely to have a child in their lives again unless Juniper started a family of her own.

Ava wiped her palms across her face. She wasn't here to revisit the past. Today marked Fawn's debut as a writer. They should be celebrating that. And what better way to celebrate than with a cake?

Ava hadn't baked a thing since her kitchen blew away. The cooking urge had totally eluded her. Surely Fawn had cookbooks and a favorite recipe that Ava could make for the celebration.

Florence and Beau were both gone by the time Ava got to the kitchen. Fawn sat at the breakfast table, writing in a journal.

"Oh, so glad you're awake!" Fawn said. "Breakfast? We have cereal and fruit, or I could make you oatmeal."

"Point me to the cereal," Ava said.

She followed Fawn's arm to the cabinet, where she chose the one with the most colorful box.

"What's your favorite cake, Fawn?" Ava asked as she accepted a bowl, then poured in the cereal.

"Coconut cream cake, especially that delectable white icing that goes on it. Do you remember Grandma making that cake at Easter?"

"Yes. I'm afraid I lost her recipe in the storm."

Fawn briefly left the table as Ava added the milk and sat. Returning with a folder, Fawn opened it and paged through handwritten recipes, some on cards and some on sheets of paper. She handed over an unlined sheet of paper with browned edges.

"Mom gave it to me years ago. I can't make it like Grandma did, but I can get the general taste. For some reason, it's always heavier. I do not know how to make a light cake."

Ava felt like Fawn had issued her a welcome challenge along with one of the recipes she had lost. It wasn't in her grandmother's handwriting, but it was in Aunt Lila's.

After breakfast, Ava and Fawn headed to the grocery store. To get the cake done before they went to the play, Ava needed to bake it this morning so it would have time to cool before frosting.

Fawn drove and chatted in her typical stream of consciousness about life in Indianapolis until she rambled over to the subject of writing.

"I think there might be more in me that's going to emerge after this premiere," Fawn said.

"More plays?"

"Or songs, or even a novel. I feel like the door is opening for me tonight. I need merely to walk through and see what's next."

Ava understood that feeling of being on the precipice. The difference was that Fawn had a view of where she was going, and Ava felt like she was looking into a bank of clouds that obscured the future.

"I have ideas all the time," Fawn said. She laughed and pointed to the glove box of the car. "I have a notebook there, another in the kitchen drawer, a third in my purse. If I could ever get it all organized, I might find out that I've already written the next Grammy award–winning song." She laughed again. "Or at least, I tell myself that. No one else is encouraging me to write, so I have to be my number one champion."

"You should call Linda Mueller. She's on her umpteenth book."

"Romances, right? I read one of them. It was okay. Still, even if I called, I don't think she would help me. Do you remember when I dated Mark Van Wyler?"

Ava nodded as she watched the businesses along the street roll past. An insurance agency, a clothing boutique, an electronics store. They stopped at the light next to a bakery. The inviting window was filled with colorful cakes and cookies.

"I stole him from her, as teenage girls tend to do. Maybe she's beyond that now, yet she's never shown up to one of our reunions, so I don't think she's interested in any of us."

Ava returned her attention to Fawn.

"She stopped me the other day and asked about the suitcase I found. I think she was looking for a story idea. I didn't give her much. You can have that inspiration."

"I have so many ideas, Ava. They really do come all the time."

"What's stopping you from going all in?"

Fawn sighed and stayed silent for longer than she'd been since they got in the car.

"Well, there's Florence and Beau. Brad doesn't need me much anymore, and he's totally supportive of my writing."

She shook her head repeatedly and stayed focused on the road.

"I don't really know. It's hard to figure out how to do it."

"How to do what? It sounds like you have everything you need to be a writer."

Fawn glanced at Ava, an uncertain crinkle in her nose. Her voice came out softer this time.

"I'm not sure how to shift. I gave up my career when the kids were small, and it never seemed the right time to go back, other than a small contract job here and there. I worked part-time for that agency for a few months. I couldn't balance it with getting the kids from school and to practices and lessons. And now I don't want to go back to it, but it's really the single thing I'm equipped for."

"What does it mean to be equipped? We both have a lifetime of experience. If you're talking about equipped with education, then accounting is what I'm equipped for. I don't see myself going back to it."

"Why not? You've invested so many years."

Ava squinted as she considered. Writing sounded like a romantic thing to do. That fit Fawn. The farm was definitely right for Juniper. *If I'm not doing numbers, who am I?*

"I've been feeling like it isn't right anymore. I don't really know why," Ava said.

"I get it. I know what does feel right, but I guess I don't know how to transition from what I've been doing for twenty years to becoming a writer."

"I know it doesn't sound like me, all touchy feely. Still, there's something moving through me, Fawn. Whatever it is happens to be telling me to do things differently. The other day I even called my former neighbor, who I never particularly liked, to come do my makeup for me."

Fawn laughed. "I do not believe that. You mean the neighbor with the lecherous husband?"

"Lecherous?"

"Oh yeah. I went to see you and Donovan one day right after you got married. You weren't home, so he offered that I could wait at his place. It was clear what he had in mind."

"Creeper," Ava said. "His wife is Connie. She wanted to help after the tornado. And it was nice. She is a nice person, not whatever I assumed she was. Plus, I looked good when she finished with the makeup."

Fawn drove into the parking lot of a large grocery store. Pulling into a spot, she turned off the car. Neither of them moved.

"Ava Marie Winston, if you can get a stranger to do your makeup and not feel like it was the worst day of the week, then the earth is definitely tilting. We're adjusting along with it, I suppose. You better be ready for anything, and I better get ready to embrace my writerly self."

"Keep in mind, my comparison for worst day at the moment is a tornado that took my house."

"Yet you still had the gumption to drive up here. And now you want to make me a cake. You're obviously not in the depths of depression."

"That's the thing, Fawn. The loss doesn't feel oppressive or depressive. The rift with Juniper does. If it weren't for that, I think I would be perfectly fine."

Florence came directly home after school. Brad arrived a few minutes later from his last class of the week so everyone could go to the play together. Florence wore her dress, jacket, and hat, all in shades of green that not many people could pull off. Yet she looked like she was born for that style.

"How'd it go over at school?" Ava asked.

"Oh, they're all used to me by now. I get a compliment once in a while. Mostly people pretend I'm dressed like they are because they don't know what to say. I have a knack for knocking people off balance."

Florence wrapped her arms around Ava.

"I'm so glad you're here. You are my favorite relative. I assume you know that."

"I did not. I am honored."

"Good, because I don't hand out compliments to most people."

Florence gave a sassy wave, then left the room.

Ava shook her head fondly. If she was Florence's favorite relative, she certainly didn't want to embarrass her by dressing inappropriately for the play. Ava went to the mirror. She felt like she should amp up her own look. Curl her hair? Put it back in a headband? She didn't have a curling iron or a headband, so she pulled out the makeup Connie left her.

"If you don't know what you want to be, make yourself into a pleasant picture until you figure it out."

The advice came to Ava as if she had heard it yesterday. But she knew it was coming from farther away. Who had said that?

There was a knock on her door, and Fawn walked in wearing a short black skirt with tall black boots and a fuzzy, baby-blue sweater. She seemed almost as young as her teenage daughter.

"Do I look like a playwright?" Fawn asked as she stood back and twirled.

"You need a beret."

Fawn laughed. "Don't say that too loudly, or Florence will find one for me!"

She sat on the bed as Ava made an attempt with the makeup. Fawn played with her bracelet, then tugged at the sweater, pulling the arms down over her hands. She breathed deeply.

"Are you worried?" Ava said.

"This means so much to me. If it's not good, I'll be second-guessing myself. I already feel like a fraud."

"The playwright is one part of making a successful play. I think it takes courage to hand your work over to a director and actors and hope they make it what you intended."

Fawn smoothed her palm over her hair and plucked at her sweater again.

"True. And you know, there's a character in it inspired by Lizzie."

Ava glanced at Fawn, who was now unzipping and zipping her boots, too distracted to offer to help with the makeup. Ava brushed the powder over her nose to dim the shine like Connie had shown her. She hoped she looked presentable.

"Anyone else in the family going to make an appearance?"

"That's the problem with writing. People always think it's about real life, even when it's labeled a play or a fictional story. The character was inspired by Lizzie; it's not her."

Ava ran a comb through her hair one more time, then turned to face Fawn.

"I'm sure it's going to be good."

Fawn nodded and stood. Ava followed her to the living room, feeling frumpy even in the new leggings with the leather stripe and the blue-and-pink floral blouse Bernadette had insisted she buy. She was relieved to see Beau and Brad both wearing crisp jeans and plaid button-down shirts. She could be part of the regular folk with them while Fawn took the spotlight.

"When you coming back to Kentucky?" Ava asked Brad as she sat on the couch next to him. He had always seemed the most at home on the family farm. Ava sometimes wondered how such a country boy at heart could survive in the city.

"I'm thinking of spending the summer with Grandma. She needs someone to help her with the farm. She called me the other day and said her neighbor isn't going to rent it this summer."

Aunt Lila had mentioned nothing about that to Ava. Certainly it would be a blow to Lila's income if she didn't find another interested farmer.

"Maybe Juniper could use some help too," Ava said.

"That'd be great. You think she could pay me? If it's a real job, I can get an internship credit for school."

"Approach her with a business proposition, and see what she says."

Brad launched into the pitch he would make to his adviser about turning his summer work into an independent study in botany. He remembered the lady's slippers that grew on the farm and proposed to study them.

"They're an incredibly complex plant. It takes seven years to produce its first flower," he said.

Ava had walked past the plants near the creek but didn't know that. Maybe she should spend time communing with her fellow late bloomers.

Brad's enthusiasm filled the space as he went on. "Then they make so many seeds and hang on to them for years before the wind scatters them. If they don't land in the right habitat, they won't bloom."

Fawn walked past, ruffling his hair. "Don't be in such a hurry to get away from here."

Ava fixated on what he'd said, repeating it to herself. *Their habitat has to be right, or they won't bloom.*

Brad smiled at Ava, and she wondered if he knew how much he resembled his great-grandfather. Maybe Brad also took after him with his deep love for the farm, even if it was for different reasons.

Beau drove them all to the theater, which was in an old building downtown. Below the space was a restaurant filled with round, café-like tables. They walked up the back staircase to the theater. In the front of the room was a slightly elevated stage with a blue curtain as a backdrop. Ava counted ten short rows of chairs with seven round bar tables as the back row. Fawn settled the five of them around one table. They'd made themselves comfortable when a man in his forties with a day-old beard and golden ringlets approached Fawn and kissed her cheek. She introduced him as Mick Baldridge, the director of the play.

"And the lighting designer and the chief publicist," he said. "We're a small operation, but I know quality when I see it."

Mick moved in closer to their circle, next to Fawn, and lowered his voice. "Fawn's play is the best. Don't tell the other playwrights."

Ava noticed how Fawn beamed and didn't move away from Mick, though he stood closer to her than Beau was. What a charmer. Ava wondered if Mick would say the same thing to every playwright in the house.

When he left, Florence leaned toward Ava's ear. "I think he's crushing on Mom."

Ava could see where that might be the interpretation. In the theater tonight, however, Beau held Fawn's hand and gazed at her as if he could see no other woman.

Fawn peered past Ava at the doorway and raised her free hand to wave at someone. Beau pulled over another chair, scraping it against the floor until it reached the table. He nestled it between his chair and Ava's. Suddenly, Donovan filled it.

Ava glanced at Florence, who shrugged, suggesting she knew nothing about this. Donovan greeted everyone like he was still part of the family circle.

"So, Ava, you made it for Fawn's opening night. This is a good show of support for the artist in the family."

"One of the artists," Florence corrected.

Ava scrunched her eyes at him. "In the family?"

Donovan glanced at Fawn and Beau, who looked at each other and avoided Ava's glare. Beau nodded to Fawn.

"We usually see Donovan when he comes to town for business.

And that's been more often recently," Fawn said.

Ava sat back in her chair, adding a few inches more space between them. She shouldn't be surprised that Donovan and Beau had continued their friendship beyond her marriage; they'd bonded instantly. She had never thought about what that friendship consisted of or considered that it would bring Donovan into her circle while she was in Indianapolis, though he had told her he would be in the city. She was there for some "in with the new," not "back to the old."

"It's looking more likely that we're going to open a plant here," Donovan said.

"What kind of plant?" Ava asked.

"Solar panels, like we have in Colorado. It's going too well not to expand and diversify with some more landscape-friendly options. This will be a tougher market, but I like the idea of coming closer to home."

"So why not take the plant to Kentucky?" Brad asked.

"There's a good infrastructure here, and I have connections," Donovan said. He sounded so much like a legitimate businessman that Ava didn't think she would recognize his voice if she were sitting with her back to him. When had this happened?

Donovan and Beau continued to talk business, and Ava realized this Donovan must have emerged during the years they'd been apart. When they were married, she'd participated in very little of his professional life, except for paying the bills for some of his new ventures. Still, she was sure he wasn't this solidly confident before. Oh, he could spew the sparkle; he just didn't have anything for it to stick to. Now that he had success, a true success that had grown roots, the confidence was real.

"Oh, oh, look," Florence said as she handed Ava her phone. There was the photo of the suitcase along with a few comments under it.

"Anything promising?" Ava asked, trying to read the small print.

"This one says she has an idea for you to check out."

"Who's it from?"

"Bernadette O'Donnell."

"I already asked her!"

At the motel, Bernadette's behavior had been a little like Donovan's fake certainty in his earlier years. Ava didn't quite buy that Bernadette was clueless. That day, there had been so much going on that Ava let it go. Now, when she replayed Bernadette's reaction, she could see her hesitation.

"Do you want to message her?" Florence asked, her energy bouncing in her leg.

"I can see her when I get back."

"I won't be there with you if you wait. Let's ask her now."

"Sure, why not."

Florence typed something, then stared at the screen as though expecting an immediate reply.

"She's my age, Florence. She's probably not sitting with her phone in her hand, waiting to answer you."

Florence put her phone on the table. "Plenty of people your age are as glued to their phones as I am, but you don't happen to be one of them."

Beyond their little group, the low-tech venue was filling. Some audience members were so casual that they looked ready to stretch out on the couch at home for the night and watch television. Others had that Florence and Fawn flare. Born with it? Ava wondered. It came so naturally to them.

Ava studied the program. Fawn's one-act would end the first group of plays.

Donovan wasn't talking to her, yet Ava found her ear pulled to his voice. That was what he'd always done—drawn Ava out of herself and to him as if he were the most important thing in the room. Then he was gone, and Ava was on her own, focusing inward so that no one could pull on her like that again.

Fawn smiled at her knowingly. But she didn't know what Ava was feeling. Fawn must have intuited the pull as positive, or she wouldn't have arranged the chairs just so. Ava wondered if there was an inconspicuous way to trade seats with Florence.

The lights dimmed. Mick stepped onto the stage and into the spotlight, then introduced the evening. Ava was glad to focus on something besides her own table. As the plays proceeded, Donovan's movements, Donovan's laughter, Donovan's everything distracted Ava from the stage. She didn't want to be connected to him anymore, but now that he was next to her again, it was obvious that she was. They no longer had the tie of a growing Juniper whose parents had to consult about her. Juni was on her own, so Ava should be too. How did he maintain that power over her that made her feel incomplete without him?

Or maybe that wasn't really it. After all, she didn't long for him when they were apart.

Her head buzzed as if Donovan's presence sated some sort of addiction. When he hadn't been around, she'd channeled that energy into Juni and into work. Now she had neither. Was he merely filling a void she hadn't had the opportunity to fill with something else?

Then came Fawn's play. Ava refocused on the stage. The lights illuminated two characters, a brother and a sister on a farm who were trying to catch the animal that was getting into the chicken coop. Donovan faded as the story blossomed on the stage.

Was it a fox? A coyote? A dog? They couldn't tell from the tracks, so they decided to sit out and wait one evening in the dark. And in the dark, as so often happens, their secrets came out—secrets about a common friend who had disclosed troubles to them separately, secrets about what they heard their parents arguing about, secrets about the farm that gave them life, a farm that might be leaving their family.

It was a lot for ten minutes, and it absorbed Ava like none of the other plays. Ava didn't pick up on any Lizzie influence. Instead, she wondered how Fawn had managed to convey so much story, so many feelings, in so few words. That was a gift. Fawn definitely needed to keep writing and show the world her talent.

The theater erupted in applause, more than any other play received. Mick announced intermission. Beau and Donovan offered to get them all drinks, so Fawn and Ava stayed at the table while Brad and Florence wandered off.

"Well?"

"It was the best one tonight," Ava said.

Fawn's smile glimmered. She leaned toward Ava and lowered her voice. "I thought so too, but it feels better to hear it from someone else."

Standing, she bounced excitedly on her feet. She gazed at the stage before returning her eyes to Ava.

"I think I may have found my one true thing," Fawn said. "For years I've flitted from this to that and had some successes, though I never felt I was there yet. It was more like I was trying things out and putting them on a list. 'Might volunteer at the library again.' 'Never sponsor the scouts again.' I hadn't listed anything in the 'This is it' column."

"I didn't know you were searching for something."

"I don't think I knew either, until I found it. Does that make sense?"

Yes, it did make sense to Ava. Maybe that would happen to her. When she finally hit upon it, she would know, and that would be that.

Florence returned, sat next to Ava, and showed her the phone. Ava picked it up and held it closer to her eyes to see it clearly.

"I THINK IT'S SOMEONE WE BOTH KNOW. CALL ME."

It was from Bernadette.

"Do you want to call her now?" Florence asked.

"Not in the middle of the plays," Ava said.

"We're not in the middle. We're at intermission."

"Tomorrow, Florence."

Florence sighed. "Why put off until tomorrow what you can do today? Think about it."

With that, she stepped down from her stool and fell into a heap on the floor.

Chapter 7

Florence squeezed her eyes shut and grimaced.

"Sweetie, are you okay?" Fawn was kneeling next to her.

"I turned my ankle," Florence said in a voice that was little more than a whisper.

Ava scanned the milling crowd for Beau. He stood at the bar, so she threaded through the bubbling conversations to find Beau and Donovan with drinks in their hands.

"Couldn't wait, Ava?" Donovan asked as he handed her one.

Ava ignored his question.

"Florence fell," she told Beau.

She turned to lead them back through the crowd. Florence was sitting up with Fawn holding her close. Both of Florence's legs stretched in front of her. One foot was bare, her ankle puffed like a pillow.

Florence looked up at Beau. "It hurts, Daddy. Like, really hurts, not dramatic hurts."

Fawn moved out of the way so Beau and Donovan could help her to her feet.

"One, two, three, up," Beau said.

She stood on one foot and tried to put weight on the other but then let out a cry and sank into her helpers. If they hadn't been holding her, she would have crumpled again.

"We need to get her to the hospital," Beau said. "Fawn, pull the car around front. I'll carry her out."

Ava and Fawn hustled out the door to the parking garage across the street. Fawn didn't say anything. She kept looking at Ava, seeming to seek assurance that it would be okay. When she broke the silence, her voice wasn't worried; it was angry.

"Of all nights, why tonight? This was supposed to be my time, my play, my accolades," Fawn said.

The whining was the same Ava had heard so many times growing up. Nothing was ever for Fawn because Lizzie was always first and always better at everything. The praise went to Lizzie, while Fawn remained in the background. But this wasn't Lizzie; it was Florence, Fawn's only daughter.

"What happened exactly?" Fawn said. Her boots clacked on the pavement as they strode toward the car.

"She stepped off her chair and collapsed."

"Why couldn't that girl be more careful?"

"Fawn, she didn't do this on purpose. It was an accident. And judging by the pain, a serious one."

"Of course, everything is serious with that girl. I wish she wanted to go stay with Mom for the summer."

Ava stopped next to the car and stared over the roof at Fawn.

"Fawn, are you okay? Should I drive?"

Fawn closed her eyes and shook her head. She took a minute before speaking.

"I must sound horrid. Maybe I am horrid, Ava. Maybe I'm the worst mother ever."

Ava saw the anguish in Fawn's eyes.

"Florence is a dream, really. She's sensible. She's fun. She's creative. I have no reason to think the worst of her or to be jealous of her. Still, I look at the past eighteen years of my life, and I see that I haven't provided any sort of professional role model for her. That's why she takes on the movie-star personas. Now I'm fifty-four, and if I do want to get back into the workforce, I have nothing to start with. I'll be at the bottom with a tall ladder to climb."

"What happened to pursuing writing?"

"There is that."

Fawn shrugged, then unlocked the car so they could both get in.

"Ava, you know me well enough to ignore me. I'm having a fit about nothing, and as soon as the doctor says Florence is okay, I'll be fine."

"So, let's get her to the hospital."

Ava considered something Fawn had said earlier about putting herself first for a change. That wouldn't happen yet. It was the life of a mother to readily jump to the back seat every time one of her clan needed the front one.

Ava sat with Brad in the emergency waiting room while Donovan wandered off with his phone to his ear. Brad appeared more bored than concerned.

"Have you ever broken a bone?" Ava asked him.

"Nah. Florence is the one who's in for that sort of drama."

"It's not like she did it on purpose."

"Yeah, but I guarantee you she'll play it up like crazy. Just wait. You should have seen her last year when she got strep."

Ava sat back and closed her eyes. What an evening. High to low, family to the invasive species named Donovan. Ava wrapped her arms under her breasts and tried to imagine herself tucked into bed with no alarm set for the morning. She had planned to stay longer, but with this accident, it might be better for her to drive on back to Lexington.

It was also possible that when she woke up, everyone in the house would have restored their equilibrium.

Florence had a severe ankle sprain. They sent her home with it tightly wrapped and told her it might be weeks before she could walk without crutches. They would know more after they saw the orthopedist.

Fawn settled Florence into her bed. As Ava slid under the covers of the fold-out couch and wondered if she should read for a few minutes before trying to sleep, there was a knock on the door. Fawn came in wearing shiny lavender pajamas. She sat at the end of the bed and crossed her legs like they were at a sleepover and it was time to tell secrets.

"Is she okay?" Ava asked.

"Yes, and loving every minute of being waited on. She's unsteady on the crutches, so we made a special phone ring to use in case she wakes up in the night and needs me to help her to the bathroom."

Fawn seemed to have returned to herself, but Ava wondered about the anger in the parking garage.

"And you? How are you, Fawn?"

Fawn pushed her hair out of her face and stared at her hands.

"Ashamed. Embarrassed by my behavior. And if I'm honest, also a little bit green-eyed."

Ava waited for more. Fawn scooted around to resettle herself.

"She's so unafraid to be who she is. I don't know where she gets that."

"She is a marvel," Ava said.

"She makes me feel like I missed something, like I chose the path I was expected to follow. Maybe it wasn't the best one for me. Except that I love Beau and Brad and Florence and can't imagine what I would have been without them."

Fawn leaned forward and took Ava's hands.

"I am so sorry, Ava. You're the one charting a new course, and I'm babbling when I have everything I need. Sometimes I see clearly how coddled I really am, and that's precisely what's always driven me crazy about Lizzie. She's always had everything and still never been satisfied."

Lizzie looked like she had everything. Ava knew that could be entirely different from actually having it all.

"I want Florence to have everything, too," Fawn said. "I know you want the same for Juni."

Ava was glad it wasn't her daughter who had an injured ankle.

Juniper would be impossible to live with if she couldn't get around the farm.

"If Juniper got hurt, I might not hear about it. We are on a Juniper-mandated separation. Did I tell you that?"

"Mom filled me in about the house dispute. Tough call."

That was what no one seemed to get. For Ava, it wasn't a difficult decision.

"Juni's not ready to let the past be the past."

"And you?"

"I'm ready. I don't know what I'm doing tomorrow. I feel more drawn to the mystery of what's next than to anything in the past."

"Including Donovan?" Fawn said. Her expression was filled with a hope that Ava didn't feel.

"We talked at your mom's when Juniper brought him with her to discuss the house. That didn't lead to anything, and neither will this."

"Oh, come on, Ava. I could see that spark is still there. You cannot deny you felt it."

Ava wanted to give her a quick retort; she held her tongue. She did feel the spark but hadn't realized it was visible to anyone else. And it wasn't necessarily a good spark. Sparks started forest fires.

"Stay another couple of days. Go out to dinner with him," Fawn said.

"Are you his confidant now? Or his counselor?"

"Very funny."

"I will not go to dinner with Donovan," Ava insisted. She settled deeper under the covers and pulled them up to her chin.

Fawn flicked her neck to throw her hair over her shoulder, the same move she had used as a teenager.

"Ava Marie, you are more stubborn than you used to be. If you could channel that stubbornness in the right direction, you would be queen of the universe."

"I have no desire to be queen of the universe. Queen of my own little kingdom is all I need, thank you."

"You don't want to be alone for the rest of your life, do you?"

It was a fair question and one Ava had been able to avoid when she had a routine to keep her busy.

She pushed back against the pictures of herself and Donovan together. If she let him reside in her thoughts, he might become a permanent condition. And she had no reason to believe he would have any more staying power than he had all those years ago.

"How about coffee? Or maybe breakfast? That's not the same commitment as dinner. You could text him. That makes it easy to ask."

Maybe she should text him. Then Ava would be calling the shots. *Be the inviter for a change*, she told herself. *Pursue the new.*

But Donovan was the old.

Ava was still wondering what to do when she fell asleep.

In the morning, Ava found Florence in bed with her foot elevated on three sagging pillows. The girl stared out the window, not a hint of happiness anywhere in her expression.

"I'm sure Saturday in bed isn't what you had planned."

"Alas, I am a captive in my own home."

Ava sat on the bed facing Florence. Without the Doris Day makeup and clothes, her skin was smooth and flushed with the bloom of youth, reminding Ava how young Florence was.

"I wanted to take you shopping at Lula's today. You have to rebuild your wardrobe, so you should do it with style," Florence said.

"You're saying I don't have style?"

Florence sucked in her cheeks.

"Did you think you did?"

Ava laughed. "Never."

Florence studied Ava's face, making Ava as self-conscious as she had been when Connie made her over.

"You're Vivian Vance," Florence said.

"What?"

"Vivian Vance, Lucy's sidekick. Lucille Ball had all that frou-frou about her with the pretty hair and the red lips and the big eyes. Vivian was the sensible sidekick, sort of in the background with the intention of not allowing her beauty to overshadow Lucy's. When you look at her old photos, the glamour shots they did of her as a young actress in Hollywood, you see that Vivian was a knockout."

Ava hadn't felt pretty, much less like a knockout, in so many years that she couldn't reconcile the word "beauty" being associated with her. Leave it to Florence to try to create that picture out of the little that was there.

"I don't need to be a beauty," Ava said, feeling like it was true. Sure, she wanted to look okay, but she was beyond the days of longing to be as attractive as Fawn. That, she decided, was one of the gifts she would give herself for the second half of her life. Ava needed to feel comfortable with her appearance. They didn't have to please anyone else.

That included Donovan. He accepted her invitation to meet for coffee at ten. Coffee—no food, no lingering. She would meet him without anyone else in the family around. That would be a better way to see how it felt, to let the conversation go wherever it would. She couldn't imagine it would leave her with any more than relief that she was no longer married to him. He had kept popping up since the tornado like they were playing a game of whack-a-mole.

Fawn recommended a place not too far away so Ava didn't have to drive in the downtown traffic. She parked in the lot and wondered which car Donovan was driving.

As she opened the door, she saw him chatting with the smiling barista. He never put his salesman away.

Ava approached, and he turned toward her.

"Ava, good morning. What would you like?"

"Coffee, black."

"I should have known it wouldn't be anything fancy for you."

Donovan placed the order, and Ava felt the warmth of him next to her. The broad expanse of his shoulders made her feel delicate, a sensation she rarely had. It was one of the things she most liked about him.

Ava picked up her coffee and cradled it between both palms. They went to a corner with two cushy chairs and a small table between them. He still had those light-blue eyes and that dark hair, a combination that tipped Ava off balance when she gazed at him. The gray at his temples didn't diminish his looks. It made him appear steadier, more reliable.

Most women would be thrilled to have coffee with him.

He asked about Florence, so Ava updated him. Donovan nodded. Ava sipped her coffee. Now that she was with him, she wasn't sure what the purpose was. Maybe she wanted to whack him and see if he popped up again anyway.

"Juniper's been true to her request, and I haven't heard from her. How is she?" Ava said.

"She's calling me with daily reports about what's going on at the farm. Is that what she usually does with you?"

"Not daily, but frequently enough. I miss hearing about what they've planted, what Washington has been working on. No catastrophes this week?"

"No. They're moving along and trying to make it profitable, except that there's some conflict with their baker. Juniper did say they were working on that. I admire what they're doing, even though it's not an easy path."

"You are the person to recognize the least traveled and most hazardous journey."

He grinned at Ava. She couldn't stop her own smile.

"She does have a lot of your spirit, Donovan. I also admire what she's doing. I will say, though, that it scared the breath out of me the first time she told me about it."

"And now?"

Ava paused. She didn't know if she had gradually come to accept what Juniper was doing or if acceptance had suddenly come and Ava just hadn't been paying attention.

"Everything's different now. Maybe I'm happier for her because I saw how quickly it can all go away. I've long admired her willingness to take risks. Plus, she doesn't have to stick with what she's doing forever. If it doesn't work out, she'll have other choices."

"And what about your choices, Ava? If you don't rebuild, where will you live?"

Ava sat back and readjusted her hands around the mug.

"Has Juniper said anything about rebuilding?"

"She asked me if I had the original architectural drawings. She wants to show them to a builder to get an estimate."

Ava's throat tightened.

"Does she want to live there? Because I do not."

"I'm not getting between you two, Ava."

He sounded sincere, which eased Ava's throat. If it was only mother and daughter working it out with no one else's interference, they would get there. Eventually.

"If you don't want to be there, where do you want to be?" Donovan said.

"I haven't gotten that far yet. Aunt Maud told me I should get an apartment, but that sounds like an old-lady decision. Besides, I'd like to have a nice kitchen for baking, and I haven't seen many apartments that have that."

"I miss your cakes," he said. He motioned to the shop's bakery case. "Nothing in there looks as good as what you make."

It was nice that he missed something about her. Donovan drank his coffee and seemed to be measuring Ava. He continued to watch her, and she squirmed. He had never shied away from saying exactly what was on his mind. In that way, they were a good pair.

"I'm thinking about moving to Indy to get the new plant up and running."

He fell silent, and she could tell he was letting it sit there, allowing her the time to pick up that idea, turn it over, and examine it. Indy wasn't Kentucky, but it was next door.

"It's nice in Colorado—beautiful parks, good hiking. Juni and I always had a great time when she came to visit. But she's not a kid anymore. She has her own business. She can't get on a plane at spring break and summer vacation. I could move closer, drive down to see her and help her learn the business skills she needs."

Ava took that to mean he didn't have a woman to keep him out there. He hadn't mentioned bringing anyone with him.

"Juni would like that."

Donovan continued, talking about the business, listing things he liked about Indianapolis. He would be closer, close enough for Ava to see him if she wanted. The drive hadn't been that difficult.

In all these years, there had never been another Donovan. She'd gone on a few dates, but no one was worth the trouble. No one made her feel aglow clear to her bones.

She listened to the timbre of his voice, losing herself in its depth as if she were at a symphony and not thinking at all about the rest of the world. She was so absent that she didn't catch his words. She took a long drink of her coffee. She needed to pay attention before she nodded at the wrong thing.

Donovan continued to talk, and something abruptly clicked in Ava's brain. She wished he would stop. *Why am I letting myself fall like this?* Her brain was a word jumble where all the letters had uprooted themselves and were tumbling and jumping over one another on the page. She needed them to stay in one place so she could assess the information, put all the ideas and feelings into neat lists where she could rank them in order of importance, attend to one thing at a time, not let this man sweep away her common sense. She needed silence to do that.

"That means we're dissolving the partnership. He'll be in charge out there, and I'll have the expansion sites in Oklahoma and, if it works out, Indy."

Ava refocused on Donovan, wondering what else about the business she had missed. Obviously it was a considerable chunk if they had gotten to Donovan beginning again without his longtime partner. That must be the real impetus for the move. He wasn't as settled and steady as he seemed. And he was still taking risks.

"Oklahoma and Indy? So, your choice is to live in one or the other?" Ava asked.

"I could stay in Colorado. We've been running the Oklahoma plant from there already. But I like the idea of Indy, close to people I care about."

"Oklahoma sounds dry and hot to me."

He smiled, then leaned toward Ava.

"And you? How would you feel about me moving to Indy?"

There it was, that giddy dance he had so often started in her stomach when she was younger. He could still do it. But which column should she put that feeling into?

"I don't think the ex-wife has a say."

He gazed into his cup, then slowly up at Ava. She could see the uncertain twenty-year-old in his face. It reminded her of his marriage proposal. He'd kneeled, and his natural confidence had temporarily dimmed under the possibility that she would say no.

"I'm asking because I would look forward to the move if I knew I would see you more often."

There, he'd said it, simply—what was in his heart. And it made Ava nervous because nothing sounded wrong in that. He wasn't asking her for more than a possibility.

Ava's pulse quickened. "This is not a good time for me, Donovan. Everything is so uncertain, and I'm trying to move forward, not go back."

"We can't go back. We'll never get back the years when we could have raised Juniper together."

Ava clenched her jaw. There was the accusation. She should have known it was coming. Even when Donovan sounded like he was saying what he meant, there was always something below the surface that she didn't initially see.

Or maybe he meant what he said and Ava was the one with unexpressed feelings. She never had shared her regrets with him.

"I didn't mean that to sound harsh, Ava."

She nodded. If she was ever going to sweep those dust bunnies out of her life, it could be now.

"It's always been hard for me," she said.

"What, Ava? What's been hard?"

His eyes were so kind yet questioning. He clearly did want to understand. But after all these years, she shouldn't have to explain. Her mother's death. The idea that risk meant loss. She knew it held her back, had known it for years, but to get the feeling out of her soul and into her head where she could label it with words that would make sense to someone else was still beyond her.

She shrugged, wishing he could say it for her.

A squeal of tires drew them both out of their seats. Outside, a car was skidding into the parking lot. It hit the car at the end of the line of parked vehicles. The crash of crunching metal sent Ava's hands to Donovan's arm as she watched the car push one car into hers and hers into the next one.

Numbly, Ava pointed outside. "That was my car, Donovan. My car that survived the tornado."

"To get crushed at a coffee shop," he murmured.

Two police cars, lights flashing blue around the parking lot, stopped behind the crash. They must have been chasing the driver. A young man got out of the car and made a feeble attempt to run before one of the officers grabbed and cuffed him.

Donovan followed Ava outside. Her car was clearly totaled, crushed between two other vehicles. Her throat tightened.

"I hope there wasn't anything in there you needed," Donovan said as he stared at the now half-sized vehicle.

"I've learned there's a lot I can live without."

Ava held her hands together to stop the shaking. There was another "out with the old."

The crowd grew as more people from the coffee shop filled the parking lot. A fire truck and ambulance both pulled in, further crowding the area.

Ava watched it all in silence. It wasn't a house, yet it was still vital to her daily life. She no longer had the option of living in her car if it came to that.

Donovan stood next to her, surveying the scene. When the police asked for the owners of the cars, he held up his arm and directed the officer to Ava. She answered his questions as he filled in a report, and Donovan went inside to refill her coffee.

The crowd got more raucous instead of quieting, so Ava and the officer walked to the far end of the lot where the row of cars was still drivable. They had almost finished when a loud, red-faced man joined them and demanded Ava's phone number. He was trying to rally the accident victims to join together in a lawsuit against the police. His car was a month old, and he wanted someone other than the insurance company to pay for his loss.

He asked a second time, and Ava still didn't answer. Donovan returned and handed Ava her coffee while he addressed the man.

"Back off. She clearly doesn't want to share her personal information," Donovan told him.

The man reached into his pocket and pulled out a card, handing it to her before retreating to the loud group.

"Here's the report number," the officer said and gave Ava a slip of paper. "Your insurance company will ask for it."

Another insurance report to deal with. At least she had some recent experience answering an adjuster's questions.

Donovan's phone rang, so he excused himself. He walked a few feet away. It jarred Ava to be without him next to her, although she had gotten through the tornado's aftermath mostly alone with little issue.

She tried shoving her shaking hands into her pockets to still them.

God clearly didn't want her to have a house, at least not the house where she had been living. And God clearly didn't want her to have a car, at least not the one she was driving.

She shared those thoughts as Donovan drove her back to Fawn's.

"They were both accidents, Ava. Like Florence's ankle."

Ava sipped the coffee to clear her head of the haze that had descended, like after the tornado.

"Two accidents of destruction within a month cannot be a coincidence. I don't know what they mean. I don't have even an inkling."

"You don't have to figure it out today."

She closed her eyes. Reckoning day—decision day—would come, and she didn't have a clue about how to prepare.

She placed the coffee cup in the holder and leaned her head on the passenger-side window. Giving in to the desire to sleep felt right.

When she opened her eyes, she saw Donovan outside her open door, extending his hand. She felt so weak, as if hearing that crunching metal had drained her blood and she needed an infusion to stay upright and move forward. He put an arm around her waist and took her hand in his as they walked to the door, where Fawn was waiting.

Donovan deposited Ava on the couch. She listened to the two of them talk and realized Donovan had called ahead. Fawn fluffed two pillows at the arm of the couch.

"Get comfortable, Ava. I'll get you a blanket."

Ava kicked off her shoes and stretched out, relaxing into the pillows. Donovan's and Fawn's voices faded as she drifted off.

When Ava awoke, she let her eyes roam the room, trying to figure out where she was. She sat up and spotted Fawn pacing the living room with the phone at her ear. Her cousin seemed as frantic as she had been the night before about Florence's ankle. Then Ava remembered the destruction of her car and Donovan driving her back. He wasn't in the room.

Ava listened to Fawn's call, wondering if yet another tragedy had occurred during this one visit. Maybe she should have holed up at Aunt Lila's, keeping her bad aura to herself and not going anywhere.

In fact it sounded like Aunt Maud was calling about Aunt Lila. Panic blasted away the remaining murkiness in Ava's brain and forced her upright, back straight. Fawn looked grim, glancing at Ava occasionally now that she was awake.

As soon as Fawn hung up, she sat next to Ava.

"How are you feeling?"

"I'm okay. What's going on?"

Fawn stared at her hand where the phone had been.

"Mom fainted while she was serving breakfast to her guests this morning. They called an ambulance that took her to the hospital, and they couldn't find anything except dehydration and lack of food. She hadn't eaten yet."

Ava fell back onto the couch. This was Aunt Lila. She was more important than any car or job or house.

"Is she back home?"

"Aunt Maud is staying with her, and Juniper and her friend Vivienne are doing breakfast for the guests in the morning. You know if Mom is allowing Maud to stay there, it must be more serious than it sounds."

Lila never droned on about health problems like some older folks did. The vivacity with which she cleaned her home and served her guests made her appear youthful.

Fawn wrinkled her brow.

"I'm worried, Ava. I've rarely seen Mom sick. She had appendicitis once and had it taken out. Other than that, she's not complained of so much as a toothache."

"I'll head back and help out," Ava said.

"I want to go too. Beau can take care of Florence."

"Can he really?"

Fawn dropped her head back. "Oh, maybe not. I mean, I guess I should wait at least a day or two and go to the orthopedist with her to make sure it's nothing more than they diagnosed. She'll have to get around on crutches, and that's a first for her."

Ava stood. Donovan and Fawn had taken care of her. Now she needed to take care of Fawn.

"Do you want coffee or tea with your cake?"

Fawn reached for Ava's hand. "Thank you, Ava. I have chamomile tea in the cabinet."

In the kitchen, Ava filled the kettle with water and found two saucers. She removed the cover from the fluffy cake she'd made for Fawn the previous day, plating two slices. The confection could have come straight from a bakery case.

Ava took the slices to the living room, then returned to pour the tea. She brought them out and placed both on coasters on the coffee table.

"I'll go on today. If you can make it in a few days, you can drive down then."

"You don't have a car, Ava. You'll at least have to stay the night."

Ava spotted a piece of paper with Donovan's handwriting on the coffee table; it showed the name of a car rental agency and a phone number.

She took another bite. *Oh, the comfort of a good piece of cake!*

"You should call Donovan. He was worried when he left you here."

Ava could still see the kindness in his eyes.

"I'll let him know I'm okay," she said. "In the meantime, try not to fret about your mom. That won't help anything. And you know Aunt Maud is capable of keeping her in line."

Fawn smiled but looked nothing like the up-and-coming playwright from the night before. Her creative self had disappeared behind worry and responsibility.

"You probably came here thinking this trip would give you a chance to reset. Instead, you got our brand of crazy."

Ava shrugged. Lots of brands of crazy, or worry or confusion, floated through the lives of people she knew. She took another bite. A little more of that creamy frosting, and she might feel ready to face the world again. She savored the light sweetness on her tongue.

Fawn tapped her plate with her fork. "Sugar can make all problems go away, at least temporarily."

"Maybe I should go to culinary school. Then I could open a bakery," Ava said.

"You don't need to go to school for that. You already know how to bake. Maybe you could open a bakery at Mom's bed-and-breakfast. Bake for the guests and sell the rest. You know how people are. They love something homemade that comes from a farm."

It took Ava only a few minutes to pack her bag the next morning. She had brought little and hadn't collected anything on the trip other than the program from the show. *It's too bad I don't want to travel the world*, she mused, *considering how lightly I pack*. She could get away with a carry-on, thereby eliminating her fear of losing her luggage.

Actually, the tornado had already done that. Losing one bag would be nothing compared to losing a house.

Ava went to tell Florence goodbye and found her resituating her leg on her bed.

"Are you going to see your friend Bernadette to find out what she has to say about the suitcase?" Florence asked.

"Good reminder, Florence. Yes, I am. First priority is helping your grandma, second is seeing Bernadette."

"Let me know."

"And you keep me up on your progress," Ava said. She leaned over to kiss Florence on the cheek. "I expect you'll find a movie star who walked around on crutches and turn her into your current look."

Florence grinned.

"Mom's play was really good, wasn't it?"

There was such adulation on that fresh face. Ava wondered if Fawn understood how much Florence loved and admired her. *Mothers never know what they have in their daughters until they're gone.*

Ava pulled her phone out of her pocket. No messages. Nothing from Donovan since dropping her off. It would feel so good to hear from Juniper. This forced separation was like a conviction of sorts. That was probably why Donovan had been such a comfort. Ava needed her family; she needed her daughter. Especially during this time of trying to figure things out.

Beau and Fawn were drinking coffee at the kitchen table, so Ava helped herself to a cup and joined them.

"What's next, Ava?" Beau asked.

"First, see to Aunt Lila, then solve the mystery of the suitcase. Bernadette has an idea, so I'm going to see her when I get back." Ava glanced at Fawn. "You remember Bernadette?"

"Sure. I haven't seen her for, oh, ten years or so. When I last saw her, I admired how calm she was with all of those kids running around her."

"She's a good mother," Ava said.

Beau took their coffee cups and refilled them before returning to the table.

"I've been pondering that whole suitcase situation. I might take your advice and use that in my next play," Fawn said. "I could build a plot around a mysterious suitcase."

"Be sure you invite me to the premiere."

Fawn ran her fingers through her hair. "It might be sooner than you think. Mick asked if I could write something longer for the playhouse."

"That's huge, Fawn. So, a play, not a novel?"

"Maybe both. Who knows."

Beau leaned in to kiss Fawn, then stood. "Brad and I are off to look at the golf clubs Donovan wants to let go. Good to see you, Ava."

"Thanks for sharing your family with me," Ava said.

Fawn sipped her coffee as Beau left. "What's really next for you, Ava? After the suitcase?"

"Juniper and I have to get together about the house. There are still four more weeks before that discussion. I don't know how I'll make it so long without seeing her."

"Call her."

"No, it was her request. I want to respect it." Ava tapped her cup. "Maybe I'll text her? Or if I'm lucky, I'll see her when she's at Aunt Lila's."

"You're a sly one, Ava."

She shrugged. "It does occur to me that I could give in, get a bid on building a new house. My neighbor, or former neighbor, is a builder. Maybe I could avoid the next disaster that's awaiting me if I go back to the old normal. After all, when has a tornado struck the same place twice?"

Fawn shook her head. "You would rather take the easy route? You would go back to your job instead of pursuing the baking idea?"

Ava turned up her hands, empty of answers.

"You could retreat at Lizzie's place in the DR. Hang out on the beach, soak in the sun."

Ava's hands shook at the idea, or maybe from anger. Fawn knew she didn't fly and never would. It was a cruel thing to suggest.

"I'm not getting on a plane."

"If you're tired of people pigeonholing you, then you should leap beyond the expected. Travel. By air."

Fawn's voice was so gentle that Ava had to tame her irritation. It wasn't an intentional taunting; the suggestion came from a good place.

"There's so much to see, Ava. People to meet, foods to try. Maybe new cakes to learn to bake."

Ava's chest tightened. She met Fawn's eyes and slowly shook her head.

"You are so stubborn." Fawn frowned. "What's a food you used to hate that you now love?"

"Easy. Ham. It was always too salty for me, but now I can't get enough."

"And you had to take the first bite to learn that, yes?"

Ava pushed back from the table.

"Of course. And I see where you're going with this. It's not going to work. I'm not going to Lizzie's."

Fawn started to say something else, but Ava cupped her hands over her ears. Once her cousin stopped trying to speak, Ava removed her hands. She swiftly changed the subject.

"By the way, you said last night that Lizzie inspired your play. How so?"

Fawn laughed. "Every time she had a sleepover, Lizzie took an unsuspecting friend outside, with the creatures of the night making noises that could scare any city girl. She would take whatever girl it was to watch the chicken coop, making out like they could rescue the chickens by finding the animal thief. There never was an animal thief. Lizzie liked to scare those sissies. Prissy as she could be, she was still a farm girl."

Fawn's smile disappeared.

"I'm worried about her, Ava. She hasn't been home in three years. She and Max supposedly have all of this money and this grand new house in an island paradise, but when I talk to her, she doesn't sound happy. I think something's going on that she won't tell us about. You could put my mind at ease if you go see how she's doing."

"Not getting on a plane, even for Lizzie."

Yet Lizzie kept popping into Ava's mind as she drove south on Interstate 65. Lizzie had experienced her share of difficulties, but they never stopped her from moving forward. Of course, it had been years since Ava had spent substantial time with her. And she was older than Ava. Maybe she had gone through her own turnabout as she entered the second half of her life. As she was the closest thing

Ava had to an older sister, she might be the perfect person to advise Ava about moving forward.

The silence in the rental car cloaked Ava in a loneliness she hadn't felt in years. That was the problem with spending time in a house filled with family. Ava felt the absence as soon as she left. Fawn and Beau reminded Ava of her own parents. William, like Beau, was the steady one you could always count on. Jeannie had charisma, like Fawn.

Unlike them, Ava was alone. Her brother was across the country. Her family was Juniper.

Ava shook her head at her moroseness. *And I have Aunt Lila. And Fawn and her brood.* They were all she needed, all she wanted. And once she got back, she would feel okay. She wouldn't sense the loss so sharply. She wouldn't still be wondering about Donovan and whether he would move to Indianapolis. And whether she would want to see him more often if he did.

Maybe what came next would have nothing to do with Donovan or any other man. Maybe Ava should bring some of her mother's spirit into her life. As Jeannie's daughter, she must have some of it in there, buried beneath instructions and columns of numbers that kept everything where it should be. In her new house, she could resurrect the home museums of her childhood. She could take up photography and have revolving exhibits. Host opening parties like an actual gallery. Make delicious desserts for all of her guests.

When the farm came into sight, Ava felt like she was sipping a cool drink she hadn't realized she needed. Her head naturally fell to the headrest. There was the lane of trees, now green with the leaves of true spring. The dogwoods had opened more of their pink-and-white blossoms, providing a colorful contrast to the occasional redbud and its purple flowers. Spring couldn't possibly be more beautiful anywhere outside of Kentucky.

Ava spotted the cars in the driveway and wondered who they could be. One was Aunt Maud's. The other had pulled directly up to the front steps. Maybe Aunt Lila's guests were checking out. She parked by the garage, pulled the lever for the trunk, and hefted her suitcase. As she walked to the front steps, she peered again at the car. A magnetic sticker on the side said MICHAEL REALTY.

Chapter 8

A realtor? That realtor? Their television ads always pushed Ava over the edge with their unrealistic portrayals of family life, with kids running around a white home that sparkled as if it were brand new. That state would likely only last through the first hour after a family arranged their furniture and moved in—on a day when, realistically, boxes were still cluttering the space.

As Ava entered, she heard the male voice from the commercials. He might have been a native Kentuckian, like Ava's own father; however, unlike her father, he exaggerated his accent. He didn't have the soft curves of central Kentucky but rather the sharp edges of another place altogether.

"I would be happy to work with you and get it into the right hands," Mr. Michael was saying. "I can already see a bidding war for such a beauty."

Aunt Lila sat in the recliner in the living room, and she glanced up at Ava like a child who had been caught playing in her mother's closet. Aunt Maud stood. At least Mr. Michael was smart enough to follow her cue. He nodded to Ava as Maud walked him out the front door.

Ava set her suitcase at the bottom of the stairs and went to the couch where Aunt Maud had been sitting. *The farm, gone?* That couldn't be the plan. Lila had a sweet business that made her happy. Besides that, it was the family home. They couldn't sell it.

"I'm not selling tomorrow," Aunt Lila said. "And before you ask, this has nothing to do with me fainting. Maud has been bugging me to get this real estate appointment scheduled to see where I stand."

"You mean she wanted to know how much you can get for it. I thought you were happy here. I didn't have any idea you wanted to move. To an apartment like Aunt Maud recommended?"

Ava heard her own voice reaching a higher pitch than usual and recognized her childishness. Aunt Lila was pale, clearly not well. Ava needed to stop.

Lila shook her head slightly. "It's not that I'm unhappy." Her voice was quiet, lacking her usual energy. She looked down.

Ava wondered how it would feel to have time to say goodbye to a house.

When Lila raised her eyes again, Ava saw the age in her expression. For the first time, Ava recognized how difficult being the spine of the family might be for Aunt Lila. Maybe it wasn't something the older woman had the energy to own any longer.

"Lizzie doesn't want the farm. I'd always hoped she might tire of that highfalutin lifestyle of theirs and come back, yet I don't see that in the cards. And Fawn and Beau are happy in Indianapolis."

"Brad loves this place. He wants to come help you this summer and turn the visit into an independent study for college. He said something about studying the lady's slippers if they're still here."

Lila gave Ava a tired smile. "They sure are. God love that boy. He's so much like my daddy."

She reached across the side table to the couch, and Ava offered her hand. Lila's skin was cool and her clasp light.

"Ava, I'm nearly eighty years old. A farm like this, away from town, isn't the place for an old woman to live alone. And I know I'm not alone all the time. The guests are almost always sweethearts, and I so enjoy them, but they're not family. They were good to call the ambulance yesterday. I hate that this might have put a damper on their vacation."

"And what was the fainting about?"

"When you get to be an old woman, you don't always have the same appetite as when you were young. I hadn't eaten anything, and I'd been on my feet making breakfast for the guests. It's as simple as that."

The front door opened, and Aunt Maud joined them with a resolute expression and enough determination to bulldoze a house.

"She can't keep doing this, Ava. And Mr. Michael says this place will sell overnight, especially if we divide it into parcels. He's sending out an appraiser tomorrow," she said. She pressed her lips together so her smile couldn't escape, but Ava saw it lurking. Maud had been waiting years for this day.

Lila grimaced. Ava wasn't sure if it was an emotional reaction to Maud or a physical pain. Ava lightly squeezed her hand as she gazed at her grandfather's desk in the corner of the living room—such a symbol of stability, of hard work, of constancy. It looked so right in this house.

Ava narrowed her eyes at Aunt Maud.

"Given a choice, Grandpa would never let this farm go outside the family. And he certainly wouldn't cut it up to get more money."

Maud started to say something, but Lila cut her off with a wave and regarded Ava thoughtfully.

"Have you decided what you're going to do about your house?" she asked.

The choices had circled Ava's mind during the drive. She sighed.

"I was thinking about getting a price on rebuilding. I don't know if it's worth it. As much as I try, I can't gather any excitement about that prospect," Ava said.

"So where will you go?"

Ava shrugged. "I don't have that answer yet. I would love to talk with Juniper about it, but you know about that."

"Not easy being a mother, is it?"

Ava considered Fawn and Florence. What was it between mothers and daughters? Their lost hopes? Dreams deferred? Were those the things that kept them apart? Ava never got the chance to find out with her own mother. She assumed they hadn't been close because they were so different, but then, Ava had only been fifteen, not old enough to have a mature relationship with the woman who gave her life.

Ava clasped Lila's hand in a connection that excluded Maud. It was impossible to picture the house without Aunt Lila.

"Will you keep thinking about the farm like I'll keep thinking about my house?" Ava said.

"No doubt. I don't want it going to strangers who would turn it into a subdivision, that's for certain. I'll stew on it awhile."

Ava turned to Aunt Maud, who now wore a sour expression. "What should I do to take care of the patient?"

"She needs to rest. She has an appointment with her doctor tomorrow for blood work, and until then, she's restricted from doing anything."

"Which is about to drive me batty."

"You know what Dr. Dorchester said." Maud looked at Ava. "The guests are gone, and Juniper is bringing over some supper tonight. That girl's a doll."

"And she's sentimental about houses, so don't tell her about Mr. Michael. Thinking about losing two family homes might break her," Ava sighed.

She left her aunts and carried her bag upstairs, wondering what this house meant to Juniper. For Ava, the place had been a part of her for longer than Juniper had. She could close her eyes and picture the entire family gathered around the Christmas tree in the old living room. There were her parents, laughing behind their mugs of hot cider. In this house, Ava still felt their spirits.

Spirits. Spirits filled Natalya's suitcase, embedded in those photos and the blouse with the tatted collar. Instead of unpacking, Ava reached under the bed for the suitcase. It was a good thing she had left it there rather than in the trunk of her car.

Ava wondered how many homes this suitcase had been in. She opened it and perused the contents again, hoping to spot something she had missed. She brushed her palm over the white blouse's collar.

It had obviously been made with much love and care by someone who wanted Natalya to look nice. Ava unfolded the dark-brown skirt and saw that Natalya must have been a small, short woman. Even in Ava's younger days, the skirt wouldn't have fit her.

Ava tried to reconcile the contents with the actual suitcase. Some of the clothes seemed older than the blue American Tourister, which Ava guessed dated to 1980 or so. Someone had saved these timeworn items and moved them from one suitcase to another. Maybe a mouse had gotten into the other one, or perhaps it had been otherwise damaged so the owner had to replace it.

Why would these things be so important that someone would keep them and include them in a go bag with clothes she could wear? Was this a woman who truly didn't have any place that felt like home?

Ava pulled out her phone and called Bernadette.

"You're back from your trip. Did your new clothes work?"

"Sure. Listen, you said on the message that you had an idea about the suitcase?"

There were voices in the background, but Bernadette was silent.

"Bernadette?"

Ava didn't hear anything. She wondered if Bernadette was moving to a more isolated place to talk. There wasn't much privacy at the motel, and perhaps this needed to be a secret exchange.

"Ava?"

"I'm still here."

"Everyone's here now. We found a place to move until our house is ready, so the kids are helping us load up and get over there. Can you come see me tomorrow?"

"You can't just tell me? I need to take my aunt to the doctor in the morning."

"Three-Eleven McDoughney Avenue is where we'll be. I think I can work it out by the afternoon, so come after twelve."

With that, she hung up, leaving Ava to wonder why Bernadette maintained the mystery instead of simply telling her what she knew.

Aunt Lila promised to lounge and read. Ava was too restless to do something similar. Until the Michael Realty car had appeared, she'd been able to stay relatively calm because she still had a home, of sorts. The thought of losing the farm made her feel like a puzzle whose pieces had been scattered across miles.

So Ava took a drive. Without making a conscious decision, she headed toward her property.

During her time away, more of Lexington's trees had sprouted baby leaves, their branches showing promise of summer shade. Ava's street was lined with new life. Ellen Slater was planting pansies in her flower garden. Larry McBride drove his riding mower, giving the yard its first trim and the neighborhood its own spring theme song. Ava saw no signs of Marvin and Connie Gaines at their house, though a new half barrel filled with purple-and-yellow pansies stood by their front stoop.

While her street was alive with the colors and sounds of spring, Ava's own lot provided a lifeless contrast. Most of the debris was gone, leaving only the standing house corner. Ava parked and got out. She trudged around, peering into the former basement and marveling at the destruction. A couple in Versailles had died in their mobile home when the tornado turned it over. With the ferocity of that wind, Ava was surprised more people hadn't lost their lives.

She glanced around and realized someone had mowed her yard. The task wasn't something she had considered now that the house was gone, so she was grateful for the help.

She moved away from the house remains and toward the downed tree. Maybe she should leave the tree and fill in the hole to make it a park. Or Juniper could turn it into a neighborhood garden. Or Juniper could build her own home there on the land where she'd started life.

The place pulled Ava back into memories of her young life with Donovan and Juniper, but she fought against more remembering. She still couldn't picture herself there in the future. She could conjure a blurry image of herself in the years ahead, as an older person with grayer hair, but there was no reconciling that portrait with this place.

She knew it would disappoint Juniper; still, she didn't see that fact changing her mind, even if she got a decent bid for rebuilding.

On her drive back, Ava meandered, first past the remains of Bernadette's home, then out toward Juniper's farm. Ava pulled into the end of the long driveway. The farmhouse windows were alight with a welcoming golden glow. She hoped Juniper felt as comfortable inside the old place as it seemed on the outside. She wished for Juniper a fulfilling day's work, a sense of satisfaction, and a profitable enough business to continue pursuing her dream.

Ava heard the gravel crunch behind her and reached for her lights to turn them off, but she knew it was too late to avoid being seen.

The truck stopped, a door slammed, and footsteps approached. Washington stood outside her car.

Ava rolled down the window.

"Hey, Mrs. Winston. How you doing?"

"I'm getting along."

"Come up to the house. Vivienne's experimenting with some new quiches, so we're taste-testing tonight," he said. "I think Juniper went to take one to her aunt's house."

"You're kind, Washington. I shouldn't. I don't think Juni would want me here."

He shook his head. "I know I shouldn't tell you, but she's missing you bad."

"She said that?"

"She mopes around like her best friend threw her over for someone else."

Oh, for the warmth of that girl's hug. Still, Ava had promised her, and it was not yet time. But Washington might have more information.

"Has she said anything about the house?"

"Not directly. She goes over there about every day. I don't know what she does."

Ava pictured Juniper lying on the tree, hugging it to her body.

"Don't tell her I was here. Please."

Washington held up his hands, silently confirming he wouldn't say a thing. Ava thanked him, then waited for him to drive past before she turned around and headed back to Aunt Lila's—driving slowly so she wouldn't run into Juniper.

The next morning, Ava cleaned the bed-and-breakfast to prepare for the new guests: two couples from Ireland. Aunt Lila sat arranging flowers in vases at the kitchen table and gave Ava precise instructions about what needed to be done in each room.

As Ava moved from room to room, she marveled at her aunt's attention to detail. Soft towels hung in the bathrooms, which were complete with herbal soaps and luxurious body cream. The beds hosted a pile of fluffy pillows in various shapes. She pulled back the curtains to allow the soft spring sunshine to welcome the guests.

After the rooms were complete, Lila and Ava headed to the doctor's office. Something about sitting in the car and being out of her own environment made Aunt Lila seem smaller and weaker than she had even in the recliner. Her wrists were so thin, and her hands, when not in motion, looked wrinkled like fallen yeast bread. She was old, and Ava had never paid attention. Maybe she wanted so badly for Aunt Lila to be the Lila she had always been that she couldn't see the woman who was really in front of her.

Lila did not want Ava in the exam room with her, so Ava watched the television in the waiting room without absorbing what was on. Lila's health was yet another change, one more motivation to adapt her vision. Ava could not picture her aunt in an apartment. She could not imagine lacking the family home as a refuge. Ava scooted around in the vinyl-covered chair, trying to get comfortable. It didn't feel right. Nothing felt right.

"They'll call me with the results," Aunt Lila said as they walked to the car. "He doesn't think it's any more than what I said. If I eat, I'll be fine. And he said I could go back to work."

Ava kept pace next to her, a hand extended behind Lila's back in case her aunt needed steadying.

"And maybe if you do a little less work, you'll be more than fine. I can help out."

"I appreciate that, Ava, but I'm not your burden."

"No, you're my aunt, who I love, so let's keep it at that. Now you need to call Fawn and update her."

They got in the car and fastened their seat belts.

"I don't need that girl coming down here. She has her own family to care for. And poor Florence, breaking her ankle. Gracious."

"It's a sprain. Fawn's your daughter, and you know she's going to do what she wants, regardless of what you say. She wants to hear from you."

Aunt Lila stayed silent.

After lunch, Ava settled Lila on the front porch with a glass of iced tea and put the suitcase in the rental car's trunk in case Bernadette's information was enough to make the delivery. Ava followed the directions to Bernadette's rental. It was on the south side of Lexington, on a street that was too new to have trees lining the sidewalks. The brick houses looked neat, and the lawns were mowed. It appeared vastly more livable than the motel.

Ava parked behind a familiar car. She couldn't quite place it.

Bernadette met her at the door with a somber expression. Her eyes opened wide as if she were trying to convey something to Ava before she entered. Ava couldn't interpret.

Bernadette stepped back. Ava walked in, and there was Connie Gaines.

Ava glanced from Bernadette to Connie and back again. Bernadette motioned toward the couch.

"I should have told you," Bernadette said.

Ava was still confused.

"Told me? I'm not sure what's going on."

"It was my go bag that I stored at Bernadette's," Connie said in a small voice.

Why would Connie Gaines need a go bag? Ava wondered. *And why fill it with old-fashioned things?*

"She came to me three months ago," Bernadette said. "Marvin is a rooster who fluffs his feathers and then spurs his hen."

Ava held her tongue; he had never appeared desirable or trustworthy in her eyes.

"I saw it in your yard when we walked over after the storm, but he was with me. I couldn't say anything."

Connie's voice jittered, and her eyes shifted to Bernadette, then to Ava, then to the floor, then the window, never stopping their movement.

"He's that bad, Connie?" Ava said. While she didn't care for Marvin, she had never detected anything amiss between the two of them.

Connie pulled up her sleeve to reveal a deep-purple bruise on her forearm.

"Did you bring it with you? I need it. I need it now."

Her rapid speech pushed Ava to stand. "It's in the trunk. I can go get it."

"No, wait," Bernadette said.

Connie was hovering on the edge of the couch like she might jump up and flee at any moment. Ava regarded her cautiously. *Does she think he's on his way over? Or is it the opposite?* Maybe Connie was ready to go right back to him before he knew what she had planned.

Or maybe she had someone else waiting for her somewhere. The letter had been written by someone for whom English wasn't her first language. Connie might have family overseas.

Ava settled back down and shook her head to clear her thoughts. She was being too much like Florence, letting the drama of the situation push her wonderings to extremes.

Bernadette laid her hand on Connie's arm and gazed at her with such tender care that Ava knew their friendship had been a close one for some time.

"You have the car. You have the basics in your trunk, and Ava has your suitcase. Don't get on the road and drive willy-nilly without a plan. That could send you careening back to that oaf."

Connie scooted across the couch so Bernadette couldn't reach her, twitching like a rabbit cornered by a cat. "I can't slow down. He'll find me."

Her voice was so faint that Ava leaned forward to hear her.

"He doesn't have to find you. We can hide you, can't we, Ava?" Bernadette turned to Ava, inviting her back into the conversation.

"Aunt Lila has guests coming, but the small single room is still open. You could stay there, with us, until you have a plan," Ava said.

Connie shook her head. "It's too close. He could drive by and see the car."

"We can put it behind the garage. Between the garage and the fallen tree, he won't see it. Besides, we're off the road, and he's not likely to drive back there."

"What if he's tracking my phone?"

Ava held her hands up. "Sorry, not my area of expertise."

Bernadette reached for the phone. "Give it to me. I'll ask my son to look at it and get it back to you."

Connie reluctantly handed over the device, her shoulders and hands trembling. She put one hand atop the other in a seeming bid to still herself. Her eyes shifted around the room as if searching for an escape route. Ava was sure Connie wouldn't leave without her suitcase. As long as it stayed in the trunk of the car, they could try to calm the poor woman and help her consider where to go and what to do.

Chapter 9

"**Thirty-six years.** Our anniversary is next week. I can't take one more."

Connie's blue eyes filled with tears, but she appeared determined to hold on to any asset that might help her get to the next step, to life beyond Marvin. Even her tears. Her cheeks remained dry.

"Do you know what you want to do next?" Ava asked. "I don't have a clue for myself. The house is gone, my daughter's mad at me, I quit my job—"

"You what?" Bernadette said.

"I quit my job," Ava said defensively. She didn't know why Bernadette, who hadn't worked outside the home full-time since her first child was born, was aghast at the idea.

"How will you get along? Does Donovan pay you alimony?"

"No, he doesn't. I don't know how I'll get along except that I'll be happier. Or I'll go back if I'm desperate."

As she said it, Ava realized that having the answers would make her happy. Unlike Connie, she had many options. She didn't need to escape from anything.

"It looks like we're both in solo boats, floating along and hoping we don't get swept into a whirlpool before we find our oars," Connie said, her voice stronger and her eyes on Ava, who sat stunned at her analogy. Maybe Connie was a poet. She had hidden a lot of herself behind the makeup mask.

She stood and focused on Ava. "I don't want to impose. I can pay for my room. I have a sister in Missouri who might take me in, but I haven't told her yet."

"*Take her in.*" Connie made it sound like she was a lost package rather than a person. She needed more than a place to stay. She needed a confidence boost and to be with people who cared.

"I'm sure that Aunt Lila won't take a penny of your money. Truly, she might be happy for someone to help keep things up in the house while the guests are there. I told her I would help, but I'm not the most thorough cleaner."

"Keeping up appearances is my specialty," Connie said without a trace of irony.

Bernadette and Ava both rose.

"You will follow her, Connie, right? You won't pull off in another direction?"

"She has my mother's photos in the suitcase. I will follow her."

"Your mother? That's why I didn't know the name," Ava said. The time period of the letters made sense for Connie's mother.

Connie turned to Bernadette. "Thank you for keeping my secret. It means a lot that you've been such a true friend."

"I'm still here for you. Go with God," Bernadette said. "Both of you."

Ava called Aunt Lila to let her know about Connie.

Lila had the room ready with a vase of fresh flowers when they arrived. She showed Connie around, then left her to her privacy while Ava filled her aunt in about what she knew. Ava still felt like there were missing pieces to the puzzle, but it didn't matter. What was important was that Connie was safe in a place that might give her enough peace to figure out what she could do with her life without Marvin.

Ava didn't have the same motivation for moving on as Connie; she had choices like Connie had never known. Rebuilding and going back to her job would give her the freedom that routine allowed. But she couldn't help but remember the joy in Fawn's voice when she talked about her writing. *What has ever made me that excited?* Ava asked herself. *What did I dream about as a girl, before I became a wife and mother?*

She couldn't identify it. In her mind her early years were merely divided into the life of adventure her mother had provided and the somber afterlife in which Ava strove to stay safe and within the lines because veering outside of them could lead to tragedy.

Aunt Lila had veered outside the lines. She'd been forced to when Uncle Frank died. To keep the farm, she had to generate income. She'd figured out how to do it and discovered skills she hadn't fully utilized before.

Ava again felt drawn to her grandfather's desk in the living room. She carried a chair from the dining table and sat at the rolltop, running her palm over the ridges, closing her eyes, and imagining her grandfather there with her.

He had spoken passionately about farming, but Ava never asked if it was his choice in life. Maybe he grew to love it. Still, a man with such a spark must have had other interests. Besides bills and ledgers, his desk had also housed history books. Three remained stacked inside, all of them about Kentucky's past. He could have taught it or served as a tour guide at one of the prominent historical homes. He likely would have chosen Henry Clay's home, Ashland. It still included vast grounds with gardens, so it wasn't too hard to imagine what it must have looked like when 125 acres of farmland surrounded it.

The front door of the B and B opened, pulling Ava out of her reverie. Juniper walked in with a tray covered in foil.

"Oh," she said. She stopped and stared at her mother. "I didn't know you were back."

Ava nodded, noticing that Juniper's work on the farm had browned her skin like a perfectly baked yeast roll.

"Is it against the rules for us to talk?" Ava said.

"I guess not, unless it's about the house. Let me put this away."

Juniper proceeded to the kitchen, and Ava followed, wanting to say the right thing, whatever that might be.

"I brought Vivienne's egg muffins for breakfast," Juniper said as she moved things in the refrigerator to make space for the tray. "I don't know why she insists on calling it a crustless quiche, because it's really an egg muffin."

"Not easy to get along with, is she?"

Juniper closed the refrigerator door and turned to her mom. "No, but people like her food, so we keep her."

She leaned back against the silverware drawer. Ava stood on the other side of the kitchen table. When Juniper spoke, her voice was hard as granite.

"What did you want to talk about?"

"I want to know how you are, Juni. I miss you."

Juniper inspected her fingernails. She didn't answer. She used her thumbnail to dig out a little dirt under her other nails, then turned and washed her hands in the sink. When the water stopped, Ava tried again.

"I went to see Fawn and her family. It was a good visit until Florence fell and sprained her ankle."

"Was she wearing heels she couldn't walk in?"

Juni's lack of compassion was out of character. Perhaps she wasn't going to let any of her true self through today.

"I really have work to get back to, Mom."

Ava reached for something to make her stay, maybe prompt a smile.

"How many more farm subscriptions have you gotten?"

Instead of smiling, Juni crooked her mouth down, pushing her lips forward.

"We're up to twelve. We need twenty to break even, more than that to profit. If we go through the summer with our profit coming from Vivienne's baking and nothing else, we'll be in trouble."

Ava rubbed her hands together. She'd been in that situation so many times with Donovan, fretting as they calculated a profit margin.

"Give me more postcards, and I'll spread them around."

Juniper nodded and started toward the door. Then she turned back toward her mom, her brows furrowed.

"I was at the house at lunchtime, and Marvin Gaines came over looking for his wife. He said she'd disappeared."

Ava swallowed hard. Having seen Connie's bruise, she didn't want Juni anywhere around the man. But if Juniper encountered him again during a trip to the house, it was better she not know about Connie.

"I hope she's okay," Ava said.

"Weird. It wasn't like he was worried about her safety. It was more like he was mad that he'd lost something that was his."

She watched Ava as if waiting for something more. When she didn't get it, she turned and left.

Connie came in the back door as Juni headed out the front. The older woman seemed relaxed. That was what a walk on the farm could do. She joined Ava at the kitchen table.

"What's wrong?" Connie asked.

"Juni was just here, not acting like herself. And she saw Marvin."

Connie froze.

"He asked her if she'd seen you. Of course, she doesn't know anything."

A desperate "Ohhh" escaped from Connie. She looked to Ava imploringly.

"It's going to be okay," Ava said, trying to convince herself.

"I need to get away. This is too close. I don't want you and Lila to be in a bad position." Connie paced from the sink to the back door and back to the sink. "I'll get in the car and drive west. There's more space out there, less likely he would find me."

"No, you won't."

Connie stopped at the command in Ava's voice.

"Like Bernadette said, you don't need to drive willy-nilly without a plan and in this state of mind. Be sensible, Connie."

When Ava said it, she knew she was talking about herself too. She'd always been sensible, until the tornado. Now she was flitting from place to place with no purpose, and even her daughter didn't want to be with her.

She and Connie were more alike than not.

The front door opened again, and Connie scampered out the back. Of course, Marvin wouldn't walk in without knocking, but in her state of mind, Connie wasn't thinking clearly.

It was Juni again. She entered the kitchen and handed Ava a plate covered with foil.

"I nearly drove off with this in the back seat. It's a two-layer flourless chocolate cake. Aunt Lila said she wanted an evening dessert for her guests."

"I could have made her something," Ava said, balancing it in her hands. It had been years since she last made a flourless chocolate cake. They took so many eggs. That must be why Vivienne made it.

"You weren't here, Mom," Juni said.

Ava heard the accusation and sensed it was for something more than being unavailable to make a dessert.

"I miss our talks, Juni. The day doesn't feel complete when I haven't heard from you."

A softness washed across Juniper's face.

"I do too, Mom. But we still have more than three weeks."

"Unless we've already reached our conclusions."

If it would ease Juniper's burden, Ava would stop this drawn-out pondering and make an immediate decision. If Juni needed her, Ava wanted to be there.

Juni considered her mother with a long, searching look before skirting past Ava to open the fridge. She made more space for the cake and tucked a small container in the door.

"I need more time, Mom. Things at the farm are taking all of my focus, so I haven't been able to do what I want before I reach my decision. I'm researching options." She took a few seconds to recompose herself before continuing. "So, there's strawberry jam between the layers and fresh strawberries to top the slices."

"I'll take care of it. Thank you, Juni."

Ava heard footsteps, and Aunt Lila appeared. She smiled at Juniper and hugged her, but her color was still pale. She wore weariness like a beekeeper's hood. Ava would be serving the cake to the guests.

"Ava, where's Connie? I thought she might like a little lemonade and a talk on the porch."

Juniper set her mouth in that hard line as she leveled her gaze at Ava.

"You didn't trust me to tell me?"

Ava swallowed hard. "Honey, it wasn't trust. Connie's in quite a predicament, maybe even a dangerous one. Her story isn't mine to tell."

"I asked if you knew where she was. I didn't ask for her story."

Thankfully, rather than storming out of the house, Juni dropped into a chair. She removed her ponytail holder, shook her hair free, and rolled the elastic band onto her wrist. Ava caught Aunt Lila's eye and motioned to the back door, where Connie had gone.

Ava sat next to her daughter as Lila left.

"Juni, my heart stopped when you said Marvin asked you about Connie. It's easier to stay uninvolved if you don't know anything."

Juni's concern showed in her eyes. "Do you think he's dangerous?"

"To Connie he is. I don't know about to anyone else, but I certainly won't take a chance with you."

Juni tugged at the ponytail holder.

"I better stop going over there every day. Then he can't ask, and I don't have to lie."

Ava's stomach lurched. Juni had been there every day since the tornado. Her love for that spot was as deep as Ava's love for the family farm.

"Juni, if you must go over, please take someone with you. I don't trust that man."

Juniper bit her lip and nodded. A crease split her eyebrows. "Did you know, Mom? About Marvin?"

Guilt washed over Ava like a bucket of ice water. She rubbed her arms to get rid of her goose bumps. She shook her head. "I feel terrible. I never gave them much thought, even though they were our neighbors."

The couple had been there when Ava and Donovan first moved in. Their kids were in school, and they seemed like a typical busy family. After their kids grew up and left, Ava was busy with Juniper, and she didn't pay enough attention to realize that Connie might be lonely. She might have needed a friend.

"I guess she would have been happy if her house had blown away in a tornado. Maybe it would've given her an easy way to leave him," Juni said.

"She's doing it now, even if she doesn't know how."

"Sort of like us." Juni stood and sighed. "See you in a few weeks, Mom."

Ava searched for something else to keep Juni in the room, but it wasn't there. Juniper was gone.

Ava wanted that glass of lemonade and time with Aunt Lila on the porch herself, but she needed to let Lila work her calming magic with Connie.

She rose and opened the refrigerator to check out the egg muffins. Bread would complement the eggs—sweet bread. Ava rummaged through the fridge for ingredients before moving on to the cabinets, where she found a container of cinnamon. Cinnamon rolls would be the perfect accompaniment. That was something she could contribute.

In the morning, Ava helped Aunt Lila serve breakfast to the Irish visitors. Though not quite as engaging as usual, Lila still prompted plenty of conversation with her inquiries about where they'd been. The previous day it had been the Kentucky Horse Park, and today they had tickets for a horse farm tour that included a picnic lunch. Kentucky already felt like a second home to them.

"I could close my eyes, breathe in the air, then open them and look at the green grass, the rolling hills, and the stone fences and feel certain I was back home," said one of the young men, his soft brogue drawing in Ava. "It's no surprise why some of our people moved here. They must have thought they'd found the other end of the rainbow."

"Especially when they found the bourbon. Everywhere we go, they want to take us on a bourbon trail tour. In Ireland, that tour is through the bars in every town, naturally—no formal guide needed," his young wife said.

The foursome chuckled, and Ava was reminded of the warmth she'd felt at Fawn's house. She pulled the cinnamon rolls out of the oven while Aunt Lila poured the coffee and tea, all the while listing other places the group might want to explore. Ava glanced at them and saw how attentively, almost adoringly, they regarded her aunt as they listened.

"McConnell Springs is a lovely place to get away from the noise of the city. It's right inside of Lexington," she said. "Sugar and cream are both here. What else might you need?"

"That cinnamon smell is tantalizing," the second woman said.

Ava carried over the plate and placed it in the center of the table.

"Just out of the oven, so they're still hot," she said.

"Can we take you two home with us?" the first young man asked. His wife swatted his arm. "What, love? Then you could be served breakfast every day, which is fitting for my queen of the castle."

"I know what you intended. You don't like my cooking," she said. She looked at Ava. "I can't bake at all. This is a treat."

"I'll keep you in treats while you're here," Ava promised with a satisfied smile.

Later that day, Ava found Aunt Lila showing Connie photos of Lizzie's place in the Dominican Republic. It did seem like a dream home, with colorful tiles around the doorways, an in-ground swimming pool, palm trees, and a patio overflowing with potted flowers. The sun brightened everything as if to say nothing bad could happen there.

"Looks like the perfect place to forget about the world for a while," Connie said wistfully.

"Have you been to the Caribbean?" Lila asked. Ava filled a glass with iced tea as she listened.

"We went to London on our honeymoon, though I would have chosen Paris. We went to Florida once, the Mississippi coast another time. Always for sales conventions. Marvin would go do his business and leave me on my own. I explored, but it's not so much fun when you're alone."

The sadness in Connie's voice cracked Ava's heart. *When did all this sappiness start oozing in?* she wondered.

"Have you been there?" Connie asked Lila.

"Two years ago, with my daughter Fawn and her family."

Lila described the trip, painting a picture of paradise. The sunset from the beach restaurant was the most beautiful she had ever seen. The flowers had glossy leaves and large blossoms in vibrant colors.

"I would like to see that," Connie said.

"I'm going to see if Lizzie wants visitors. It would be perfect for you," Aunt Lila said. Then she peered at Ava, who was still hanging back in the kitchen.

Ava shook her head. "You know I'm not getting on a plane."

"As I recall, Juniper got you a passport for a Christmas present. Did you rescue it from the house?"

When sorting through her portable safe to find her home insurance policy, Ava had indeed come across the passport, so new that it was stiff to open.

"She must have known you would need it. I'm calling Lizzie," Lila said. "And by the way, Fawn's coming in a few days. That will free you up to travel, Ava, because you won't have to worry about me."

Connie excused herself, and Ava sat at the breakfast bar across from Lila. A tautness in the air told Ava that Aunt Lila wasn't going to let this go.

"Ava, your mother wasn't scared of anything. She would never have wanted you to fence yourself in because of her accident."

"Maybe not, but she's not here to tell me that, is she? And neither is Daddy because he couldn't face up to anything without her."

Ava took in a sharp breath. Even as a grown woman in the middle of her life, those feelings were still tender. She so rarely allowed herself to go there.

Lila's eyes conveyed the sadness Ava felt. Her father had never been the same after her mother was gone.

"You know he tried, honey. People deal with tragedy in different ways. For men like him, it takes a toll on their health. I always assumed Will married Jeannie because she had enough courage for the both of them."

"I guess I take after him."

"You're almost fifty-five years old. You take after whoever you decide to take after."

It had never occurred to Ava that she had an option—that she wasn't a paper doll who could only fit into the slot she was cut out of. She could change her shape.

Ava liked the idea. When she was a teenager, she had wanted so badly to be more like her mother. Jeannie didn't care about anyone's opinion of her and had a slew of friends, likely because she was authentic. Ava rarely saw her mother alone—except during that magic hour before she went to bed. That's when Jeannie would shower, then sit on the back porch to simply be. If Ava wanted to talk with her about something, she knew she would get Jeannie's full attention during that time.

"I think Connie needs to get away for a while, gain some perspective for herself," Aunt Lila said.

There was another sharp breath, this time fueled by guilt rather than sadness. Ava tried to imagine herself back in her house, tried to remember the occasions when she had seen Connie. Since the Gaines children moved away, she had only ever seen Connie with Marvin. It made her wonder how Connie had gotten away to do Ava's makeup when Donovan came to visit.

Ava's cell phone rang on the kitchen counter. It was Bernadette.

"Marvin is prowling around for Connie. He's been driving past our new rental for twenty minutes, Ava. I don't know how he found out where we are!"

Bernadette pushed her words breathlessly.

"If he knows about me, he probably knows about you too, and I wouldn't be surprised if he knows about your aunt's place. Connie needs to get out of town."

"Slow down, Bernadette. You haven't told Connie, have you?" Ava said.

"Heavens no, Ava. I'm scared enough for her. I don't want to put this on her. You need to get her out of here before he goes to the police and puts in a missing person report. Then the police will be looking for her. They'll show her picture around like she's a criminal."

Ava wondered if Connie should file an emergency protective order. She didn't know what evidence might be required for such a thing. Or maybe Ava should call Marvin and tell him to leave Connie alone. There must be an answer. Bernadette was too stressed to help her figure it out.

"I'll take care of it, Bernadette. Don't worry."

Bernadette sighed her relief, as if she had total confidence that Ava could handle this. Ava wished she had such confidence in herself.

Chapter 10

Connie refused to file an emergency protective order. She also didn't want to step outside the house. She got up every day, did her makeup and hair, and dressed like she was going out. Then she cleaned. At first it was a typical vacuuming and dusting, but on the third day, she began a deep spring cleaning of the entire house. She moved all the furniture, washed down the walls, shampooed the carpets—all the things Ava had never done in her own home.

Ava watched without knowing what to say. Connie didn't ask for anything as she focused on her tasks, so Ava decided to make herself useful in the kitchen. She discovered Aunt Lila's shelves of cookbooks and paged through them, searching for something new to try.

She baked muffins and coffee cakes for the guests. She decorated cupcakes and made a tray of three kinds of cookies for a late-afternoon snack.

Putting a few cookies on a plate, Ava took them to the breakfast bar, where Lila was reviewing a gardening notebook. For years she had grown a luscious cutting garden of flowers, but recently, on a fundraising tour she and Maud had taken through some of the prettiest gardens in town, she had come across one house that boasted a walking garden planted with a visually pleasing mix of flowers, vegetables, and herbs.

"The guests would enjoy it—a sort of meditation walk among the growing beauties," Aunt Lila said. It would also give her fresh produce to cook for them. People loved hearing that something was homegrown.

Ava scanned the sketches Lila had made of garden designs. In one, a serpentine path lined with low-growing flowers like violets and marigolds circled through spherical mounds of perennials, with an herb tucked in here and there. Lila would have to stay at least through the growing season to bring the plan to fruition.

"I take this to mean you're not really thinking of selling?" Ava said.

Lila gazed steadily at Ava. "I don't know. I guess having you and Connie here makes me forget about selling. Though I know you won't be here forever."

It felt so right to be at the farm, but permanently? It would be presumptuous for Ava to invite herself.

"I'm worried about Connie," Aunt Lila said. "Don't get me wrong, I'm thankful for her work. She's cleaned the entire place better than I have for years. What will she do when she's finished with the house? You have to do something, Ava."

"I went to school for accounting because I can handle numbers. I've never been as good with people."

"Honey, she trusts you, or she wouldn't still be here."

Ava nibbled at a cookie. She could try to talk Connie into going car shopping with her. That was one way to get her out of the house, and Ava was driving a rental, so Marvin wouldn't recognize that.

However, the rental car argument didn't convince Connie that it was safe to leave the property. She declined and returned to scrubbing the front porch.

Ava set out on her own. She wanted something practical with good gas mileage, maybe in silver or black.

Yet at the first dealership, a red car with an ivory interior momentarily took her breath. That was certainly something different. But studies showed that red cars got more speeding tickets. No, she needed gray, plain gray. Ava wasn't in a position to go into debt over traffic fines.

As she drove from dealership to dealership, Ava kept her eyes on the rearview mirror, watching for Marvin. It was unlikely he would find her, but Ava stayed alert. If he wasn't following her, she could reassure Connie that it was okay to wander out.

Instead of Marvin, Ava spotted someone who looked an awful lot like Juniper, which struck her as odd since it was 2 p.m. In the spring, Juni's habit was to work on the farm from sunup to sundown and leave the property for errands after that. Nonetheless, that small blue car behind Ava resembled Juni's, and the woman inside with the strawberry-blond ponytail appeared to be Ava's daughter.

After staying behind Ava for two stoplights, the car turned left, into the public library's parking lot. Juni did like to read, but more likely she was researching something for the farm, which she could have done online. Ava passed the library before she could confirm it was Juni getting out of the car.

Ava's phone rang. She was annoyed she hadn't turned it off. People who talked on their phones while driving made her nervous. She glanced at the screen. *Donovan.*

"Hello," she said after she pulled over in front of a medical office, her pulse quickening with worry. "Is something up with Juni?"

"Juni? She sounded good last night."

"Okay," Ava said, even though it wasn't. Her motherly instincts insisted that something was off with Juniper. But Donovan didn't know Ava had seen her going to the library in the middle of the day. "So why did you call?"

"I wanted to check on you. How are you, Ava?"

Until Indy, she'd gone years without Donovan "checking" on her. Maybe it was his way of following up on crash day.

"I'm shopping for a car."

Donovan was quiet. She knew her response had come out sharp as a knife, though he had done nothing wrong. But he would have to deal with it.

"Is there something else?" Ava said.

She closed her eyes and shook her head. *Why can't I be as kind to him as I was to Connie?* She took a deep breath.

"I'm fine, Donovan, really. Thank you for asking."

"I did want to talk with you about a job. It sounds like this isn't the right time. Can we talk later?"

"A job? I don't know what you mean."

"I'm going to need someone to manage the accounting office when we get up and running in Indy. I thought of you."

She did need a job, just like she needed a place to live—a place in Kentucky.

"I might not have a house, but that doesn't mean I want to move to another state," Ava said.

"Don't give me an answer now, Ava. Explore the idea. Ask me whatever you need to know. We'll talk in another week or two."

He said it like a man in charge of his business who knew what he wanted. The tone made Ava sit up a little straighter. Perhaps he truly had left the reckless gambler behind.

"Good luck with the car search."

Ava hung up and stared at her phone. *A job. With Donovan. In Indianapolis. Why would he think I would be interested in that?* It was hard enough to drive there to visit Fawn. An entire move to a new place would shake her to the core. Besides that, her life was in Lexington.

Juni was in Lexington.

She shook her head again to clear her thoughts. First she had to take care of necessities. A car was something she could easily mark off her list. A job could wait. According to Mrs. Alvarado, she was still on leave, even though in Ava's mind, she'd already left. And she didn't miss it at all. It was strange to realize that after all those years at the agency, she had quickly relegated her job to the past. No one from the office had called to check on her or to ask her guidance about anything.

If she worked for Donovan, she could be a manager. That was what he offered her. That was what she had missed out on in her own agency.

There was no way she could move to Indianapolis.

Ava pulled into the next dealership, where a slick-haired young man greeted her with a white-strip smile. She veered away from him to peruse the lot alone, then found him again when she identified one to test-drive. After the drive, it didn't take much negotiation before he left her seated at a desk and went to draw up the papers.

He returned with the salesman panache still in place, encouraging her to sign up for yet another warranty or service with each page. "The car, that's all I want," she said to him. "Let's get to that signature and be done with it."

He nodded with a serious expression, then told her they would clean up the car and have it ready for her in the morning.

In her happiness about completing her task, Ava almost didn't notice the car parked at the end of Aunt Lila's driveway. She assumed a traveler had pulled over to check directions, perhaps a new guest. But when she turned into the driveway, she saw she was wrong. It was Marvin.

She sped past him, hoping he wouldn't recognize her, praying he hadn't narrowed in on Connie's real location. In reality, there was no other reason for him to be there.

When Ava reached the house, Aunt Lila was sitting on the porch. Ava approached and saw through the front door that the guests were inside, gathered around the kitchen table with the cookies and cupcakes.

"You look worried," Aunt Lila said from the porch swing.

Ava sat on the rocker and leaned in so she could talk softly.

"Marvin is at the end of the driveway."

"I'll call the police. They patrol for me when I need it. And you need to go up and see Connie."

"I can't tell her. She'll freak out."

Aunt Lila put up her hand like a traffic cop. "No, I don't mean tell her. Bernadette brought Connie's phone to her earlier and said her son fixed it so no one could track her location and that he blocked Marvin from calling her."

That sounded exactly like what Connie needed. But Lila's worried eyes told Ava that wasn't all.

"She was cleaning the back porch, and her phone rang. She put down the mop, went upstairs, and hasn't been back since."

"How long ago was that?"

Aunt Lila glanced at her watch. "Three hours."

Ava stood. She had brought Connie to this house. She had to find out what else Connie might need, even if it wasn't something Ava could provide.

Ava greeted the guests as she walked inside. They responded with praise for the cookies and cupcakes. Her happiness warmed her like a blush over a compliment from a crush. If baking to make people happy was her purpose, life might be simple, and she could be happy. *Is it that easy?*

She stood outside Connie's closed door, the weeping on the other side spilling out like a creek overflowing its banks. Ava winced. When Juni cried, Ava felt pulled to do whatever she could to comfort her. Around any other crier, Ava preferred to bake a cake to help ease the pain instead of offering personal reassurance.

She found Connie sitting on the edge of the bed, her mascara streaking her cheeks.

"Don't look at me. I'm a mess."

Ava took the seat from the vanity and turned it toward Connie.

"What's happened?" she asked.

"It's Heather. I got my phone back, and there were messages from Heather and from Tyler. I called them both. Marvin had already reached them each with a story about me going crazy."

It hadn't occurred to Ava that while Connie was unable to use her phone, Marvin could tell their children his own version of the story.

"And?"

"Tyler understands. He and his father always had a contentious relationship. Heather is Daddy's little girl. She told me if I don't call Marvin so he can help me get medical treatment, she will tell him where I am."

To have a traitor as a daughter—that wasn't something Ava could imagine.

That's when Ava noticed the blue suitcase by the door.

"Did she give you a timeline?"

"The weekend. I hope she waits that long; I can be gone by Sunday afternoon."

Ava's heart pounded. Two days. That might be too long, considering Marvin had already figured out Connie's location or at least suspected it.

"You're not in this alone, Connie. We'll figure it out together."

Connie nodded, then wept with tremors racking her small body; Ava eased next to her and put an arm around her shoulders.

Fawn arrived on Thursday, ready to stay for as long as her mother needed her. Florence was still wrapping the ankle and trundling around on crutches, both of which she had mastered. However, the injury had temporarily halted her creative fashion choices.

Fawn sat on the porch with her mother and Ava, who updated her on Connie's situation. Connie was mostly staying in her room for fear of putting a damper on the guests' vacation.

"I'm telling you, go to Lizzie's. Sun and sand can burn away all the problems of the soul," Fawn said. "You've got a free place to stay there. Lizzie has a cook and housekeeper, so it will be like you're staying in a hotel."

"You should go with them, sweetheart. It would be good for your writing to get away," Aunt Lila said.

"Really, Mom? You know I came here for you. And I know that neither you nor the guests require twenty-four-hour minding, so I'm sure I'm going to have time to write."

Ava cast about for another solution, though she'd already done that for hours and come up empty. When she had left to pick up her new car, Marvin was driving past the farm yet again. Upon her return, she stayed at the end of the driveway to see if he would make another pass. Twenty minutes later, he hadn't reappeared. He must have been figuring out his next move.

Aunt Lila put her hand over Ava's. "Ava, the truth is that Connie needs you to be brave so she can do the same. She's walking away from a long marriage. Getting on a plane seems like a small thing to do next to that. But big or small, you also need to do it for yourself."

"For me? Why for me?"

"Oh, honey, relax a little. Dream a little. Let yourself go, and see where you land on the other side."

Fawn nodded to Ava, her eyebrows raised. It was two against one.

Ava wondered if she could get in to see the doctor the next day. Maybe he could give her a prescription to put her out as soon as she got on the plane.

She abruptly stopped her thought process to marvel over it. *Am I actually considering this?*

Ava was surprised when Connie said yes to the idea without hesitation. Aunt Lila called Lizzie, and Fawn helped them book tickets for Sunday.

Ava was more surprised to get an appointment with the doctor the next day. She entered the waiting room to find Bernadette with her younger daughter, Erin. Bernadette glanced past Ava.

"Well, no one brought you in, so I suppose it's voluntary," Bernadette said. She glared at Erin, who looked pointedly at Ava, then continued to read a magazine.

"Have you gone batty too, Ava?" Bernadette said.

"Batty?"

"My family thinks I've lost it because I'm trying to replenish what was lost in the storm. Some sort of post-tornado trauma, they say."

Erin closed her magazine and looked pointedly at her mother, her lips pushed forward as she spoke. "You can't replace memories, Mom. Even you admitted that. Only one family was living in our house. It looks like you're buying for four families! And you don't listen to any of us."

Erin turned to Ava, her reddish-brown eyes ablaze.

"Sheila said they ran into you on shopping day number one. Since then, Mom has maxed out two credit cards, and number three appears to be near its limit."

"We need pots and pans and plates, unless we're going to eat out every day. And I know you don't want me wandering around the house—or the town—buck naked, so I do need clothing."

Erin ignored her mother as she spoke to Ava.

"We had to ban her from using the car so she couldn't shop. Then boxes started arriving because she had to try out the top shopping sites. Now the dining room in the temp house is so filled with unopened boxes that we have to stand at the kitchen counter or sit on the living room floor to eat. She's bought so much, but not a kitchen table."

"The living room floor is carpeted, and I did purchase pillows," Bernadette said. "And as you said, we have a counter in the kitchen. Your brothers eat half of their meals standing anyway."

Ava felt like she was peeking around the curtain into a place Bernadette never would have invited her. Bernadette had always been such a paragon in the community, a mother supreme with a beautiful family and a loving husband. Everything she did supported that characterization. The tornado unleashed a different Bernadette.

Ava hadn't felt the slightest need to replenish what was lost. Unless it was a necessity, like clothes, she was glad to not have to keep up with it. In fact, she hadn't thought at all about the items in that storage unit.

"Well, Ava, are you going to stand up for me?" Bernadette's eyes seemed larger than Ava had ever seen them as she challenged her. "You've known me longer than my children, longer even than my husband. Am I a loony?"

Ava remembered Bernadette's reaction when Ava told her she had quit her job—like Ava was the one who had lost her mind. Maybe Bernadette needed a change of scenery, to be in a place that could wipe out the pictures of what she had lost.

"Would you like to get away, Bernadette? Connie and I are going to see my cousin. You could join us."

"Where is she?"

"The Dominican Republic."

Bernadette closed her eyes hard and waggled her head as if trying to shake away a fog. Her eyes popped open, aimed at Ava.

"You're joking, right? You don't fly. You've never flown, not once."

"That's why I'm here. I'm hoping I can get something to knock me out on the plane. I don't know if I can do it any other way."

Erin set the magazine on the reading material table. "Mom, let's ask the doctor what he thinks. It might be what you need, you know, to get away, break the habit."

"You think I won't shop if I go to another country? Shopping there is probably much more enticing than any of the stores here."

"Bernadette O'Donnell," announced the nurse at the door to the hallway.

Erin nodded to Ava and stood with her mother. "We'll call you."

Ava pulled her seat belt tight. Next to her, Connie refreshed her lipstick while Ava fast-forwarded through every possible way the plane could go down. *A door could blow off. Lightning could strike. The pilot might have a heart attack. Freak midair collision. Terrorism.*

Ava imagined Juniper saying to her, "Calm down, Mom. You're not going into space." But Juniper had flown by herself since she was a teenager visiting her dad in Colorado. The experience didn't give her so much as a queasy stomach, whereas Ava was sorry she had eaten breakfast; for her, it *was* like going into space.

"Toodle-oo, girls," Bernadette said as she strolled past them. She hadn't found an adjoining seat but managed to get a ticket for the same flight.

Ava felt Connie's eyes on her, then a patting on her hand.

"There are lots of things that are scarier than this in the world," Connie said.

"Like tornadoes? I guess I did survive that. I do not think hearing about other scary things will help me right now."

"Do you want to pray?"

The "Our Father" had been on repeat in Ava's brain since she'd left home that morning. It had not calmed her.

"Something else."

Connie removed her hand and faced the window. Ava grew antsy. This wasn't a time for silence. Thankfully, Connie turned back, her expression serious.

"How about the story of Natalya Kerminskaya?"

"I've been hoping you would tell me."

Ava settled against the headrest and hoped Connie was an engaging storyteller.

"She was my mother. I like to picture her as a young girl in the hills of Belarus, running wild, happy, and free. In truth, she never talked about her childhood."

Connie stared at the seat pocket in front of her.

"When she was fifteen, she felt like her life was over. That's what her sister, Katya, later told me. They both endured years of abuse from one of their older brothers. He was born a bully. His mother, my grandmother, didn't try to control him, and my grandfather was too sickly to do anything about it. It was worse for Mother because Katya didn't spend much time at home after she turned thirteen and got work as a nanny. So, their aunt approached Natalya and asked if she would be interested in changing her life, in going to America."

Ava was vaguely aware of a voice providing instructions to the passengers over the intercom. She tuned it out, feeling an urgency to learn more about Natalya.

"And she said yes?" Ava said.

"Of course. She didn't ask questions. She didn't want to leave her parents, yet even her mother urged her to get away and start a life of her own."

Connie clasped her hands together.

"Her aunt made her a match through an underground agency for foreign brides. She corresponded with the man for three months or so, which was two or three letters apiece because the mail wasn't fast with America. Then, at sixteen, her aunt bought her the plane ticket and sent her away to a new life. She never saw her parents or her brothers again."

"What about her sister?"

"Oh yes, she followed the next year. She matched to a man in St. Louis. Mother's match was to a man living outside of Lexington, in Mount Sterling."

Ava pondered the bravery of the sisters. To leave home for a foreign land and an unknown spouse, life must have been harder than Ava could imagine.

"Were they happy?" she asked.

Connie shrugged. "What is happy? That's what Mother used to say. 'As a woman, you are here to care for your man and your babies. Happiness is a figment of the imagination. Duty is what's real.' She told me that repeatedly."

Ava sank back in her seat, considering that idea. Duty. She had felt duty-bound for years. It was her duty to make sure her brother went to school. With Donovan, it was her duty to pay the bills and ensure he didn't overextend their modest resources with one of his business schemes. It was her duty to care for Juniper, to make her doctor appointments, to be sure she was eating. The duties never ended.

She'd moved beyond most of those duties, though she still felt that drive to protect Juniper. That would never change; after all, some duties were fueled by love. But Ava toyed with the idea that she had arrived at a time when duty was no longer as important as happiness. Maybe that was what made middle age different.

Connie rustled beside her, and Ava felt guilty for thinking of herself. Connie had left her home and her husband, causing a rift with her daughter. She was the one making seismic changes in her life, and she didn't have the luxury of waffling about her decisions.

"Connie," Ava said quietly. "You don't have to answer this, but is that why you're still with Marvin? Is it duty?"

Ava felt like she was staring into the eyes of a sixteen-year-old who regretted committing to a choice because she knew it was the wrong one.

"He's not a nice man, Ava. That's why I packed the bag. After thirty-six years of fulfilling my obligations to him, I couldn't take it anymore. I was afraid to tell him, afraid he would hold me captive in my own home. He's done that to me psychologically for all the time we've been together, so I don't think anything would stop him from doing it physically as well."

"He comes across as a reliable businessman. I would never have guessed he was so terrible to you."

"We learn to put on a public face. That was another lesson from Mother. Maybe it wasn't a good skill to develop."

This time it was Ava who patted Connie's hand. "Now you're here. And I'm here, and we're two women out to relax, to see some of the world. We're actually going to a tropical island paradise. And

Bernadette will be there with us, so it's sure to be a trip of surprises."

Connie squeezed Ava's hand. "Thank you for helping me get away. I know you've thought for a long time that I'm a foolish woman, and it was good of you to put aside your opinion."

"It was your suitcase that helped me do that."

Connie bit her lips. "Did you read the letters?"

"I read one. I was more drawn to the pictures. I could see the love between the mother and her children. I knew whoever she was, she had to be reunited with the contents, which were clearly so dear to her—or, as it turns out, so dear to you."

"Maybe you have a future as a jet-setting detective."

Ava glanced out the window and spotted the white fluff of a cloud. They were flying. *She* was flying, and it felt marvelous.

Chapter 11

A middle-aged woman paired with a young man wheeled a cart down the aisle to offer snacks and drinks to the rows ahead of Ava. She watched and wondered at the choices. She wasn't hungry but was determined to take advantage of everything she had paid for.

Beside her, Connie slept with her head against the window. Maybe it took being on a plane headed out of the country to relax her. Marvin certainly couldn't reach them where they were going.

In the row in front of Ava and Connie, a woman sat between a man—likely her husband—and a small boy who was eagerly peering out the window. The woman had a book open, but her husband was talking to her. Ava didn't hear any other conversations around and wondered whether the man was breaking an unwritten rule of airplane silence by talking persistently, and somewhat loudly, while his wife clearly wanted to read.

The boy turned to his mother, tapped her hand, and pointed out the window to where a white cloud transitioned into a dark gray on its underbelly. Ava strained to see out the window past Connie. The cloud seemed ominous.

The flight attendants rolled the cart slightly beyond Ava, then retreated to the family's row to get their order.

"Coffee. No, I'd rather have juice," the husband said. "Or a mixed drink?"

Ava couldn't see the wife but imagined her rolling her eyes. Or maybe she was used to his indecisiveness. Perhaps he was the kind of man who had so many ideas bouncing through his brain that he had a hard time focusing on one or committing to something that would provide stability for his family. Ava stopped herself. Every man wasn't a Donovan clone.

Connie didn't stir when the flight attendant got to their row. The capable and friendly flight attendant served Ava with the right mix of assuredness that she would take care of her and friendliness that made Ava think they could have a nice chat.

Ava chose coffee and cookies. She fiddled with the tray in front of her until it dropped open. The boy bounced in his seat, jiggling the seat back. It was a good thing Connie didn't have coffee on her table.

Ava sipped her coffee, but before she set it down, the plane dipped. A few drops sloshed onto her cookie as she let out an involuntary "Ohhh."

The flight attendant grabbed onto Ava's seat back. Ava looked to her for answers. *Will those face masks drop next?*

"It's a little turbulence. There's nothing to worry about," the woman said.

Then they fell again.

Ava's breath was shallow and fast. She peeked at Connie, who rearranged herself but didn't open her eyes. The intercom crackled.

"Flight attendants, please close service and return to your seats. We're encountering rough air. I ask everyone to remain seated with your seat belt fastened."

Ava sought another word of reassurance, but the woman had already pushed the cart to the end of the aisle. Outside, all the clouds had turned a dark gray.

Ava finished her coffee quickly, then folded up her table and refastened it, holding her remaining cookie and napkin. Table up and seat belt on would be the safest option. The plane quaked, and Ava closed her eyes, willing herself not to scream. She wondered if her mother had experienced this before she went down. Had there been time to realize what was happening, or had Jeannie been in the middle of a big story that suddenly ended with no warning? No investigator could answer that sort of question.

Ava should have stayed home. She should have put Connie in her car and gone somewhere they could reach on land. *Should have, should have, should have . . .*

. . . gone to Colorado with Donovan. She wouldn't even be on the plane if she had done that. Who knew how her life would have gone, or Juniper's?

But that was the thing. Juniper was happy. She seemed like she was where she was supposed to be. And if Ava had gone to Colorado, Juniper would have gone too, and it was unlikely she would currently be on a farm in Kentucky.

And Ava would be moving from Colorado to Indianapolis with Donovan. Or would she? Maybe his career would have taken a different turn if she had been in Colorado with him. Maybe her career would have been vastly different. Maybe it would never have worked out and she would've ended up back in Kentucky anyway.

None of it mattered if they didn't get safely to the ground. None of it meant a thing if they crashed.

The little boy in front of Ava had grabbed his mother's arm and buried his face in her body. Her husband said, "Hon, what's going on? Should we be worried?"

He definitely sounded worried. He had lowered his voice as if only now aware that his words could disturb someone around him.

"It's a little turbulence. We'll be fine."

The plane bounced again. Ava grabbed her armrests. She never had liked roller coasters, and a roller coaster in the sky was worse. She closed her eyes again to try to calm herself. Instead, all the decisions she needed to make swirled around her like a funnel cloud. She hadn't thought about them when Connie's problem was absorbing her. Now it was solely Ava and the storm and her decisions, decisions from years ago that might have been wrong and new decisions she had put off through her nondecisions. And she wanted a chance to choose her own way, to discover a passion like Fawn had. It would be hard, but she wanted the chance to try.

Ava glanced at Connie; still asleep. She should have warned Connie and Bernadette that she had already encountered two disasters, so a third was likely coming her way. She should have been that considerate. Now they were stuck in this storm with her, their fates all linked.

Ava squeezed her eyelids as if that could change the picture and automatically put her where she should be at fifty-five. Somewhere safe. Somewhere she wouldn't have to leave, wouldn't be driven from. She had never imagined that in the middle of her life, she would be starting all over again. She should be happily settled, waiting for Juniper to get married and give her grandchildren. *Should be.*

The light penetrated Ava's darkness, and she didn't know if that was a sign things would be okay or if actual daylight was returning. She looked out the window, and the clouds were once again white, the sun sending a few rays from a distance.

"Would you like a refill?" The flight attendant had returned with the pot of coffee like nothing had happened. Ava reached for the cup crumpled against the armrest. The attendant pulled a new one from her apron, filled it, and handed it to Ava.

"We should be on the ground in an hour. Another cookie?"

Ava held out her still-shaking hand for the welcome distraction.

Before she moved on, the flight attendant asked Ava whether she was going on vacation. Ava nodded.

She leaned a little closer to Ava. "Relax. The turbulence is past, and it's not worth fretting over anyway. Overthinking kills happiness."

She went on to the next person, and Ava repeated it to herself: *Overthinking kills happiness.*

In front of her, the little boy was gazing out the window again. The husband was silent, maybe sleeping. The mother was finally reading her book.

As the most experienced traveler of the three, Connie led Ava and Bernadette through customs. Ava quietly took in the people, the signs, and the lines while Bernadette babbled on about her seatmates.

"The woman was average. You should have seen the man. He was so delicious," she said. "I love my husband, but if I were a younger woman, he would have tempted me."

Connie giggled. "You're the one of us with a good man of your own, so leave the handsome ones to us," she said.

"Why, Connie, are you already in pursuit of a new man?"

"I don't feel like I've had one who cared a bit about me for years, so maybe I am ready."

Ava considered the text she had gotten from Donovan. She had been unnecessarily rude the day he called her in the car, but he didn't mention that. Instead, he was incredulous that she was taking the trip, and so supportive. And he reminded her about the job offer. They could talk more about it when she returned.

That was where things stood today. There was no reason to reach back farther and wonder how things might have been different. There was no reason to project forward to determine her next step at home. She was on vacation, and that was exactly where she needed to be.

In the airport arrival area, they found a man holding a sign with Ava's name. He welcomed them in accented English and said Lizzie had sent him to retrieve them.

"Our own driver. Very fancy," Bernadette said.

"Lizzie has long done everything with class," Ava said. "I'm sure we're in for a luxurious getaway."

She watched the countryside through the van window. There were slight hills, some areas of green and others of brown, small houses here and there, a few animals—goats or small cows. It didn't look totally foreign. The warm air and the sunshine created an atmosphere of welcome, of possibility. Ava was in a new place where something exciting, something unexpected, could happen.

The music on the radio made her want to dance. She had never been a skilled dancer, but she enjoyed trying a few steps, especially with music that challenged the very notion of sitting still.

The song ended, and an announcer came on speaking in rapid Spanish. The one word Ava understood was "*huracán.*" Huracán Adolfo.

"Excuse me," Ava said to the driver. "Did they say a hurricane is coming?"

"Sí. Huracán Adolfo."

"When?"

"One week. Maybe. Maybe not."

Ava stared at both Connie and Bernadette. Bernadette was frozen, her eyes big. Connie patted Ava's hand.

"Can you believe this? We've gone from being smack in the eye of the tornado season to directly in the path of a hurricane," Ava said. Maybe the airplane turbulence hadn't been disaster number three but a prelude to something more.

"It might not hit," Connie said, her voice wavering with reassurance.

"I hope your cousin has a basement, or whatever you need for shelter in a hurricane. I do not want to go through all of that stuff flying at me again," Bernadette said.

"You two shouldn't be traveling with me. I'm obviously bad luck," Ava said. She squeezed her fists, sending her fingernails into her palms.

"Or good luck. You survived the first two. I don't think the third will get any of us," Connie said.

They stopped at a gatehouse, and the driver said a few words to a uniformed guard, who then opened a secured gate. The houses they passed sprawled across large lawns or stood two or three stories tall. Ava could easily imagine what they would look like after hurricane-force winds.

She closed her eyes to calm herself. When she opened them,

she willed her mind not to conjure up destruction. Instead, Ava saw vast lawns and pictured Juniper planting an orchard there. The traffic islands were filled with flowers and appeared movie-ready. Everything was just so, including Lizzie's front yard, where a grove of bougainvillea glittered in deep pink.

The door swung open, and there was Lizzie, beautiful as always. She had pulled back her mass of strawberry-blond curls with a headband. Freckles dotted her fair face, and she wore a flowing sundress. It reached her bare toes, which peeped out from bejeweled sandals.

"Welcome to Casa de las Flores," she said as she stood back to let them in. The driver followed with their luggage.

Lizzie settled her hands on Ava's shoulders. "No worse for the flying?"

Ava glanced at Connie, who bit her lip to keep from laughing.

"Connie kept me calm during takeoff. Then when we hit turbulence, she slept through it. It was like riding a roller coaster!" Ava said. "Could I book a cruise to get back? By sea would surely be a better way to travel for me."

"You made it, Ava. Your first flight, your first foreign country, all before the age of sixty. What an overachiever you are."

Bernadette raised her eyebrows, and Connie cast her eyes to the floor. Fawn had mentioned Lizzie hadn't seemed like herself recently. Still, Ava didn't expect it would show itself as soon as she stepped into her cousin's home.

"Now that you've achieved this goal, surely there's nothing to stop you from enjoying your stay."

"Only that a hurricane is on the way," Ava said.

Lizzie put her arm around Ava and patted her, maybe apologizing for her greeting. Maybe this was still the cousin Ava knew.

"If it actually becomes a hurricane, it will be the earliest on record. You don't have any worries," Lizzie said.

"Only that I need to figure out what I'm going to do with the rest of my life. And more immediately, where am I going to live," Ava couldn't help adding.

"And where I'm going to live," Connie said.

"And how I'm going to live without my home. We're quite the gang you've taken on, Lizzie," Bernadette said. "Maybe you're the one set up to enjoy, if we can at least be decent company."

"If anyone can be decent company."

Lizzie said it under her breath as she turned away, so Ava assumed she was the only one who heard.

Lizzie motioned for them to follow her. The tile floors shone. Potted plants with gleaming leaves sat here and there. Through the large window was an inviting patio with a rattan couch, chairs, and a table; a pool sparkled beyond it. After all, Lizzie was living in a vacation paradise, not a permanent home.

"It's sort of like a spring break trip for the mature friends," Lizzie said. "Make yourself at home while you're here. You're in the rooms upstairs, and the entire house is yours."

They followed Lizzie up the stairs and onto a cool tile floor. She pushed open one door to reveal a bedroom with a large bed and a window overlooking the pool.

"I'll take it," Ava said.

Lizzie took Connie and Bernadette to the next room.

Ava checked out the bathroom and found it better appointed than a hotel. There was a Jacuzzi tub and a separate shower tiled in various shades of blue, green, and brown. On the white marble vanity was a glass tray filled with items to make Ava feel beautiful: face cream, lotion, shampoo, conditioner, body butter, and sunscreen. Next to all of that was a large vase of purple bougainvillea.

Ava turned back to the bedroom, where a love seat was positioned behind a coffee table that held more flowers and two books, one an ornithological exploration of the Caribbean and the other a book on the history of baseball in the Dominican Republic. A luxuriously soft peach throw was draped across the love seat.

Ava flopped down on the bed. She sank in a bit before she felt the comfort of the mattress. It supported her while also giving her a little embrace. And those firm yet soft pillows—there were six of them.

Ava closed her eyes. She had done it. She'd flown to another country without catastrophe. Now that she was settling into the room, it felt good, like someone had unwrapped a bandage that had been binding Ava together since the tornado. She sighed, reached for a second pillow to increase her feeling of extravagance, closed her eyes again, and crossed her feet. This was a good idea.

Ava might never leave her room.

The next morning, they went onto the patio for breakfast. The air felt fresh, and the sky was a crisp blue. The wooden table that would hold the spread was painted with oversized flowers in orange and pink.

Araceli, who appeared to be the cook and the housekeeper, served them like a sprite who didn't want to be seen. Lizzie carried on a monologue about all the places she had lived and traveled while Araceli carried out a tray with a pitcher of freshly squeezed juice and four glasses and put it on the table. Lizzie talked about the Chanel showroom in Paris, the top-rated restaurant in the world in New York, and the Palace of Holyroodhouse in Edinburg. Araceli filled the glasses and placed one in front of each woman's plate, all without Lizzie stopping once to thank her. Next came warm croissants, then a bowl of boiled eggs and one with freshly cut pineapple and mango.

"Coffee or tea?" Lizzie asked them.

"Coffee," Ava replied as Connie said, "Tea."

Lizzie nodded to Araceli.

"What's on the agenda today? I'm ready to explore the country," Bernadette said. She'd sprayed her hair and put on coordinating earrings and necklace as if she were going to work at Sheila's store. "And we can find a man for Connie!"

Connie blushed and ducked her head. "I was joking, Bernadette."

"No, you weren't. You haven't had the loving attention of a man for too long," Bernadette said.

Connie bit into her croissant and didn't raise her face from the plate.

"We can drive into Santo Domingo for shopping, walk the *malecón* so you can see the beach, go to a museum if you like. It is a city with all the headaches of city traffic and crowds. Or we could drive to the national park down the highway and explore the trails there, get a guide to tell us about the plants and wildlife. Or we can stay here. If I wanted to get away from the world, I probably wouldn't leave the compound."

To Ava, that sounded out of step with Lizzie's long travel list.

"Shopping!" Bernadette called out.

Ava and Connie simultaneously shook their heads at Bernadette.

"We need to stay away from the shopping. Bernadette was possessed by a shopping demon after the tornado, and her family sent her with us in hopes of breaking that habit," Ava said.

Lizzie described what they would find in the compound: shops with touristy trinkets and beachwear, plus a grocery store and four restaurants—and, should they be interested, a pirate ship to tour, an indoor concert hall, and an amphitheater.

"The compound?" The term made it sound like they were prisoners in a secret place. Ava suddenly lost the desire to stay cloistered there and not venture out.

"Gated community, same thing," Lizzie said. "It's a world set apart, or they wouldn't have so many big names owning houses and visiting here."

"Big names like who?" Bernadette asked, leaning eagerly toward Lizzie.

"I would rather not say. Let's keep it at a baseball player, a pop singer, and a multimillionaire. Discretion is highly valued among the residents."

There had been a time when Lizzie would drop names like crumbs from a shortbread cookie. Now she didn't want to call out even one. Ava found the change disconcerting, like when jealousy had temporarily turned Fawn into someone she wasn't.

Connie put down her cup of tea. "I'm happy to be here. I'm content to stay, at least for a couple of days. What about you Ava?"

Ava put up her hands. "You all know I'm not the traveler. I've accomplished my goal by getting here. If you want me to lounge on the floating chaise in the pool for the rest of the trip, I can do that and be happy."

Lizzie laughed. "Oh, Ava, you'll never get the Kentucky out of you, will you?"

"Why would I want to?"

As soon as she said it, Ava felt the tension. Lizzie appraised Ava, avoiding her eyes.

"There's a lot to explore in the world, Ava. It makes a person well rounded and stretches us into new shapes. I hope you encourage your daughter to travel."

Lizzie sounded like the big sister giving advice. It didn't affect Ava the same way it had when she was younger. She felt something inside close rather than open as it would have way back when.

Ava had encouraged Juniper to travel to her dad's house in Colorado. She didn't have to encourage travel beyond that; Juni took to it naturally. After high school graduation, Juni and her friends had taken a trip to Cancún. During every spring break throughout college, she went somewhere. One spring, she and a group of friends took a cross-country driving trip to the Grand Canyon. Every time she traveled, Ava paced until Juni called to tell her she had arrived safely.

Yet Ava had long felt that Juniper was much like her; her strength came from home. Home might not challenge a person in the same way travel could, but it didn't lack opportunities for growth and learning.

"Are you planning to go see your mom anytime soon?" Ava said. "I'm sure Fawn filled you in on her hospital visit the other day."

Lizzie sat back. She had eaten a couple pieces of pineapple. She cradled her coffee cup, not sipping from it.

"Fawn's taking care of things." Lizzie's voice softened slightly, which relieved some of the tension. "And I should thank you, Ava. I understand you were a big help."

"Your mom is special to me. I'll do whatever I can for her."

"Fawn brought her whole brood to visit two years ago, along with Mom. Max was here, and the guys spent most of their time on the golf course."

Lizzie's husband, Max, had always seemed like a dream to Ava. Good looking, smart, constantly moving up the corporate ladder, which always made Lizzie sit up with pride. Of course, that did mean they moved frequently, leaving Lizzie unable to settle into her own career.

"Fawn and I enjoyed the beach. Not Florence, who is a little sunphobic. She either stayed back at the house with Mom or came with us and stayed under an umbrella. She couldn't believe that I used to slather baby oil all over my skin so I could bake out on the lawn, all for the sake of beauty!"

All of the women laughed.

"Then she would not understand a tanning bed. The things we did when we were young," Bernadette said as she gazed beyond the group. "I thought when I got to be this age, I would have it all figured out. And it felt that way until my house was gone."

Connie patted Bernadette's hand.

"It never gets figured out," Lizzie said. Her mouth turned down as if she had eaten something bitter.

She sipped her coffee, then put it back on the table.

"Araceli, the coffee is cold."

Araceli hurried back to the table with a steaming silver coffee pot. She was about to pour it into Lizzie's cup when Lizzie stopped her with a cold stare that hit Ava at her core.

"It won't help if you pour hot coffee into coffee that's already cold. Get me a new cup."

Araceli curtsied and retreated with the coffee pot. Ava couldn't hold back any longer, but she tried to be diplomatic.

"I've helped your mom with a few guests while I've been at her house," Ava said. "I've never heard anyone be so curt with your mom when she's serving coffee."

Lizzie closed her eyes and shook her head before she opened them. She picked up the napkin from her lap and laid it on the table as she stood. "You're right, Ava. I haven't been myself, and that combined with my sincere desire to help Araceli improve isn't working out well. Employment here is a good option for her, but it's her first personal service position, and she's so untrained."

Lizzie pulled her hair behind her shoulders, took a step toward the kitchen, then stopped and turned back to the table. "Can any of you drive a golf cart?"

Connie raised her hand and didn't say anything.

"It's in front of the garage, and the key is in it. The main road makes a circle around the complex, and there are signs for the beach and village. Help yourselves."

Then she went into the kitchen and spoke quietly with Araceli.

"Let's go exploring, girls. What do you say?" Bernadette resembled a child who had been given the run of the entire playground.

Ava glanced one last time at Lizzie, who was filling the sink with water and putting the dishes in it while Araceli found a clean cup for coffee in the cabinet.

"Exploring, but no shopping for you," Ava said.

"Not to worry. They gave me a credit card with a low limit." Bernadette rolled her eyes and laughed. "I'm sure they're happy to have me off their hands for a while. And I'm happy too. I don't think I've ever taken a vacation with girlfriends."

They headed for the garage. The golf cart had two tan vinyl-covered benches for passengers and another on the back facing the opposite direction. The vehicle's exterior was painted aquamarine, and large yellow-and-pink flowers decorated the front. As Ava settled into the passenger seat, she felt like she was perched on a float for the high school homecoming parade.

Connie leaned toward Ava from the driver's seat.

"You're good to bring me with you, Ava. I hope I won't be a burden while we're here."

Ava laughed. "Are you kidding? Apparently, you're the one who will get us around."

They rolled down the driveway, and Connie turned left, toward the end of the street. The closest place for recreation was the beach and the small street of shops that Lizzie referred to as the Village. The shopping area was built to mimic the hills of Tuscany, according to Lizzie. Although Ava wasn't a world traveler, she'd seen the movie *Under the Tuscan Sun*. It seemed odd to bring its flavor to the Caribbean community, which had a culture all its own.

A golf cart with two men and their golf clubs drove past the women. Then there was a car, then another, all going slowly to obey the speed limit.

"It all seems so civilized," Connie said. "I hate to admit it, but I thought the Dominican Republic was going to be something else."

"Like what?"

"Marvin took me to Mexico once. Not to the fancy tourist resorts but to a town about an hour or so from Mexico City where he was looking at investment property. It seemed to me like there were fewer laws, or maybe fewer people to enforce them, so the traffic was fast, the garbage was prolific, and some of the restaurants looked like they could never pass an inspection."

"Did it scare you?"

"No. I was mostly curious about how it all worked—whether people were happy living like that," she said. Her expression became contemplative. "It seemed wildly freeing to me."

Ava remembered asking Mrs. Alvarado to take the barrette out of her hair. When she quit her job, Ava had wanted to feel a wild freedom for herself every day. She wasn't sure what that would be like. She imagined lightness as a constant companion, maybe even a strength in the wings that had remained neatly folded for so many years. She wasn't there yet. She'd been away from the office for longer than she had since Juniper was born, yet Ava felt something continuing to hold her down.

Bernadette hummed behind them. Ava guessed she couldn't hear the conversation over the purr of the golf cart.

Connie continued, "I spent one day alone while Marvin was in meetings, and I meandered around the town. People were friendly. There was a different feel about things than I had walking at home. I'm not sure how else to explain it."

Ava turned to include Bernadette in the conversation.

"I don't know if we'll get anything like that inside this compound. I had no idea that Lizzie lived like this. I assumed she lived in a real neighborhood with Dominican neighbors. This is sort of like the Disneyland of the Caribbean. Do you suppose they own it?"

"I don't know who owns it, but I feel like I'm hobnobbing with the rich and the famous," Bernadette said. She tried to smooth her hair. The persistent breeze ruffled it again.

"It's disorienting to see those buildings," Connie said as she pointed ahead. "I might prefer to stay at Lizzie's house where I'm not so confused about where I am. I was picturing a beach vacation."

Ahead stood the pinkish buildings that mimicked Tuscany. It did feel like a major disconnect.

"Maybe we should pretend we're in Italy for a while," Ava said.

"I'm good at pretending," Connie said.

She went on to talk about how in her marriage, it was her job to make sure no one knew what happened in their house. She kept things as normal as possible for the kids. Then, after they left, it was such a habit that she kept it up. "I forgot that there could be anything different. I forgot that I had simply to walk out my door, talk to someone, and things could change."

"Did you ever think about walking out and never going back? Picking up and leaving him?"

"How could I, Ava? He controls the bank account, pays all the bills. At one point I didn't even know how much it cost us to have electricity and running water every month. I didn't have a car or a driver's license until the kids started school, and he was only amenable to that because he couldn't leave work every time one of them got sick."

Donovan might have been difficult to live with, but certainly not like that.

Connie pulled into a parking place, then touched Ava's forearm and looked her in the eye.

"I left twice before and went to my sister's house. I couldn't make it stick. But not this time. I'm done with all of that now. I can't go back. Thank you." Connie turned back to Bernadette. "And thanks to you, too. Without you, I might not have been reunited with my suitcase or come on this trip."

"We have to look out for one another," Bernadette said.

"I wish I'd done something years ago so you could have thanked me then," Ava said.

"We are where we are, and where we are is good," Bernadette said. "Look around. We're in Tuscany!"

Ava couldn't tell if the building colors came from the stone or a trick of the light. Next to them was a two-story structure with wrought iron flower boxes in the second-floor windows. Flowers billowed down. Ava expected to see Juliet appear any minute.

At the ground level, the door opened into what looked like a coffee shop. An older man sat at a table outside, reading a newspaper. The three strolled forth, taking in the street. Two young women speaking rapid Spanish walked past them. Beyond the buildings ahead, they glimpsed the beach.

"I haven't been to Italy, but I don't think they speak Spanish there," Ava said.

"Come on, Ava, don't let reality get in the way. Let's enjoy," Bernadette said.

Ava stopped and gazed through the window of a shop that sold bathing suits.

"I brought nothing to swim in," Ava said.

Connie pointed to the beach. "You take your time, and I'll meet you at the beach when you're finished. Bernadette, are you coming?"

Bernadette reluctantly joined Connie, glancing back longingly. Connie pulled her hand, and they moved on.

Ava opened the door to the shop and ambled past displays of bathing suits and cover-ups. She rummaged through a rack and found they were all bikinis. They would be nice for Juniper, or for Lizzie, but not for Ava. She needed a modest one-piece, preferably navy blue or black, that wouldn't draw attention. Without it she would be sitting on the beach in shorts and a T-shirt. If she'd had a bathing suit packed away in the house, it likely didn't fit any longer.

Ava scrutinized a rack displaying a few one-piece suits with high-cut legs and cut-out sides. Even the cover-ups weren't really for hiding anything. They were mesh or some other sheer fabric. Their primary goal was apparently a game of peekaboo.

Ava never had been much of a swimmer anyway.

Next door were locally made arts and crafts: ceramic animals, handwoven place mats, fans of woven palms—Dominican crafts sold behind a Tuscan storefront in a gated community built to keep the locals out and the foreigners in. Ava laughed. She felt like she had walked into the middle of an absurdist play and didn't know who would stride onstage next.

When she wandered into the next store, there he was. Before he spoke, he reminded her of the actor Colin Firth. She and her girlfriends had pegged the actor as the perfect boyfriend when they saw *Bridget Jones's Diary* all those many years ago. Twenty years, was it? Or thirty? The man examining the jewelry—undoubtedly shopping for a gift for his wife—was several years older than the

Colin of that movie. His maturity made him more attractive.

Then he spoke to the cashier, and Ava moved closer, expecting to hear that high-toned British accent. Instead, what emerged was a smooth English tinged with curls of what Ava guessed was Italian.

The store was filled with clothes Ava assumed she couldn't afford. They seemed like the kind of dresses Lizzie would wear to impress her neighbors or when she wanted to outfit herself for a trip to Santo Domingo. Ava pushed through hangers on the rack of low-cut sundresses in front of her. She wanted to watch the man, listen to his voice. That deep resonance drew her in. Had his features been a little less than average, she still would have fallen for the voice.

"No, no, my sister is two years older than me and several inches shorter. She likes something delicate to not overpower her, yet big enough that it will be noticed," he said.

Ava wondered if he worked in the fashion industry. He had the language for it. That blue-and-white-striped shirt tucked into dark-blue cuffed pants made him look ready to walk down a runway with a model. Or maybe he was the model.

He glanced up and caught Ava studying him. He smiled, and Ava turned away. He had that leading-man charisma.

She should flirt with him.

Ava made her way around the store as the man inspected a few necklaces before choosing one. If the saleswoman would just step away, Ava could sidle up next to him. Or could she? It sounded like something out of a movie: Plain Jane meets Prince Charming on a vacation in the Dominican Republic. Plain Jane usually bumped into Prince Charming, or tripped and fell into him. This situation didn't offer those opportunities.

By the time she meandered back to the door, he was still talking with the cashier. Ava slipped out and contemplated whether—in this absurdist universe—she might run into him again.

Chapter 12

When they returned, Ava found her cousin slouched on a lounge chair on the patio and staring at her blue-and-white-tiled pool. Lizzie quickly straightened her back and lifted her chin as Ava sat in the chair next to her, but it didn't make her face any less strained.

Araceli delivered a tray of iced sparkling water with a plate of cheese and olives. Pink hibiscus and palm branches framed Lizzie's blond elegance. The contrast with the concentration on her face was striking.

Ava waited for Lizzie to speak. The silence remained. So Ava told her about their jaunt, even about the handsome man. Lizzie's expression said she was somewhere else. Her eyebrows pushed down over her eyes as she glanced at Ava. She picked up an olive and nonchalantly dropped it into her mouth. Chewing, she turned to Ava as if realizing it was her turn to talk.

"My neighbors hired three different maids within nine weeks. One she fired for stealing their milk, another because they didn't like the way she made the beds, and the third because the woman's son was sick and she needed a day off. Can you imagine?"

No, Ava couldn't imagine. She had never hired someone to clean her house. She did pay someone to mow her lawn after Donovan left because the neighbors would have complained at the height. When Juniper went off to college and Ava had more time, though, she started doing the lawn herself.

"Araceli has been with us four months. Previously, her aunt was our maid and her husband our gardener. The aunt got ill, so she sent Araceli. She has two young children at home, and this is her first job like this. Which on a regular day would be okay. But things haven't been regular. I haven't been able to train her because I've been distracted."

Ava waited for more. As a teenager, she had been willing to listen to Lizzie talk about anything. It was like spying through the curtains at grown-up life. Lizzie knew about hosting parties, choosing the best clothes for an occasion, how to flirt with a boy without being too obvious. Lizzie liked to work out those things for herself by talking aloud, even if she was in a room alone.

"Max is preparing to submit his retirement letter."

Lizzie looked like she'd bitten into a piece of rotten fruit.

"He wants to retire here. A few years ago, one of his colleagues bought a home in the Caribbean, which is why we did. He's been here twice."

To buy a house in a foreign country because his colleague did? That was another part of Lizzie's life that Ava couldn't imagine, nor did she want to. And it didn't appear it was all that appealing to Lizzie. The sour expression hadn't left. Ava saw in Lizzie the same vulnerability she'd seen in Aunt Lila when she was sick.

"I don't want to retire here. I want to move back to New York. I have a job offer."

Ava leaned forward. "A job! Lizzie, that's great news. You loved New York when you lived there."

"It's been a long time."

Ava tried to remember when Lizzie had last worked full-time. It must have been when she was in her twenties, maybe her early thirties. Lizzie had found it discouraging to pour herself into a position only to abandon it when Max's job moved again, which was why she eventually turned to charity work, volunteering on boards and finding other ways to contribute.

"What would you be doing?" Ava said.

Lizzie fully turned toward Ava, her whole body taking on a new energy. The determination in her eyes reminded Ava of teenage Lizzie pursuing a crush.

"That's the thing: it's perfect for me. The Tenement Museum, my favorite museum in the city, is joining with a few other small museums to hire a special events and fundraising coordinator. I've raised money for them before, and I know how to do it. Learning about the other museums will be more of a challenge, so it's not doing something I've done before; it will stimulate me to expand my knowledge and experience."

"Max doesn't want you to?"

Lizzie pulled her hair behind her shoulders as she rested back in her chair.

"The offer came in last week. I haven't told him. Every time we talk, he's so enthusiastic about this place. And he never loved New York like I did."

Ava remembered Donovan moving to Colorado, but that wasn't the same situation. Lizzie and Max had a different relationship. They would be able to work it out; they would have to.

"He'll be here this weekend, Ava. I have to talk with him about it then."

Ava nodded. Another home at stake—except that it became more evident every minute that Lizzie wasn't truly living in the Dominican Republic. Yes, she enjoyed their weather, their beaches, their gardens. She basically had an American life highlighted with foreign accents and flowers within the gated community. It was probably the easiest foray outside the United States Ava could have made. For all the torture of the plane trip, it felt like she had barely left the country at all.

"We're having guests for dinner tonight, my neighbors from Great Britain." Lizzie's tone returned to "madam of the manor." "Seven for appetizers. Tell the others. And do wear something nice, Ava. They might bring a friend."

Ava's eyebrows rose involuntarily. The last thing she needed was to be expected to entertain a friend of the Brits.

In her room, Ava took off her shoes and fell onto the love seat. Her phone dinged with a text from Juniper.

"So proud of you for traveling! Maybe this means we can take a vacation together sometime."

Ava immediately answered. "Would love that."

"Say a few prayers for us, Mom. Not doing well at the farm. Makes me rethink rebuilding the house."

"I can call you."

"Not now. Still a few things to work out. Love you."

"Love you too, Juni. I'm here for you anytime."

Nothing followed, so Ava put down the phone. *Trouble at the farm.* It was probably with Vivienne. She seemed a prickly person to live and work with. Or maybe it wasn't Vivienne. It could also be lack of subscriptions. Or the weather, which even the best farmers couldn't control. It must be major if it made Juniper think twice about rebuilding the house after sounding so certain about it.

If rebuilding would ease Juniper's burden, Ava would do it and not bother Juniper with the details. It would give Juniper a place to go if the farm failed. Ava would return to work and do whatever she could to support her daughter. On weekends, she could help on the farm—if they figured out how to keep her from killing the vegetables. Maybe there were animals that needed to be fed. If Ava didn't return to her agency, she could go to work with Donovan. She could give Juniper a loan once she had a new salary to plan around.

It was settled. Rebuilding was the easiest decision because thinking about the alternatives was exhausting. Ava could enjoy her vacation and stop torturing herself.

She tried to sink into the love seat and relax. She propped her feet up on the table and rolled her shoulders. Yet she couldn't get comfortable. If she admitted what she was feeling, Ava still couldn't picture living there again, even if her head said that was the thing to do. Sometimes a mother had to push her feelings aside and do what was best for her child. Ava had failed at that when she refused to go to Colorado with Donovan. That choice had been fueled by fear, and her recent experiences had helped her move beyond some of that. She wouldn't let selfishness guide her into a poor decision if Juniper needed something else.

Ava heard the voice of the flight attendant. *Overthinking kills happiness.*

Ava wanted happiness.

She abruptly stood and rifled through her clothes for something to wear that wouldn't embarrass Lizzie at dinner. Ava didn't care about seeming unsophisticated. Maybe she would care if they were having dinner with the Italian man from the store, but then again, maybe not. At this age, she should be allowed to be herself without feeling like she had to live up to someone's expectations.

Ava put on the one skirt and blouse she'd brought with her. The outfit wasn't as elegant as the sundresses she'd seen in the shop. Regardless, the blue blouse looked good, and the skirt made Ava feel like swaying. Sprinkled with blue-and-purple flowers, it was the full sort of skirt that would float around her if she had a partner who could twirl her, maybe lift her elegantly so the fabric flowed behind her like angel wings.

Surely the Colin Firth lookalike could dance like a dream.

Ava shook her head at her reflection in the mirror and brushed her hair. What had that attractive man seen when he saw her? She imagined herself magically transforming into a princess under his gaze and realized she hadn't let herself imagine the impossible since she was a teenager. Maybe a new country where she was a stranger was a good place to attract a prince—a safer place than in a coffee shop with Donovan.

At six, Ava and Connie went downstairs to help prepare for the guests while Bernadette chatted with her husband in her room. They found Lizzie in the kitchen, giving Araceli one command after another. The long table inside was set beautifully with two huge bouquets of flowers. There were seven places set with salad plates and embroidered yellow napkins.

Connie looked nearly as pained as she had the day Ava found her at Bernadette's. She went to the patio to fluff the pillows. Ava followed.

"I know she's your cousin, Ava, but she's unkind to that girl. She treats her like she doesn't have a brain in her head," Connie said in a low voice.

Ava glanced at Araceli and saw Connie's expression on the woman's face.

"I'm so sorry, Connie. Maybe this wasn't the place to come."

"It's just that I was hoping to forget about Marvin, not be reminded of him by Lizzie's behavior. It's the same, you know, whether it's a spouse, an acquaintance, or an employer."

Ava knew it wasn't the same. Lizzie wanted to do what was right, but until she settled things with Max, she wouldn't be fully herself. In the meantime, perhaps she and Connie could distract Lizzie from the preparations and help Araceli at the same time.

Lizzie joined them on the patio, where she straightened the coasters and books on the table. Connie deftly engaged her in a conversation about their childhoods. Connie had moved from Mount Sterling to Prestonsburg and then to Richmond before her parents finally settled down.

Ava checked in with Araceli, who was setting the table with the silverware placed incorrectly. Ava demonstrated the correct table setting, and then Araceli sent her out to Lizzie and Connie with a tray of drinks. Bernadette soon joined them. She regaled them with a story about when she and Joe had visited Patrick at Notre Dame and brought bedbugs home from their hotel.

"We had to bag up nearly everything, have the place sprayed. It was terrible," Bernadette said.

"I think you're safe here," Lizzie said.

Bernadette sighed. "I didn't mean to imply otherwise. I was just thinking I would go through all of that again if I could have my house back."

The doorbell rang, and Lizzie excused herself. Ava listened to the voices. It sounded like Lizzie was greeting one man instead of the three people she was expecting.

"Leo wrenched his knee during our golf game," the man said. "He's one of those blokes who needs intensive care when he's injured."

That was the accent she heard so frequently on Masterpiece Theatre. She strained to see the doorway without getting up. She couldn't stretch her neck that far.

Lizzie rounded the corner with the guest at her side. Connie stood, so Ava followed. Lizzie introduced them.

"Lovely to meet you both. Chester Brody, Marsha's brother. She and Leo were kind enough to invite me to stay with them for a month, so here I am."

"Do come in. Now the party is complete," Ava said

Ava didn't know where that had come from; it sounded like a line from a movie. But she wanted him to keep talking. She loved the way he spoke, though she couldn't quite eke out anything intelligible that might draw him into conversation. He was beautiful, more like Colin Farrell than Firth.

What is wrong with me? Men's looks had never silenced Ava, even men like this. Was this what was going to happen as she attempted to be more adventurous? She would stumble over her own tongue and shut down? She didn't have years of flirting experience to supply her with a natural repartee. Maybe it was too late to develop it.

Nonetheless, it didn't hurt to share company with someone so easy on the eyes.

Chester handed Lizzie a bottle of wine.

"How considerate," Lizzie said without taking her eyes from his. "Please sit down and join us. We were exchanging stories about worst travel experiences."

Chester sat on the couch next to Lizzie's chair. Connie settled beside him, a respectable distance away but close enough that she could reach over and touch him if the opportunity arose. Bernadette raised her eyebrows in delight, then stared encouragingly at Ava.

"Mine would be my flight down here since that was my first flight ever," Ava said. She was surprised she had spoken up. Now all eyes were on her. "It felt like I would die the minute we left the ground."

Mentioning it returned Ava to her early flight jitters, and heat waved across her face.

"You'd never flown before?" Chester said.

"No."

She could tell them about her mother dying in a plane crash. That would certainly halt the conversation and leave more than an awkward silence.

"I was strictly a land traveler and even then hadn't gone farther than the states surrounding Kentucky. Connie there got me through the takeoff by telling me stories. She was the perfect travel companion for my maiden flight."

Chester turned to Bernadette. "Did you fly with them?"

"Yes, I was a last-minute addition. My family couldn't put up with me any longer, so they dumped me on Connie and Ava."

"And you all made it here unscathed," Lizzie said. She sat back on the lounge chair, arranged her skirt around her, and slowly met each individual's eyes before returning her attention to Chester.

"Mine was Paris—the first time I went when I was eighteen. I was naive and so little traveled, not the ideal situation," she said. That flirtatious teenager was still there.

Ava remembered that trip. It had sounded so romantic and adventurous.

"Did naive Lizzie get into trouble in Paris?" Chester said.

"Not me. Instead, I got the boys in trouble."

She closed her eyes and smiled as if returning to that space in her memories.

"It was the first time I ever went dancing in a club. As far as I knew, we didn't even have clubs in Lexington. Paris was totally different. It was like I got off the plane, and the world was waiting for me."

"Ooh la la," Bernadette said.

Lizzie gazed off to the side, toward her pool. Her face softened, and Ava saw a flash of the cousin she used to know.

"It was exciting—liberating, somehow—to be anonymous yet to be myself in a way I never had been before. No one knew my parents or where I lived. They could see me, as I was."

Her eyes snapped back to the group with an expression that said she had nearly forgotten who was listening to her.

Connie shifted in her seat, then excused herself. Chester began telling a story about buying a suit in Paris as Connie went to the dining room table, where Araceli was hurriedly arranging the food, some of it steaming. Connie spoke quietly to Araceli, who shook her head no. Then Connie followed her to the kitchen and returned with Araceli, carrying more of the food.

Lizzie glanced at them. Ava hoped Connie's assistance wouldn't cause problems for Araceli, whose eyes kept flicking toward Lizzie. Lizzie glanced at her almost imperceptibly and gave a slight nod.

The hostess invited everyone to the table. The salmon and roasted vegetables gave off an alluring aroma. Ava wondered what the Dominican neighbors were serving.

Lizzie whispered to Chester and touched his hand. Ava blinked and peered at her cousin again, though there didn't seem to be anything untoward in Lizzie's interaction with her guest.

Ava had always liked Max, though the rest of the family felt he had stolen Lizzie away from them and not brought her back for frequent enough visits. He didn't leave Lizzie wanting and worrying about the basics like Donovan had Ava, although Lizzie's basics had always been different since she didn't have children. Maybe that was what Ava couldn't understand. A marital relationship must be substantially altered without a little one to care for and grow with over the years. Maybe that was why Max had an island fantasy but Lizzie wanted to go to work.

As Ava watched the faces around the table, she wondered what the sophisticates in Santo Domingo talked about. Did they go for a drink after dinner? Or did they walk the malecón? What was the malecón anyway? Maybe they had another type of party altogether. Maybe they didn't sit around at all but rather danced until dawn.

She wouldn't find out by visiting Lizzie.

"Photography," Chester was saying. "All kinds, though of late it's been fashion photography and real estate. An Italian magazine is doing a photo shoot here this week, so I'm working with them. They want to capture Tuscany in the DR for their summer issue."

"I saw a man today who looked like he belonged to the fashion world, and his accent sounded Italian," Ava said.

"Probably Bruno, the creative director of the magazine. His sister is the editor. He came while she stayed back in Milan."

"I've stepped into a world of sophisticates," Ava said. She glanced at Connie. "This is a world away from looking through strangers' stuff on my lawn, isn't it?"

Ava hadn't intended to reference the suitcase but recognized her mistake when Connie pinked up. Chester's face was a question mark.

"A tornado blew away Ava's house and mine," Bernadette said.

"What a tragedy," Chester said. "Are you rebuilding your home? Or is it in a place that's likely to be devastated again?"

"I don't think tornadoes are as predictable as fires are beginning to be, or hurricanes," Ava said. "The rebuilding depends on what my daughter says. I'm leaning toward it."

Bernadette and Connie exchanged a meaningful look.

"I thought you were still considering, or had even decided not to," Lizzie said.

"Rebuild, go back to a job, be there for Juniper—it might be easier. I got a message from her saying there are problems at the farm."

Concern wrinkled Lizzie's forehead. "You'll keep thinking

about it, right? Because you just got here, and you might see things differently after a few more days of vacation."

Chester smiled at Ava and locked onto her eyes.

"A woman at the crossroads of life who's exploring. That sounds like a good place to be," he said.

The way he said it made Ava think he might like to explore with her.

"Chester, since you've done real estate photography, do you think you could photograph this place for me?" Lizzie said.

"It would be my pleasure, if you'll allow me to get some garden shots. You have the most beautiful flowers I've seen since I've been here."

Chester nodded toward the flowers on the table, all of which Lizzie had cut and arranged earlier in the day.

"I agree to your terms," Lizzie said.

She offered him her hand, and they shook to seal the deal.

The next morning, Lizzie and Bernadette both turned down an invitation to go with Ava and Connie to a nearby ecological park and cave. Ava didn't mind. The company concerned Ava less than getting out of the compound and into the real country.

Araceli's brother, Mauricio, arrived as promised at ten o'clock to drive them to the park. Ava and Connie settled into the back seat to take in the scenery. The highway system didn't seem so foreign, despite the Spanish-language signs. The plant growth along the roads, though, was different from at home—wilder, less manicured. That was what Ava was missing at Lizzie's: a wild freedom to blossom into whoever she was to become. Lizzie's place, despite its beauty, imposed a structure that Ava had previously been comfortable with but now made her squirm. Or maybe it was Lizzie herself, who appeared to be filling a role that someone expected of her. Or, at least, that she thought was expected.

Ava wanted to be that errant plant bursting from the crack in the sidewalk against all odds.

When they arrived at the park, Mauricio walked in with them to be sure they got their tickets.

"Would you like to go with us?" Connie asked.

"No, señora. I wait. It is no problem."

He spoke significantly more English than Araceli, which Ava assumed was necessary for his work as a driver.

The crowd gathering for the tour had a more down-to-earth quality than the people Ava had seen the previous day in the compound's shops. No one was as handsome as the Italian, though everyone was friendly, smiling even if they couldn't converse. A tall woman with red hair stayed close to her blond husband and their two children. Ava thought they were speaking German. Another family with five children chatted in Spanish while an older Asian couple spoke English. A third man joined them, and Connie struck up a conversation with him, looking quite entranced. Ava examined the displays explaining the history of the cave from its discovery to the day it opened to the public.

That would be quite something, to discover a natural phenomenon that had always been there but no one had noticed. It made Ava want to scour her aunt's farm. Maybe there was something there equally as interesting to prove it should stay in the family. Brad would be game to help her.

"Good morning. Please gather 'round," said a short, round man, who then repeated himself in Spanish.

The group of twenty or so people clustered together as he motioned them to come in closer.

"Very good. You passed your admission test. Now that I know you can follow directions, you are all admitted to one of the most beautiful paths on this island. We'll first walk through the forest, where we'll identify the plants that have grown here for centuries; then we'll make our way to the cave, and as we exit, we'll walk through the iguana sanctuary."

"Sanctuary?" an Asian man asked. "Aren't iguanas common on the island?"

"Aha. They are, my keen friend. In our country today, they are too often killed for food or sport, and they have fallen into a state that inspired a local naturalist to create this sanctuary so we don't lose that part of our heritage."

He again repeated himself in Spanish. Then they followed him into the forest.

Ava listened to him describe the growing habits of the native flowers and plants. She had so often strolled past natural beauty at home and never asked the names, never wondered at the growing habits. Her nephew could label every growing thing.

When they got to the cave, Ava's curiosity deepened. The writings, the guide said, had been there before Columbus arrived. Ava wondered if anything she had ever done would last that long. And what did the writings mean? Certainly they weren't written for posterity; the people didn't know they were creating something that would last so long that people would pay for a tour to see them. Yet there they were, survivors of the natural and manmade changes around them. Life could be so strange and impossible to predict.

Ava turned to look for Connie. Her former neighbor was lagging behind, still chatting with the man she met at the beginning of the tour. There was a flirtatious smile, a laugh. Connie needed to be away from everything familiar so she could flower into herself.

When the two of them returned to the car, Connie was as giddy as a teenage girl.

"He liked me," Connie said in a soft voice intended only for Ava's ears. "We talked so easily, and it felt good."

"Do you have a date?"

"No, silly. However, I did strike up a conversation, totally on my own, with a man I didn't know." Connie sounded incredulous, like she'd climbed a mountain that no one expected she would even approach.

"No other person introduced us or kept the conversation going.

It was all me. And I didn't have to do anything for him. He was happy to talk, nothing more."

Ava wondered if she would be as giddy if a man interacted with her like that. She didn't think so. She had been on a few dates since Donovan left, but they never seemed worth the sacrifice of her independence. She wasn't sure she was up for more than a little flirtation.

She was, however, up for exploring Aunt Lila's farm from a different angle. Maybe there was a way to set up tours there to discover the native plants of Kentucky growing by the creek. Perhaps the lady's slippers were worth preserving and sharing.

Of course, that assumed the farm would stay in the family.

Ava and Connie returned to Lizzie's, satisfied that they'd experienced something most people within the gated community had likely never taken the time to see. And it was fascinating. It was history. It was beauty.

Lizzie didn't care. She sat on the chaise on the patio, sipping a drink and staring at the pool again.

"Plans for the rest of the day?" Lizzie said as they walked in.

"No," Ava said. "You?"

"I thought we could go to the beach restaurant for dinner tonight. It's a lovely place to see the sunset. And I sent Araceli home. She needed a break, so we won't eat here."

Lizzie's words sounded flat next to the beautiful picture she was trying to create.

"Sunset on the beach sounds like a good plan to me," Connie said, then left for her room.

Ava sat.

"Guests tonight?" she said.

"If you want to invite someone. Your Italian fashion man or Chester?"

Ava sensed the teasing in Lizzie's words. Connie's new friend would be more likely.

"When will we see Max?" Ava asked.

Lizzie lowered her eyes to her hands.

"Two days. I have two days to figure out how to approach him about the job—and this place."

Ava had never seen Lizzie looking so tense.

"He loves you, Lizzie. And he's a good man."

Lizzie nodded. She didn't appear convinced. And Ava knew that being a good person didn't guarantee the selflessness marriage called for at critical moments.

"Ava, I need your help," Connie called from the stairwell. Ava couldn't imagine what she might need, unless her daughter had given Marvin her number.

Ava excused herself and went upstairs. Connie was in the doorway of the room she shared with Bernadette. Ava peered over Connie's shoulder and spotted two dozen shopping bags covering Bernadette's bed.

Bernadette held up her hand to silence them. Yet Ava had been quiet before when her friend was buying so many clothes, and that hadn't been helpful.

Bernadette opened a large bag and pulled out a woven blanket in primary colors. "I think I'll do one room to remind me of our trip. I also got some candles and a painting."

She laid down the blanket and rummaged through the bags until she found the painting. She proudly held it in front of her. Neither Connie nor Ava spoke.

"And I had to get souvenirs for everyone."

Worry chased Bernadette's voice to a higher register. She opened one small bag and poured out a dozen or so wooden animals, all small enough to fit in her palm and painted in a riot of primary colors.

Connie stepped closer to Bernadette. Ava watched Connie's expression transform from enchanted tourist to demanding mother.

"Bernadette, put it all in the sacks. I'll help you return everything."

Bernadette's eyes opened wide, and she stamped her foot. "You cannot tell me what to do, Connie Gaines. It's not your business."

"My life wasn't your business either, but you jumped right in. Now I'm doing the same for you. Pack it all up, and we'll return it."

Connie's voice was firmer, though it retained the gentleness of friendship.

Bernadette shifted her eyes to Ava, who crossed her arms over her stomach. Bernadette pushed out her lower lip, and a tear rolled down her cheek. Ava wondered if that was how she had gotten her way with her husband for so many years or if the tears were genuine. One tear followed another and another until she was bawling.

Connie sat next to Bernadette on the little space remaining on the bed. Ava removed bags on the other side of Bernadette and joined them. They each put an arm around her. Bernadette cried and shook like someone having a seizure.

Between deep breaths and tears, she glanced from one to the other. "My house will never be the same."

"You can make it however you want, Bernadette. It can be better," Ava said.

Bernadette wailed. Ava obviously had a different relationship with her house than Bernadette had with hers.

Bernadette pulled a handkerchief from her pocket and wiped her face.

"I don't want better. I want my memories back."

She took a few deep breaths, and her trembling eased.

"I'm sorry, Bernadette," Ava said.

Connie wore a somber expression as she spoke.

"It's not going to be the same for any of us. We're all three moving on to something new. The best we can do is be there for one another as we shift."

Bernadette nodded and wiped at her cheeks again.

"I'll pack it up," she said softly.

Chapter 13

Lizzie wore yet another lovely dress that flowed around her tall frame when they went to the restaurant. While the business had an indoor dining room, they opted for a table on the patio's edge, where they could gaze at the water reflecting the sunset.

Ava settled back into her chair, beheld the scene, and felt like a wealthy woman. To have this opportunity, in this place, with these friends was so unexpected but welcome. They'd returned all of Bernadette's purchases, except the blanket, and Bernadette seemed resigned to no more shopping. A little of her sadness lingered, though she was more herself.

The waiter greeted Lizzie with a "Your favorite drink, señora?" and they chitchatted in light Spanish. Lizzie's shoulders dropped, and the tension in her face relaxed.

"One of the benefits of the community," Lizzie said as she looked around. "The food is superb, and the view, well, you can see."

"Your mother could do something like this at the back of her house for her guests. The view would be different but still beautiful," Ava mused.

"Spring is pretty there, sometimes fall as well. This is guaranteed pretty year-round, as Max likes to remind me. We do get the occasional hurricane threat, but not often enough to dissuade him from this place."

"What happened to that hurricane we heard about when we arrived?" Ava asked.

Lizzie shrugged. "It turned and moved north. Nothing's ever certain."

Ava glanced at Connie, wondering how she was feeling in the land of uncertainty. Connie hadn't mentioned any conversations with her children since the day at Aunt Lila's—hadn't said whether Heather followed through on her threat.

Bernadette stayed in close contact with her family, talking to them almost as frequently as she did Connie and Ava. They called or texted multiple times during the day. She would always be the heart of her family, even if she lost her balance for a while. They would help her regain it.

Then there was Ava's own Juniper. How Ava missed their conversations. She wondered if the spring crops had come up well and about the nature of the problems Juniper had texted about—and whether Juniper still visited the remains of the house to hug the tree.

"Has he reached out to you, Connie?" Bernadette said.

"Last night Marvin sent a string of texts through Heather, begging me to come home."

"And?" Ava said.

"Surely you won't," Bernadette said. "You left him for a reason."

"I obviously don't know the man, but I have to say, he sounds horrid," Lizzie said.

Ava felt the same way, though she wouldn't say that to Connie. She didn't know all the details, didn't know if there was room for forgiveness and reconciliation. She had gathered that the domination had gone too far to reverse.

"More than anything, I would like to be with people who allow me to be me, just who I am, without putting on a show or being worried that I'll say the wrong thing. It's not good to always be on guard. No one should have to do that," Connie said.

"We're the right friends for you," Bernadette said.

That anxiety was something Ava realized she'd rarely experienced. She wasn't on guard. She simply said what she felt without thinking about the consequences. Yes, it might have gotten her into trouble more than once, but it didn't confine her like it had Connie.

Ava noticed a tall, stylish woman approaching them, her step bouncing with confidence. *She must be a friend of Lizzie's.* She took another couple of steps, and Ava saw she was wrong. It was Linda Mueller.

Linda stopped at their table and took in each face. "Refugees from the storm come to the DR. That was a brilliant decision!" she said. Turning to Lizzie, she extended her hand. "I'm Linda Mueller, novelist. I went to school with Ava and Bernadette."

Lizzie pulled up her chin and shook the proffered hand. She didn't say anything. Lizzie had been close enough to them in school that Linda should know who she was.

Ava intervened. "Linda, that's my cousin Lizzie, Fawn's older sister."

Linda studied Lizzie more carefully, then smiled. "Of course! It's been so long since I've seen you."

"And I am oh so changed?"

"Actually, no," Linda said, her words stumbling. It was obvious that the lack of recognition insulted Lizzie. "It's been so long."

"I have a house here," Lizzie said. "And you?"

It sounded like a challenge, like a declaration of standing that Lizzie assumed Linda couldn't match.

"I'm here doing research for my next novel. With all the construction going on next door to my house, it's too loud to work at home."

Bernadette raised her eyebrows at Linda, who ignored her and turned toward Ava.

"By the way, I talked with Juniper at the library the other day. I didn't know she handled events there. She's setting up the local launch of my new book for me."

Ava swallowed hard. Juniper had taken a job off the farm. *Is that her move to save the co-op?*

Linda's gaze flicked toward the entrance, where a dark, handsome man waved to her. She turned back to the group, landing on Lizzie with her own nod.

"Excuse me. My date's here." She gave a little wave and left.

They were all looking at Ava, but it was Bernadette who spoke.

"I never did like her. She's such a showy know-it-all." She mimicked Linda: "'It's too loud to work at my house because of all the construction next door.' At least the woman still has a house!"

Connie filled in Lizzie about Bernadette and Linda being neighbors.

"I think that woman was born under a different moon than any of us," Bernadette said. "In all these years I've known her, she's never had a crisis. Not one."

Lizzie glanced over at Linda. "At least, not one you've seen. When people expect a lot from you, it's hard to admit your life isn't all it looks like."

She smoothed the napkin on her lap, then let her eyes drift over the water toward the sunset. The others followed her lead, except for Ava, who felt restless.

"How long do you think it will be before our food gets here?" Ava said.

"As I'm sure you've noticed, 'hurry' isn't in the vocabulary here. It's actually one of the things I like about the island. Do you have someone to meet?" Lizzie teased.

"I would like to walk along the beach before it's too dark."

Bernadette narrowed her eyes at Ava.

"You don't want to talk about it? We all heard what she said about Juniper."

Ava shook her head.

"It's your vacation. Do what you want," Connie said warmly.

Ava went to the edge of the patio and removed her sandals.

At the water's edge, she pushed her feet into the cooling sand. It was quiet, peaceful. No expectations, not really. Connie's words had given her permission to not worry about when her food arrived. That was less important than Juni, anyway.

Ava sighed, then took a deep breath. *Don't overthink. Don't overthink.*

She angled her face toward the setting sun and closed her eyes. Enough warmth remained to brush her like the tenderest of kisses. She felt the sand against her soles. The beach asked nothing of Ava. What a reprieve from the world.

The breeze tickled her slightly browned skin as gentle waves rolled in. They had small peaks, like in a tide pool at an amusement park—enough movement to stir her imagination yet not enough to overwhelm her. She imagined a wall of open doors; she could walk through whichever she chose. Or she could carve out her own entry to a path previously unknown.

That was more appealing than falling back into the same routine. Perhaps it was also a better example for Juni.

Ava pictured the drive to her aunt's home. Ava's Avenue—that was what she would call it if it were her place. There were possibilities on that farm that Ava could capitalize on to make the business better. And there were connections that made Ava feel needed and wanted, also loved.

She wondered if Lizzie knew that her mother was thinking of selling.

Ava didn't know what her own property looked like now. Maybe the neighbors were accustomed to it. Maybe if it became a picnic area, that would help people get to know one another. Of course, if she had tried, Ava could have known her neighbors better. After all, she was in the Dominican Republic with Connie Gaines. She would never have predicted that.

The cool water washed across her feet, then returned to its home. Although she enjoyed this place, it didn't feed her like home did. Maybe she was like the water and had to rejoin herself, return to where she came from, to figure out what was next—who she would be at the age of fifty-five. Her own mother hadn't lived to see fifty, but Lizzie had made it through. So had Aunt Lila and Aunt Maud.

Ava walked, wondering what her mother would have looked like at this age. *What would she have been?* Most likely, her spirit would have soared. Jeannie wasn't the kind of woman who faded away.

The water approached again, and Ava scurried higher up the beach to miss it, already plenty chilled. She watched the water recede. And just like that, she knew.

As long as she continued to walk the same path, the water would discomfort her on some days and tickle her on others. But she didn't have to walk the same path. She could escape what disturbed her, or better yet, she could immerse herself fully in it and get over her fears, discover what was there to help her grow, and learn a new way to thrive. She could make the choice. She could jump right into the unknown with Juniper, and they could figure it out together.

A return to some ordinary might give Ava the strength to do what she must. A bag of microwave popcorn for her meal while watching an old movie. Preparing Sunday supper for Juniper, then hanging on to her until she insisted on getting back to the farm. Unpacking the plastic tub marked SUMMER CLOTHES and finding items she had forgotten. It was all so normal, and she craved it.

Ava could cook for Juniper in a new place. Maybe they would change the night. Maybe instead of watching old movies, she would ask Florence to recommend a television series she could binge on. And perhaps she could learn to live with ten outfits that would serve her all year long. She didn't want to have so much stuff that she needed plastic tubs for storage. Some of those old habits would become sweet memories.

Ava arrived back at the table as the waiter made a show of placing each dish on the table. The three were talking about Aunt Lila.

"It's time for her to move into something more appropriate for a widow of her age," Lizzie said when Ava returned to the table. She must have spoken with Maud.

"It's her home. It was your home. Wouldn't you miss it?" Ava said.

"Like Juniper misses her home?" Lizzie replied. "You seem to be more concerned about my childhood home than your own daughter's."

Ava shouldn't have told Lizzie about the ultimatum Juniper had given her. Still, that wasn't the same. Aunt Lila's farm had been in the family for generations. Ava had been in her house for twenty-six years.

"That's not what we're talking about, Lizzie. Don't redirect the conversation."

"You think Juniper doesn't have memories there like you have at Mom's house? Ava, it's the house your daughter lived in until she moved out. Sure, she had her dad's place in Colorado, but that wasn't the same."

It was true that Ava hadn't fully considered the situation from Juniper's point of view. Nor had she considered how Donovan might feel about the house being gone. He had memories there too. She hadn't once asked him his opinion about the situation.

"Donovan offered me a job," she blurted out.

"What?" Connie and Bernadette said in unison.

"Before we left, he called and offered me a job with his new business in Indianapolis. It sounded ridiculous at the time, but I am going to have to find a job somewhere."

"You wouldn't move, would you?" Bernadette said.

"I don't want to move," Ava said, certain that was true.

"Ava," Lizzie said, drawing Ava's attention back to her. Her voice and face had softened into someone more familiar to Ava. "Think about this. Mom's place is too much for her to keep up with. If you think it's so important for her to stay there, then move in with her, help her with the business, lift some of her load."

Lizzie put words to what Ava had been feeling. It seemed strange to hear it come from Lila's own daughter, who should be the one lessening the load for her mother. It also sounded like an invitation. If neither Lizzie nor Fawn were in a position to take the pressure off, then maybe Ava was the one to do it.

The next morning, the group had gathered for breakfast when a knock at the door interrupted them. It was Chester, who had come to take the photos Lizzie requested. He joined them for coffee, then went to work, setting up a couple of lights to illuminate the darker interiors.

Ava remained at the dining room table after the others excused themselves. Chester had migrated onto the patio. He moved assuredly as he slightly angled a table and placed a vase barely off-center. Ava had never known a photographer before. She realized they must be used to finding the beauty in all sorts of situations and scenes. Unless they photographed the news. That would be totally different from still-life photography.

Chester turned to Ava with his camera in front of his eye. He snapped a picture before she could protest. When he removed the camera, he was smiling, so she couldn't scold him.

He peered around as if ascertaining whether they were alone, then went to the table and took the chair next to Ava.

"Have you seen much of the island?" he asked.

"No. Lizzie's too distracted to be any kind of tour guide. It's easier to hang out here."

He placed his camera on the table and reached for Ava's hands. "Will you honor me with your company this evening for dinner?"

His hands completely covered hers with a gentleness that surprised her. And oh, that accent. It tickled something deep within her. Ava would accompany him anywhere.

She nodded and smiled.

Chester kissed her cheek and stood.

"I'll pick you up at seven. There's a lovely restaurant on the beach in the next town. We can go there."

Ava nodded again and felt, for the first time ever, that some of Lizzie's magic fairy dust had sifted onto her life.

Ava fretted about her date, feeling like a teenager again and suddenly caring very much how she looked. She'd already worn the one nice outfit she brought when Chester joined them for dinner.

Lizzie rescued her with a flowy dress without a waist. And it was blue, which Ava was beginning to recognize as her color. Once she pulled it on, she needed to figure out what to do with her hair. Lizzie walked into the room as she was brushing it.

"Do you know that you look like Grandma Marsh?"

Ava studied her reflection and tried to see her grandmother but couldn't identify that part of her. She had always assumed she resembled her father's family because she didn't look like her mom.

"I always thought that was why you were Grandpa's favorite," Lizzie said, taking the brush from Ava's hand. She swept it through Ava's hair in long strokes.

"I wasn't his favorite," Ava said.

Lizzie rolled her eyes.

"Didn't you say you still have his desk?"

"It's the one piece of furniture that survived the storm."

"I bet if you look hard enough, you'll find a photo of Grandma as a young woman. You'll see yourself."

"You know I'm not young any longer."

"Nor are you old. By the way, your hair is pretty like this. Don't do anything else to it."

Lizzie sat on the love seat, and Ava turned to face her.

"Speaking of Grandpa, do you know if he liked farming?"

Lizzie had that knowing smile. She didn't answer.

Ava continued, "When I was with Fawn, it was clear that she's been shelving her dreams for years so she could care for her family. I was sitting at Grandpa's desk, looking at some of his things. It reminded me of how much he loved history, and I wondered if he'd ever hoped to be a professor or a museum curator or guide. Because Juniper does love farming, but I don't know if she'll be able to make it work for herself."

"It sounds like you already know the answer. People sometimes do what they have to for the people they love."

The sadness in Lizzie's voice told Ava her cousin was no longer thinking about people in general or about their family.

"When Max and I got engaged, Grandpa asked me to meet him at the farm. We went for a walk by the creek, and he told me stories about the native people who had once lived there. He'd been working with an archaeologist to unearth their story."

"I didn't know anything about that."

"I didn't either until that day. I thought he was a farmer and he enjoyed that. He didn't tell me if he did or he didn't. He did tell me that women oftentimes were overshadowed by strong men. He urged me to not let that happen."

Ava tried to imagine her seemingly traditional grandfather saying that. She couldn't picture it.

"I told him I knew Max was the one for me. The signs were all there. And he told me to always look for the signs to see where they would lead me."

"And have you?"

Lizzie shrugged. "As best I could."

She stood and set the hairbrush in front of Ava.

"There's no chart to write them on that will plot your path. But I think if we both follow his advice, we'll know what the next move is. One sign at a time."

The restaurant where Chester took Ava felt low-key and local. Conversations in Spanish floated around tables that were situated in sand rather than on a deck, and the table settings boasted locally carved wooden flowers as their centerpieces. The menu was in Spanish, with a list of choices that Ava didn't think had been at the other restaurant. She settled on a chicken and rice dish with warm and sweet spices and mashed plantains.

Chester was easy to talk with and to listen to. He had a string of stories about fascinating places he'd traveled for his work. Where Ava once wouldn't have understood why anyone would choose to travel that frequently, she felt a rush at the idea of exploring the pyramids in Egypt. Learning to samba in Rio de Janeiro would be fun. Seeing great works of art, in person, at the Uffizi—what a thrill that would be. Chester had done them all.

After they ate, Chester took her hand and led her out to the beach for a stroll in the moonlight. Although she had enjoyed her solo walk the other night, having Chester for company made for an entirely different experience. The sand was hard and wet beneath her bare feet. A cool breeze ruffled her hair. Chester's hand around hers felt so strong, so capable and dependable. Ava wondered how a person who spent little time in one place could feel so steady. It was something she'd never felt with Donovan.

Ahead, Ava spotted lights and heard a drum. Then a guitar joined the music. Chester guided her in that direction. It was a dance floor with a band. Shoes lined the sand along the wooden platform. As the gathered crowd watched, a man and a woman wearing matching turquoise outfits walked through dance steps with two other people.

Ava watched and realized she was subtly swaying her hips. It had been so long since she had danced with anyone. And it wasn't something she did well, even if she managed to lose herself in the movement and music. She glanced at Chester to see if he might be feeling the music too. Before she could discern his thoughts, a hand was reaching for hers, and the man in turquoise pulled her onto the floor.

She watched his feet as he stepped through a simple pattern. He pushed her chin up so she looked into his dark eyes. He smiled. "Feel it," he said.

And so, she did. They stepped it out, moving a little faster each time.

"Hips," her partner told her.

She watched the woman who was dancing with Chester and saw

how she swayed as she stepped. Ava tried imitating her. Then Ava's partner led her to Chester, and they joined the other couples on the floor.

Chester and Ava both laughed as they tried to match the rhythm of the music. Ava felt she was doing well, though Chester wasn't as smooth as her first partner.

"I'm afraid it doesn't come naturally for me," Chester said.

"Maybe what comes naturally is the easiest but not the best," Ava said.

"You're a wise woman, Ava Winston."

Wiser and braver than she had ever realized.

After Ava showered in the morning, she found Connie and Bernadette at the breakfast table with empty plates in front of them. Connie greeted her with a big smile, and Bernadette raised her eyebrows.

"I do believe you came in quite late last night," Bernadette said.

"I didn't. It was early this morning. Don't be so Sister Alice Mary," Ava said.

She took a seat, and Araceli brought her juice. Croissants and fruit sat on the table.

Connie touched Ava's hand as she reached for a croissant.

"Was he a dream?" she said.

Ava nodded, and Connie's smile widened. Ava felt like she was in high school, talking with her friends the day after the prom. She might look like a middle-aged woman, but inside she felt like she still had her entire life ahead of her.

Then she realized Lizzie wasn't at the table.

"Max surprised her and arrived last night instead of waiting until today," Connie said.

"She looked worried," Bernadette said. "Is something up with them? We haven't seen them this morning."

"We're not the only ones trying to find our new footing" was all Ava said.

She hoped Lizzie had brought her concerns up with Max. She wanted her cousin to feel the same airiness now washing over her. A bit of bravery to step out into something new—simultaneously lifting a burden and sending Ava's mind in a thousand directions. She'd hardly slept since returning to the house, and it wasn't because she was thinking of Chester. The evening had been the most fun she'd had with a man in years. And there promised to be more. Chester had a summer assignment in Kentucky at a horse farm. She could imagine welcoming him to a room at Aunt Lila's, showing him around central Kentucky. Maybe he would take photos she could use to promote the business. Or maybe they would simply sit on the porch and get up to dance if the breeze was right.

Something about being with him helped cement her realization that she didn't have to take the easy way. Her duty to Juniper didn't limit her options. She didn't need to go back to her old job. She didn't need to rebuild her house. If Aunt Lila was willing to take on a business partner, they could divide duties. Lila could be the public face while Ava did the rest of the work. And maybe, at the same time, Ava could lessen the load for Juniper and her partners. None of them had professed proficiency with the bookkeeping part of the business.

The possibilities were still swirling through her head that afternoon when she finally saw Lizzie, without Max. Her older cousin was placid, not a word Ava had ever associated with her. Lizzie silently walked from pot to giant pot, watering the many flowers around the patio.

"Is Max here?" Ava asked.

"Gone to the golf course. That's where he goes when he wants to think. He's a person who needs time to process."

"You told him?"

Lizzie nodded and moved on to the next plant, a bright-orange bougainvillea. She continued to water, avoiding Ava's gaze.

"I'm sure you supported Max, listened to his ideas, boosted him for all these years. I hope he realizes it's his turn to do the same," Ava said.

"He's seen me throw myself into something new every time we move, so he thinks it can be that way here too. It's not the same here."

"Please invite me to your place in New York when you're there."

With that, Lizzie draped the hose over a patio chair and smiled at Ava.

"My oh my, our little Kentuckian has transformed."

"Maybe not transformed, exactly. I think I'm more like a dehydrated piece of fruit that needed water to plump it to its luscious potential."

"And now you're stunningly juicy."

For the next two days, Ava and Connie spent most of their time on the beach. Lizzie joined them when Max golfed. Bernadette stayed poolside at Lizzie's house to avoid the shopping.

Lizzie was more relaxed. Araceli came back, and the push and pull between the two of them eased into a loose string that no longer pulled taut. Lizzie even gave Araceli a morning off. Lizzie wanted to cook for everyone herself. Her favorite meal to make was breakfast.

"These crepes are divine," Bernadette said. "What's inside?"

"Mango compote." Lizzie pointed to the trees at the back of her property. "I'm still enough of a farm girl to know that when trees give you fruit, you preserve it."

"I'll preserve these days, Lizzie. Thank you for having us," Connie said.

"Thank you for putting up with me."

"They're tolerant," Bernadette said as she smiled at her friends. Then she focused on Connie. "Is the cut permanent now?"

"I couldn't go back." Connie raised her eyebrows in an uncertain expression. "I'm going to San Francisco to see my son. Then I'll go to

Louisville to see my daughter, if she'll have me. Then I'll decide what's next. By then Marvin might have gotten used to me being gone and not want me back, which will make it easier," she said.

"Have your children told him where you are?"

"No. I asked them not to, and they agreed. It feels good to come back to the house and not dread checking my phone. Sometimes I wish we could go back to the no-cell-phone days. There was a time when you could travel abroad and it was so expensive to call home that you would only do it in an emergency."

"We could all pitch them, start our own trend," Ava said.

"And what about you, Ava? Is life new for you? Is fear gone?" Lizzie said, a slight challenge in her voice.

"I didn't think I would be starting anything new at fifty-five. By this time in life, shouldn't we all be settled into who we are until we're old and close to petrification?"

"Don't mention petrification. It's hard enough to stay attractive at this age. I can't imagine what it will be in thirty years," Bernadette said.

"Whatever word you use, we'll continue to evolve," Connie said. "What's really different now is that we better understand that we have choices."

At that, Ava's phone dinged. They all laughed, but she didn't pitch it. She picked it up and saw a message from Juniper.

"MOM, I MISS YOU. BIG NEWS TO SHARE WHEN YOU GET HOME SO BE SURE TO CALL. LOVE YOU."

Ava relayed the message to the others.

"You think it's the big news I already know?" she asked Lizzie.

"Unless she's pregnant," Lizzie said.

"I doubt that. I don't think she's even dating anyone."

"Come on, Ava. You said she's living with her ex-boyfriend. And you really think he's still the ex?"

Ava peered at Connie, who had seen the two young people together.

"Did you pick up on anything?"

"I'm not the best judge, yet they seem to get along naturally, the way I imagine people relate to one another when they're meant to be."

"Maybe it's only about the job at the library. But I will not be afraid of what she has to tell me. I will not be afraid. I will not," Ava said. "Besides that, I like Washington."

"Do I hear you starting to practice fear-free living today?" Lizzie said.

"Seems like as good a time as any."

Max walked in, and the women fell silent. They hadn't seen him much since his arrival. He bent to kiss Lizzie's cheek, then took a seat while Lizzie got him a plate and coffee.

Max's blond hair edged into white, and crow's feet defined his gray eyes. To Ava, he looked too young for retirement.

"Well, Max, will I see you in Kentucky anytime soon?" Ava said.

Lizzie placed the filled coffee cup in front of Max, who served himself a crepe.

"That's up to Lizzie. We've decided that retirement for me means she's in charge. I'll have to learn to take orders."

His congenial attitude softened Lizzie's features. She appeared genuinely happy.

"We'll keep this place, at least for a while," Lizzie said. "You can come back with your families, even if we're in New York. Araceli will be here."

"Do you have a guest room in New York?" Bernadette asked. "The shopping must be fabulous."

"For you three, the door will always be open."

Chapter 14

On the flight home, Ava sat next to the window. She gazed outside without feeling sick and didn't need Connie to keep her distracted. She didn't even panic when the plane hit an air pocket.

Ava and Bernadette followed Connie through the long line at customs. Someone ahead of them stood at the window for quite some time, talking so rapidly that the person in the booth couldn't say a thing. Ava couldn't help wondering what they would ask her and whether they would inspect her luggage.

The officer in the booth in front of them waved Connie on. Ava stood behind the yellow line, waiting to be called forward. She rolled her shoulders. The hurricane hadn't hit the Dominican Republic during their visit; Ava had escaped disaster number three. She had made it safely back to her homeland. *No reason to be afraid at customs.* She couldn't think of anything that might deny her entry back into her own country. Still, she heard so many stories about crazy things happening at international borders.

A green light came on at booth 3, and a uniformed woman waved Ava down. Ava studied the middle-aged man inside the booth and wondered how many days he had spent in that small enclosure. She handed him her passport with the paperwork inside. He opened the booklet, glanced from Ava to her picture, removed the papers, stamped the page, then handed her passport back to her.

"Welcome home," he said.

Ava smiled. They were good words to hear.

Bernadette's family, every one of them, surrounded her at the luggage carousel. It didn't look like they would ever let her travel without them again.

Connie and Ava went to Ava's car and drove to Aunt Lila's. As they headed up the tree-lined lane, Ava held her breath, hoping she wouldn't see Marvin or a For Sale sign in the yard. Instead, she found Aunt Lila had expanded her flower garden. The sign read: Bloom like a flower.

Aunt Lila sat in the kitchen, awaiting them with lemonade and shortbread cookies. Some pink colored her cheeks, and her voice sounded mellow.

The air had warmed while they were gone, though it still lacked the sun-kissed heat they'd enjoyed on the island. Aunt Lila wanted to know all about Lizzie; of course, Ava only shared the good parts. Lizzie would tell her mom more when she was ready.

"It's such a gorgeous place," Connie said. "You should go visit again."

"I've never been much of a beach person. Some people love it, but that sand between my toes makes me feel all itchy. I would rather feel the mud of a good pond all over my feet," Lila said. "Besides that, I can't be pondering vacation. I've got decisions to make here. Maud's insistent that I can't keep this up, and Fawn agrees with her."

"Are you feeling better?" Ava said.

"Considerably." Lila stared out the window. "I walked out in the field where Daddy kept the goats. When I'm out there, I can see the three of us running around—Maud, Jeannie, and me. It's like I'm there again, transported by Jeannie's laughter and Maud's bossiness. What a blessing sisters are."

Ava thought of her brother, Jarvis. She hadn't seen him in so long. Maybe she would invite him and his family for a visit. Or—now that she knew she wouldn't perish in flight—she could go to see him.

"Will you miss that if you go?" Ava asked.

"When I think of it, I can't imagine going. I can't imagine staying, either. This place is so much to keep up. Maud invited me to live with her. She said she would move into a bigger apartment with space for two."

Ava made a face, and Aunt Lila laughed.

Ava went to her grandfather's desk. She sat down and idly ran her palm over the curve of the ribbed top. Then she used both hands to roll it back into its hiding slot.

She knew all the niches and the remnants of her grandfather tucked in them. She pulled out his reading glasses, which were so delicately made. He would never have believed that today he could walk into a store and find a rack of reading glasses in varying styles with whichever prescription level he needed.

Ava replaced the glasses, and her fingers traced the calendar pad she had left there. The top of it read 1987; she had never seen a need to remove it.

Remembering Lizzie's urging to search for the photo of their grandmother, Ava sorted through all the cubbies again but didn't see anything other than what she already knew was there. Then she picked up the desk pad, and out slipped two photographs. One was a photo of Grandma Marsh in her wedding dress, a simple white dress that went to her knees. She wore a small hat atop her dark hair.

The other was Ava's high school graduation photo. The two women looked so similar that there was no doubt they were related.

It was her grandfather with whom Ava had always been infatuated. She had to work harder to remember her grandmother—the one always busy in the background, keeping things together.

Maybe her grandfather had always known Ava would never be a manager or business owner. She had a different role to fill that suited her temperament. The routine of supporting those around her energized Ava. That was why she had been able to work an office job all those years. For others, routine dimmed the sparkle they arrived with falling away like fairy dust gone stale.

She couldn't let Juniper do this to herself: work at the library just to try to make enough to keep the farm afloat. Juniper wasn't meant to be dusted in ashes.

Aunt Lila appeared at Ava's side. Connie had drifted outside to the porch.

"No, I do not intend to move in with my sister," Lila said. "Love her, I do. That would be much more difficult if we lived together."

"You and I can, don't you think?" Ava said.

Aunt Lila smiled, and Ava saw the faint resemblance to her own mother.

"Yes, I do."

"I need to call Juni, let her tell me about what's happening there, and see how she's feeling about the house," Ava said. She took one more sip of her lemonade, then headed to her room, suitcase in hand. She closed the door behind her.

One thing Lizzie had been right about was that Juniper likely did feel as strongly about their ruined house as Ava felt about Aunt Lila's house. And if it meant that much to her, maybe Ava had to be willing to rebuild. It didn't feel like the right thing for her, but for Juniper, it might be.

She called Juniper.

"It's so good to hear your voice," Ava said. "I've missed you."

"I've missed you too, Mom. It seems like the whole world has turned upside down since I last saw you."

"Are you going to keep me in suspense? You know I've been wondering about your news since I got your message."

"Well, first off, we kicked out Vivienne. She'd started a side hustle where she used our eggs, vegetables, and seed money to supply two bakeries with her baked goods. I couldn't believe it. Washington had to hold me back because I wanted to pummel her."

Ava wasn't surprised.

"She left her basic quiche recipe. That doesn't matter since none of us can replicate it well enough, so we've been in a bind. We've already lost customers, though Aunt Lila has been helping. When it finally occurred to me that she cooks for her guests, so surely she knows how to make quiche, I called her. She can't fill all the orders, and obviously she's not here, so she can't take care of the chickens. Still, it's a temporary fix."

"That doesn't sound so bad."

"There's more," Juniper said.

The silence scared Ava. Juniper had been sharing so freely. But then, nothing.

I will not be afraid. I will not.

"Can you meet me at the house, Mom? I want to see you."

As Ava drove toward the house, Lizzie's pregnancy prediction returned to her. She certainly hadn't imagined grandmotherhood welcoming her into her second half of life. Even more importantly than that, what could that mean for Juniper and her dreams?

Or was she sick? *Please, God, let her not have cancer or some other incurable disease.*

Ava parked, and the first thing she noticed was that the tree was gone. There were two chairs in its place, wooden chairs that someone had made, and Juniper sat in one of them. She stood when her mom arrived and embraced her, holding her close and not letting up. Juniper's warmth filled Ava with strength, a vitality she hadn't realized was missing during her reprieve from her daughter. With Juniper's arms around her, she felt more at home than she had in six weeks.

Juniper pulled away, then spoke before Ava could.

"I had to take a job off the farm. We weren't making the bills."

"Oh, Juni. The farm's your dream. Do you think you can do it if your attention and time are on another job?"

"I don't have a choice. We pay the mortgage, or we lose all we've invested, and we have to make up for what Vivienne stole from us."

They sat, and Juni took her mom's hand.

"Washington made us the chairs from the tree," she said, her expression lightening.

"He's a treasure," Ava said.

Juni's smile told her that her daughter realized that too.

"Did you have a good time, Mom? I'm so, so happy that you went."

"It was Connie who got me there. But I don't want to talk about the trip right now. Are Washington and the others still at the farm?"

"Oh yeah. Not to worry about that. I feel so sick about all this. I've worked five days at the library and can't even sleep at night. It's not that I don't like the library. I'm a reader, right? Still, I'm inside, mostly sitting. It's not what I envisioned. And it's definitely not the farm."

Ava was afraid to bring it up, but she knew it was time. She squeezed Juniper's hand.

"Juniper, what are you thinking about our house?"

Juniper bit her lip and didn't meet her mom's eyes. She also didn't pull her hand away. She gazed around the disheveled property.

"It looks like we were never here. Like someone else's lot."

Her voice cracked as if saying it aloud broke her. And Ava did feel a stab, a pierce of reality. Though the loss was deep for Juniper, if the place already didn't feel like hers, maybe she was ready to let it go.

"We can split the insurance money, Juniper. That would give you money for the farm. It would buy you the time you need to make things work. And we can sell the lot."

"You need a place to live. And you quit your job. It's not like you have a big bank account to fall back on."

"Your dad actually offered me a job. I think it's more than I can take on, but if he has contract work I can do, I'll take it. I have a business partnership idea of my own that would give me a place to stay. You let me worry about that. And I might have an idea for you and your partners as well."

"Are you sure, Mom? You're certain you don't want to rebuild?"

"I would to help you. But I mulled it over a lot while I was traveling. Even the sun and the sand couldn't wipe away how I felt when I emerged from that basement."

"How did you feel, Mom?"

Ava wasn't sure she could put it into words. She'd been so scared but so thankful. She was alive.

"Unbelievably blessed. Gifted with another day, a chance to live better. Unencumbered. Ready to shift."

Juniper squeezed Ava's hand. "I love you, and I don't ever want to be separated from you again. I'm not fully me when you're not here."

Ava pulled away gently. "That's a lovely sentiment, Juniper. But now that I've earned my wings, I might be flying again. Lizzie's moving back to New York. I've never been there, and it sounds like another good vacation destination."

"Maybe you'll take me with you," Juniper said.

Ava felt complete once again.

Chapter 15

They all trickled in over the course of an hour. Fawn and her family. Bernadette and Joe O'Donnell. Juniper with Washington. Connie. Even Aunt Maud showed up.

It was a warm June day. The winds were calm enough that they could sit on the outdoor deck Ava had contracted Washington to build. It was almost as spacious as Lizzie's patio, and in Ava's eyes, the view was more beautiful, especially with all these people gathered around.

Aunt Lila walked out with a tray of drinks—an array of lemonade and iced tea. She would be the hostess at the house for as long as she wanted. That was her natural talent and not one Ava was ever likely to develop. Connie said she would be happy for some part-time work after she visited her children. She could be the public face for the business if Aunt Lila wasn't up to it. Ava could be the behind-the-scenes bookkeeper and baker who came out to meet the public when no one else was available.

It would have been great timing had Chester been in town. He could have taken photos of the party for Ava. But he'd postponed his trip, promising to be there before summer was over.

Donovan unfortunately wasn't able to get away from work to attend the gathering. After settling on partnering with Lila's business, Ava was interested in what business knowledge she could pick up from him.

Since there was no significant wind, Ava displayed the photos she had recovered from the basement. The photo albums were gone, but she'd found a shoebox with an assortment of pictures from life in their former house. Baby Juniper in her bassinet. The Christmas tree and presents when Juniper was three. Juniper and Donovan building a snowman out front. Donovan grilling on the front porch. Ava carrying a birthday cake into the kitchen.

Photos to illustrate their house's story.

"Thank you all for coming tonight," Ava said as the group settled. "As you know, we're gathered for an afternoon of storytelling and remembering our recently departed home."

"I want to go first," Bernadette said.

Ava wasn't sure what her friend would say. Bernadette had turned out to be more unpredictable than Ava had ever imagined. After returning from their trip, she settled back into someone closer to her pre-tornado self, though she hid a suitcase of her own from her family, containing the blanket she'd purchased on the sly in the DR. She would surprise the others with it when she decorated their new home.

"I hadn't seen Ava for nearly ten years when she moved in there. I was too busy having babies to pay much attention to what was happening with anyone else!"

Bernadette's husband turned pink as she elbowed him.

"Anyway, Ava and Donovan walked into the church with Juniper, still an infant, and that's all it took to reconnect us. And as soon as they walked in, I knew what house they must have bought. We'd driven past it at least once a week during the construction. It was such a cute place, and I thought if our family were smaller, we could buy that one."

"You didn't think it; you said it every time we saw it," her husband said.

Everyone laughed.

"Ava and I went to a Catholic girls' school. The nuns taught us to speak our piece, and I don't think either of us has ever forgotten that."

"How's your house coming along, Mrs. O'Donnell?" Juniper asked.

"They say another three months and we'll be back in, but you know what they say about optimistic contractors. They sell sunshine like you can't see the clouds. We're okay until then."

"Me next," Connie said. "I saw them moving in. Donovan and Ava were such a sweet-looking couple, both good looking and with that pretty baby. Babies always made me feel warm and welcomed, so I walked on over and introduced myself, Marvin trailing behind me."

"I do remember that. You were the first, maybe the only, people to welcome us to the neighborhood. Then I rarely saw you again."

"Now that you know more about us, you probably understand why. Watching you two always gave me hope. Donovan would grill outside on Sundays, even with snow on the ground. You both seemed to work so hard. And, Juniper, you were such a joyful little girl. I looked at your house and decided, *That's the way a family should live.*"

"It wasn't all roses inside that house," Ava said. "As you found out later. But I'll always remember that there were plenty of good times. You should have seen Donovan and me the day we painted the living room." She laughed.

"I remember that," Fawn said, joining the laughter.

Ava warmed at the memory.

"Are you going to tell the rest of us?" Bernadette said.

"Neither of us could paint for anything, and we didn't know a bit about how to paint around light switches or wood trim, so we painted it all. And we got it on the floor, which we hadn't covered well. And on ourselves. My hair was such a mess that I ended up cutting out a big hunk of it. Then I had to go to the hairdresser to get it fixed. Donovan went to the barber and got his all cut off. It's the one time I've seen him with a buzz cut."

Fawn shook her finger at Ava. "You are not telling it all, Ava. When Beau and I got there, they weren't painting at all. They were flicking paint at each other and laughing. Then Donovan walked over and grabbed Ava, pushed her up against the just-painted wall, and kissed her like no one was watching, which he obviously didn't know we were. Ava saw us and pushed him away, and when she stood back from the wall, there was her body imprinted in the new paint!"

Ava knew she was blushing. She couldn't help it. She remembered that passion from Donovan's kiss, that fire that burned out all memory of why she was dressed in those old clothes and had a paintbrush in her hand. They'd had something special.

She wondered if she would ever have it again. If she did get another chance, she would handle it differently—not take it for granted or assume it was hers to keep forever. She would cherish the passion and the man, whoever he was. She would be willing to compromise even if it felt destabilizing.

"My turn," Juniper said. "I remember the spring that I was nine. Dad brought home a bunch of flowers, and Mom and I planted them. We worked so hard to be sure the holes were wide enough and deep enough. Then Mom taught me to fill them with water first, before planting, so the roots would be drawn into the soil."

"Ava, I didn't know you knew that much about gardening," Fawn said.

"I didn't. Your mom told me what to do, so I was simply repeating her instructions."

Juniper cleared her throat.

"And so, as soon as I woke up the next morning, I put on my clothes and ran outside to see if the flowers had grown overnight. Instead of growing, they were all uprooted."

"Who would do such a thing?" Connie said.

"A mole," Juniper said. "Of course, I was nine and I didn't understand. Mom didn't either. As we walked around the yard, she stepped into a hole and fell. It was a mole tunnel."

"It must have been an entire mole village to uproot all of your flowers," Bernadette said.

"It was. We replanted, and some of them stayed, but most of them were turned up again the next day. Our entire yard was infested that summer."

"How did you get rid of them?" Florence asked.

"Donovan got someone to come out and do something," Ava said. "I didn't ask because I didn't want to have to tell Juni they died, so I left it to Donovan. I can say this: they never came back!"

"I have one," Florence said. She grinned at Juniper, who stiffened.

"My favorite thing to do when I came to visit Grandma Lila was go visit Juniper. I especially liked it when I spent the night because Aunt Ava would have to leave for something, which meant we could get into everything."

Juniper covered her face. She must have known what Florence was about to share.

"So, on this particular visit, I was somewhat obsessed with bras. Being older than me, Juniper had already moved through that phase and had her own bras, but I didn't own one yet."

Florence grinned at Ava to be sure she had her attention.

"I wanted to see Juniper's bras, to try them on, and she wouldn't show me where they were. So we went into your room and found your underwear drawer. I must have tried on every one of them, singing along to one of your old Madonna albums as we strutted around the bedroom."

"I remember that," Ava said. "I was afraid some pervert had been in the house, rifling through my underwear. But it was you!"

Florence rose to hug Ava. "Think of it as contributing to my sex education."

"What I most remember about your house was that every time I walked in, the first place my eyes went was to Daddy's desk. You didn't shove it out of sight. You put it in a place of honor in the room where everyone gathered. That right there, Ava, is why I knew you were the one," Aunt Lila said.

"The one for what?"

"The spine of the family, the one who would keep everyone together after Maud and I are gone. No, I take that back—after I'm gone. We all know that Maud would be more likely to fracture the spine than to strengthen it."

Aunt Maud threw up her hands, though she didn't say anything.

Ava had never seen herself as the spine of the family line, but so it was. Her cousins and brother had all moved on to cities, to a different kind of life than one rooted in sunrises over fenced fields and frost on the winter branches. Staying in Kentucky hadn't felt to Ava like she was choosing the farm, like she was choosing to preserve family traditions. She'd moved on, after all, to city life. She still couldn't grow a plant in her garden without lots of fuss. Yet she was the one who would preserve this place, who would keep it alive for Juniper and maybe for Brad and another generation yet to come. Maybe even Lizzie would come home one day.

Ava's eyes went through the sliding glass door and into the corner of the living room, to her grandfather's desk. She could see him sitting there, smiling at her and nodding in approval. Perhaps he had always known she was the one. Now she could also imagine her grandmother behind him, hands on his shoulders, smiling at Ava.

"Look at you, Ava. You went to visit your cousins. You got Fawn back for a visit. And now you're going to help me out so I can stay in the house where I was born until I die."

A small gasp from the group sounded like it came from more than one person.

"Oh, don't look so shocked. I'm seventy-nine years old. I will die eventually. And it makes me so happy that I'll be able to stay right here, where I can keep looking out my bedroom window at the nest the robins build every year in the oak tree. It means more than anyone can know."

"How's this going to work? Mom bakes. Other than that, she doesn't cook much. And she can't grow a thing," Juniper said.

"She can clean, even if she doesn't like to. She can bake. And she can keep the books. Maybe we'll work out a partnership with you, Juniper. You can help make sure things stay green and that your mother doesn't kill everything. And there's a field out there that needs planting."

A few guests pulled on sweaters as dusk descended. Ava ambled to a quiet corner of the porch to gaze at the twinkling stars as they popped out here and there. Aunt Lila appeared next to her and curled an arm around Ava's waist.

"You're the night sky, Ava."

"What do you mean?" Ava asked as they both looked upward.

"If the sky were filled with stars, then none of them would shine brilliantly enough to stand out among the rest. You're one of those hundreds of millions of particles that are content to stay dark so the stars around you can shine."

Ava knew that was right. Aunt Lila and Juniper were the stars.

Ava listened to the voices behind them, cherishing each one. The most important things hadn't been blown away. She had family and friends who reminded her of all that was good in the first part of her life. They would continue with her into the second half, reminding her of who she was and whom she belonged to, the people who grounded her and gave her strength, who challenged her and wouldn't let her get away with hiding, with being less than she could be.

And there was Juniper, no longer sad that her home was gone. It wasn't the house that she needed at all; it was the memories—and the promise that there would be more memories to come in many other places.

Acknowledgments

I was blessed to grow up with parents who encouraged me to do something with my life that would make me happy. It was apparent very early that my calling is writing. I can never say "thank you" enough to my mom, my number one publicist, and my dad (watching from heaven) for opening the world to me in that way and for supporting me through every step of the journey.

Many writing friends have encouraged me as I've drafted multiple novel manuscripts. I want to give special thanks to Angela Correll, Rebecca Ryland, and Emily Toadvine. The feedback these creative women have given me on my writing, especially as my first readers for this novel, has helped me become a better writer. I cherish their friendship, talents, and their giving hearts.

I also have a group of "soul sisters" whom I've grown with for more than thirty years: Deb Core, Patti Uckotter, Martha Wade, and Joan Adkins Wood. We've been through so much together, and I've always known I can count on you for insight, prayers, and a good meal.

Thanks also to all of my Lancaster, Berea, and Lexington friends for the life-giving conversations, lunches, parties, and prayers. Being in community with you strengthens me.

I am grateful to the Carnegie Center, House Writers Group, Grassroots Writers Group, the Writers' Table, Kentucky Foundation for Women, Sisters of Loretto, Wedgewood Circle, and the Women's Fiction Writers Association for providing me with opportunities to learn and to practice my art and my craft.

I am grateful to work alongside the good folks at Koehler Books to bring this manuscript to publication. Thank you to the writers who shared their publishing and marketing wisdom along the way, helping me make decisions about the process. I am also indebted to my launch team Craig Combs, John Forgy, Kathleen Leavell, Kathryn McCullough, Claire LimMingus, and Joan Wood for joining me on this journey.

Many thanks to all of my family members who have listened to me talk about my writing for countless years. Special thanks to David Dotson, Dan Dotson, Morgan Dotson, Jan Dotson, and Aunt Peg Draper for traveling through life with me and sharing my excitement about this book.

And finally, thank you is not enough for my husband, Jim Brown. He has inspired me with his storytelling, his love of farming, and his desire to see me succeed at what I love. And as he likes to remind me, he sometimes serves as my personal chef. I need eggs in the morning to stay energized and sharp and french fries in the evening when I'm overwhelmed!

To each writer out there who is still working toward your debut publication, answer the call to write. Writing is a gift in itself. Publication can happen. Persevere.

To readers of *Rooted in Sunrise*, I so appreciate that you gave this novel a chance. May tomorrow's sunrise instill you with hope.

BOOK CLUB QUESTIONS

1. *Rooted in Sunrise* begins with a traumatic event. What did you think of Ava's immediate reaction to the tornado? How did her reaction evolve throughout the book?

2. Ava's former husband, Donovan, first shows up in her recollections, then in person. How did Ava's perception of Donovan when he arrived at her aunt's house differ from how she remembered him?

3. What do the contents of the found suitcase say to Ava? How does that change when Lila examines the suitcase? Are you familiar with the term "go bag"?

4. Ava isn't the only character dealing with a life-changing event. How do the characters' reactions differ? Which character embodies a reaction you might have to a major life change or a reaction you've seen in someone around you?

5. What role does Aunt Lila play in Ava's life? Does she play the same role for anyone else in the story?

6. Fawn is a character who is trying to channel her passion and creativity into something that could establish a new path for herself. How does Ava differ in her approach to determining what's next for her own life?

7. Going through a time of crisis with someone can reveal an unfamiliar aspect of their personality. How does Ava respond to some of the new things she learns about the women around her?

8. How did the trip out of the country play a role in each of the characters taking a next step?

9. What might it require to be the "spine" of the family? Does Ava have what it takes?

10. The theme of "home" recurs throughout the book in different characters and scenes. What makes a place a home for you?

www.ingramcontent.com/pod-product-compliance
Lightning Source LLC
LaVergne TN
LVHW041701060526
838201LV00043B/528